The Vagabond Virgins

Books by Ken Kuhlken

Midheaven

The Hickey Family Series
The Loud Adios
The Venus Deal
The Angel Gang
The Do-Re-Mi
The Vagabond Virgins

With Alan Russell
Road Kill
No Cats, No Chocolate

The Vagabond Virgins

Ken Kuhlken

Poisoned Pen Press

Poisoned
Pen
Press

Copyright © 2007 by Ken Kuhlken

Large Print Edition 2007

10 9 8 7 6 5 4 3 2 1

Library of Congress Catalog Card Number: 2007937106
ISBN 978-1-59058-462-0 Large Print

Poisoned Pen Press
6962 E. First Ave. Ste. 103
Scottsdale, AZ 85251
www.poisonedpenpress.com
info@poisonedpenpress.com
Printed in the United States of America

This one is for Zoë Ada Fox Kuhlken

Thanks to Pam Fox, Gene Riehl, and Dave Knop for help and encouragement, to Barbara Peters for excellence in editing and for creating a place where the Hickeys can live, to Father Dean McFalls for inspiration, to Steve, Bev, Sam and Alvaro Havens, and to a shoeshine boy from Mazatlan, wherever you are.

Chapter One

Alvaro Hickey liked old movies and books about tough guys from the '30s and '40s, Pop's era. They were one reason he brought his work from the penthouse suite of his employers to the fourth floor office on Broadway, with its weathered paint, coffee stains, and boxes of his brother's manuscripts stacked against a wall. In that dreary room he could break from his desk work and imagine scenes like the long-legged blonde standing in the doorway, or like the phone call he would get today.

The placard on the door read Hickey and Sons, Investigations. The white paint on the plaster walls had yellowed long ago. The wooden floor creaked. Venetian blinds shaded the small window that overlooked Broadway and the city bus turnaround in Horton Plaza, a favorite hangout for the folks Alvaro grew up calling "bums" and "winos." But this was 1979, and such names had gone out of fashion like the term "wetback," which Alvaro remembered too well.

The only light came from a lamp on the ancient desk. Photos on the walls were of old Tijuana's Agua Caliente Casino, Lane Field where the Pacific Coast League Padres had played, and the tent city on Mission Beach during WW II.

Alvaro had given up squinting at the scribbled applications for green cards, visas, and citizenship, which Garfield, Robles, Patterson, Finney and Torres, LLD, paid him to translate and polish. He was checking his watch to decide whether he needed to run for the ferry. Then the phone rang.

"Mister Hickey?" the caller said.

He would've bet nobody could sound so gentle. Yet she spoke with confidence, and her diction was precise. He barely detected a Spanish accent with the hint of another language he couldn't make out. "Speaking."

"An attorney in Tijuana believes Tom Hickey and Sons can help me?"

Hickey and Sons was only a name on a door. Alvaro hadn't worked as a P.I. in three years, since he started law school. "Which attorney?"

"*Señor* Augustín Quartilho."

"Okay," Alvaro said. If Augie Quartilho even talked to the lady, she either looked as good as she sounded or she was part of the Mexican oligarchy Augie took pleasure in fleecing. "Your name is…?"

"Lourdes." She paused. "Garcia."

Even an angelic voice can lie, he thought, then cautioned himself against judging hastily. The pause could've meant a fly landed on her. Or somebody might've stepped on her foot.

"Can I come to your office?" she asked.

"Where are you?"

"I am at the Greyhound bus depot *Señor* Quartilho tells me is very close to your office."

"Wait out front," he said. "I'll be there in five minutes."

"I can find my way to you."

Admirable, he thought. "No need. I'm due for a break and a stretch." In truth, he didn't like the idea of any woman, especially one as young and lovely as she sounded, walking the downtown streets in twilight.

"I am wearing a green hat," she said.

The Greyhound depot was a few blocks south, at the corner of 1st Street and Broadway. He loped down the four flights of stairs. On the sidewalk, he walked at twice the speed of his usual amble. In cotton slacks and a sport coat over a polo shirt, which Garfield et al allowed as long as he buttoned it to the top, he got more than his share of stares. People, especially women, admired his wavy black hair and casual grace.

He stopped for the light at 1st Street and spotted the woman in the green hat. She was under a street lamp near the side entrance to the depot, standing only a couple arms' length from two hookers. Either she was tough or naive.

She appeared not much shorter than Alvaro's five feet and ten inches. Her Kelly green hat featured a wide, flat brim. She had wound her honey brown hair into a loose bun that rested on her long neck. She wore large, round glasses tinted yellow, a modest white blouse, and a yellow unbuttoned sweater with a green pleated skirt that fell just below her knees. The bare legs were the same color as her face, the brown of *café con leche*. Her waist was just slender enough to complement the generous hips and full breasts. Carrying a large embroidered canvas purse on a shoulder strap, she listed to the side where the purse hung, as if it weighed plenty. She stood flush against the lamp post beside a canvas suitcase. She watched his approach. He was still yards away when she reached out to shake his hand and said, "I believe you are…"

He nodded and took her pretty right hand. Her nails were manicured but short and unpainted. He glanced at her other hand. No ring.

From his first close look, even with the big tinted glasses that hid her eyebrows and part of her temples, he recognized her face. Though he couldn't remember where he'd seen it, she was familiar, like somebody he either saw, thought of, or dreamed about every day. Her face was rounder than oval, her cheeks soft and pooched like a healthy child's. Her mouth was wide, her lips medium-full. He had known and dated more striking women, but striking wasn't at the top of his list. This woman was the Mona Lisa kind that looked better the longer you gazed. All the pieces of her—posture, figure, voice, and the rest—matched as well as her outfit did. Besides, the way she stood perfectly still, and the way her mouth curved up at the sides but not quite into a smile, made him imagine she knew exactly who she was.

"Thank you for—"

"*Por nada*," he said. "Are you hungry?"

"I could eat."

"So we'll get dinner while we talk?"

"That would be nice."

He offered to carry her canvas suitcase. She appeared to consider a moment before she agreed.

The weight of the suitcase surprised him. At least fifty pounds, he thought, and he wondered if she carried gallons of mineral water. Or dumbbells.

A drunken conventioneer in a Hawaiian shirt and green trousers stopped in front of the Lyceum Theater across Broadway and stared, then whistled and waved. Alvaro waved back. He and the lady rounded the corner and turned toward the harbor.

The balmy night with stone gray clouds advancing off the Pacific reminded him of his birthplace in the tropics. Though summer storms rarely came to

San Diego, he felt one on its way. He remembered the Chubasco that turned city streets to rivers the day Feliz, his three-year-old niece, was born.

He wished the rain would hurry and fall. Overcast skies could grate on his nerves. But tonight it wasn't clouds that made him edgy. Though he was hardly shy around women, even the most alluring or aloof, this lady touched him in places too deep for comfort.

She walked with short steps, leaning to her right under the weight of her shoulder bag. They passed a tattoo parlor out of which Steppenwolf hard rock blasted, then a diner Alvaro had tried once and discovered the world's worst tacos.

"What kind of visa are you using?" he asked.

"I am a tourist."

"And you want a green card?"

"No." She glanced over her far shoulder. "A detective."

In the peep show arcades, sailors plunked quarters into the slots, pressed their eyes to the lenses, moaned, and sighed. Old *pachucos* stared dreamily out of a pool hall.

Beyond the Santa Fe depot and the tracks, they hustled across Pacific Coast Highway. All those eight blocks, the lady had kept her head tilted down so the hat brim shadowed her face. She said, "*Señor* Quartilho told me the Hickeys are brave. He said they are perhaps a little…" She looked up and stared at him. "Perhaps a little wild."

"The word was *loco*, right?"

She gave him a smile he might've mortgaged his duplex to see. "Yes, *loco*."

"I won't argue that point. So, you want our help with what?"

"To find someone." Even with her sunglasses blocking his view of her eyes, he perceived from her look that she was both humble and proud. He sensed all her hopes rested on his answer, yet she would refuse any help he wasn't anxious to give.

He stared too long, wondering why she looked so familiar. Maybe she acted on Mexican television or movies, he thought while he led her across the intersection to the tourist excursion docks. As they strolled past whale watching boats, he asked, "Find who?"

He had to lean closer to hear her soft voice over the creak of docks, the slap of tidewater on pilings, the whir of tires, and gulls that screeched like frantic women.

"My sister Lupe," she said.

"She's missing, or you just lost touch?"

"Missing."

"How long."

"Ten years," she said, and blushed.

Alvaro cocked his head toward the harbor, watched the Coronado ferry cut its turn toward the landing, and wondered if he should mention the odds that her sister was dead.

Chapter Two

Clifford Hickey tried to distract himself by gazing at the bay out the bedroom window. A gondola launched out from the Catamaran Resort, the gondolier singing a lament from *Carmen*.

The distraction didn't work. Clifford's almost three-year-old daughter Feliz couldn't hold still, her head ached so. While he tried to hold a cool washcloth on her forehead, she thrashed, began to sit up, then flopped back into the pillow. As close as he could measure with her thrashing, her temperature had passed 101 degrees. When she tried not to scream, her eye sockets bulged.

She didn't want to scream. She knew how screaming freaked her mom and dad. For a three-year-old, Clifford believed, she knew a whole lot about love.

◇◇◇

A newspaper vendor stood by the dock. Alvaro bought the evening edition. Tuesday, June 26, 1979. He folded and stuffed it into the side pocket of his sport coat. He wasn't a newspaper subscriber, and didn't want to miss any stories concerning the Mexican election, five days away, on Sunday. This election was worth following, even though for decades the *Partido Revolucionario Institutional* had terrorized, murdered, defrauded, whatever it took to squash all candidates but its own. But this year they had a formidable opponent.

Three weeks ago, an apparition came to four children near Las Cuevitas, a mountain village in Baja California. Since then, she had visited a different remote village every few days. Always to *campesinos.* All but once to children. On each occasion, she delivered prophecy for the particular children, the village, and the region.

In 1531, the Virgin of Guadalupe appeared on a hill called Tepeyac where the temple of an Aztec earth mother goddess had been demolished on orders of the Catholic bishop. Ever since, the Virgin returned to visit believers all over Mexico. Often she came as an image etched into a serape or an adobe wall, or as an invisible presence with a voice. Whenever she spoke, she delivered consolation. Never until this month, Alvaro believed, had she issued such urgent warnings. Spliced together they meant: The Mexican government is an abomination. If the PRI remains in control, the Lord will strike the country with plagues that will make the locusts, rivers of blood, and the rest he used on Pharaoh's Egypt feel like gentle zephyrs.

Alvaro showed the lady to a bench. They waited for the ferry to dock and unload, the heavy canvas purse on the bench between them. She kept hold of the strap even while she rolled her shoulders to relieve the sore muscles.

"Your sister," he said. "It's been ten years."

"Yes, very long."

"Tell me about her? In Spanish, why don't you?"

The ferry hit the dock. The lady startled and looked that way. She tucked her skirt around her pretty knees. Alvaro savored the lavender scent of her hair. She continued speaking English. "My father was German. He came to Mexico as a young man. He was very old. When he died." Her nostrils flared. "To my father, women are only for making sons. My mother was fourteen when she gave birth to Lupe. My father was more than sixty years. He was wealthy, my father. He acquired many gold mines."

Though dusk had long passed, for the first time she removed her sunglasses. Her eyes were dark blue, large and almond shaped, her eyebrows thick but not bushy. They didn't distract from her eyes but rather framed them. She unzipped the purse, placed the sunglasses in it and adjusted something. As she pulled her hand out, she leaned toward Alvaro, reached around so she could use both hands, and held the purse wide open.

Alvaro hadn't seen a gold bar before. This one was

about six inches by an inch and a half, with sides that sloped inward toward the top. In this light, he might've called its color mustard. It didn't shine or appear any more precious than a dirt clod. But he guessed it could pay off the mortgage Pop had taken out to put him through the University of San Diego law school.

"Shut it," Alvaro said.

"I can pay for your service."

"No kidding." He wondered how fast he could get her and the gold somewhere safe.

The ferry passengers had begun debarking. He sensed the rain would commence any minute. He hoisted the suitcase that made him walk like a pall-bearer and ushered the lady in front of him.

They boarded the ferry, climbed the stairs, and chose a bench on the covered end of the top deck. A few other passengers came to sit near them. The ferry left the dock and crashed through swells, turning the harbor into an ocean. To the southeast, lightning displayed the rolling mountains and black mesas across the border. Big rain-drops smacked the deck and the overhang.

"You haven't heard from Lupe in ten years? Not even a phone call or letter?"

For a minute the lady sat perfectly still. Then she turned away and appeared to watch the ships and boats anchored near the mouth of the harbor. She shivered and wrapped her arms around her breasts. On instinct,

Alvaro slid as close as the purse between them allowed. She didn't seem to notice. "I believe my father was a Nazi," she said.

Thunder clapped. Lightning flashed across the bay, from Coronado where Alvaro lived, toward the submarine base and missile installations at the tip of Point Loma. A bolt struck just beyond the North Island Naval Air Base, as though heaven had declared war against the U.S.

When the ferry swung around and nosed toward the Coronado dock, they went downstairs. They fell in behind a crowd of tourists whose faces or accents came from the midwest, Asia, and a half dozen parts of Europe. Most of them had jackets or newspapers over their heads and stood awaiting the gangplank with legs flexing like marathon runners' at the starting line. When the crew got the ferry lashed to the dock and the steward lifted the rope, tourists scampered off. Alvaro and the lady went last. Or so he thought. Once on the dock, he glanced back and noticed a man come out of shadows beside the lower deck cabin.

Alvaro and the lady hustled to shelter beneath the awning of a curio booth. The man in the shadows of the ferry's cabin turned his face toward the harbor and walked down the gangplank and past them. He was small and had a round bald spot like what monks called a tonsure. He was dressed in a waiter outfit of black slacks and jacket, a white shirt underneath. He sat on a bench in the rain, out of the light, gazing down at his knees. Alvaro only caught a glimpse of his face. Suede brown, clean shaven.

They were a five minute walk from Alvaro's duplex. On days when he wasn't obliged to drive across the border and deliver documents back and forth between his employers and Augie Quartilho or some other shady *abogado*, he walked and rode the ferry to work.

Tonight, he might've chosen to go straight home, to cook dinner there or dry off and go out in his car. But a suspicion about the small man warned him not to risk giving away their destination.

"Seafood okay?"

"Oh, yes," she said. Either seafood was her favorite, or she hadn't eaten in a long while.

"Do you mind getting wet?"

"I am wet already."

"Look over there." He pointed with a hand close to his chest. But when he glanced in the direction he had pointed, the small man was gone. "Never mind." He looked at her sneakers. "Let's run." He hoisted the suitcase and touched her elbow. Any other woman, he might've reached for her hand. With this lady he would've felt presumptuous.

Alvaro could run fast. He'd played halfback in high school and was still lead-off hitter in the Saturday adult baseball league he and his brother Clifford played for. But lugging the heavy suitcase, he could only trudge along. Though Lourdes listed to the right from the weight of her canvas purse, she pulled ahead and stayed ahead, following the directions he called out, three blocks on B and Third to Orange Avenue.

Farther up Orange, he led her into Bula's, his favorite of the dozen or so fern bar eateries on that mile long stretch of Orange, the commercial hub of the beach town realtors pitched as a quaint village whose property would soon out-price La Jolla's.

They took a table in the covered patio and used the cotton napkins to dry their faces and hands. From Alvaro's seat, the lady appeared surrounded by hanging succulents. Under a fluorescent bulb, he noticed her eyes weren't as dark as he'd thought in twilight. They were gray tinged with a deep-water blue. Alvaro stared, thinking, Wow.

"Is something wrong?" she asked.

"Are you a celebrity?"

"No, I am not."

"You look like an actress, a model, somebody famous."

"Oh," she said, then started another word but cut it off and turned toward the shiny cars and taxis gliding along Orange Avenue. The ferry whistle blew. The waiter came, a shy *Indio* plenty old enough to be a great grandfather. Alvaro ordered a Dos Equis. The lady chose iced tea. They hadn't looked at the menus, but Alvaro didn't need to. He had brought a half-dozen women here.

She said, "Order for me, please."

"Swordfish okay?"

"Oh, yes."

For himself, he ordered halibut. The waiter jotted and smiled wanly at the lady.

Alvaro tapped the waiter's arm. "*Es todo.*"

The waiter scurried off, and Alvaro decided to go for the truth about the sister, even if it meant acting cold-blooded. "You're sure Lupe's still alive?"

She closed her eyes and breathed deeply enough so her chest rose. "I know she is alive."

"How do you know?"

She had hung her canvas purse over the back of the chair then looped her arm under the strap. Now she pulled the purse around in front of her. She unzipped it, looked inside, and pulled out a manila envelope, which she unfolded and handed to Alvaro.

As he opened the envelope, she drew back and looked fearful as though she had bet a fortune on one hand and was about to throw the last card down.

Inside the envelope, he found a newspaper. Section one of last Monday's *Excelsior*, from Mexico City. She said, "Page three."

He pushed aside his bread plate and silverware. He lay the paper on the table and turned the page. A familiar face stared up at him. He'd admired the same color photo in a dozen newspaper articles.

In Agua Dulce, in Baja's Sierra de Juarez, the Virgin had allowed a girl to run home and return with her box of pastels. The girl was a savant. The sketch was masterful. The Virgin's folded hands lay above her breasts, a couple inches beneath her slightly down-turned chin. Her cheeks were full, her eyes deep-water blue and spaced far apart. Her mouth was wide, her generous lips a shade darker than the rest of her creamed coffee skin. Peculiar sparkles, like flakes of amber-tinted light, appeared to issue from her eyes.

The story had first captivated Alvaro not only because he shared this Virgin's opinion of the PRI. Also, Wendy, his second mamá, had believed in angels and miracles. And Pop, Tom Hickey, the wisest man Alvaro knew, had trusted his wife's wisdom and insight above his own. Alvaro wasn't about to call miracles out of the question. Besides, he wanted to believe. Belief had carried Mamá and Clifford through some brutal times.

When Alvaro looked up from the drawing at the lady's face, he blushed, embarrassed at having taken so long to know why she was familiar. He pulled the *Sentinel* from his coat pocket, opened to the world section. He folded the paper, laid it on the table in front of her, and pointed to an article.

"You're this Virgin?" he asked, not sure what he meant, whether he believed she was a spirit or a fraud.

"Lupe," she said, as the waiter arrived with their drinks and salad.

Chapter Three

"You and Lupe are twins?" Alvaro asked.

"No, Lupe is five years older than I am."

Over dinner, he didn't question her. He admired and studied her face, and wondered if two people other than twins could look so alike. If that weren't likely, he asked himself, did it mean Lourdes was the Virgin?

They had just left Bula's when she pointed at a neon sign on the Crown Inn. "I will take a room in this hotel, perhaps."

Alvaro shook his head and looked around. He said, "Anybody carrying a gold bar needs a bodyguard." Besides, intuition warned that he shouldn't let her out of his sight. "I've got a spare room. It's a mess, but I vacuumed the other day, and the sheets are clean."

She peered at him for a few seconds as if reading his thoughts. "I am grateful."

They could've reached his duplex in five minutes of swift walking. But he didn't like what he saw across the street, behind the tinted glass doors of the Orange

Arms apartments. A shadowy figure moved stiffly like the small man had. After they walked a few more steps, when Alvaro glanced back over his shoulder, the man was hustling out of the building. He went toward a Buick, either dark red or burgundy. He ducked into the shotgun seat. Then the Buick was wheeling a U-turn to come their way.

Instead of turning right toward his duplex, Alvaro gripped the lady's elbow and led her across the intersection and up against the wall of a liquor store, out of the glow from a streetlamp and the store's neon sign. The Buick had pulled to the curb in front of Bula's.

Though he preferred not to alarm the lady, he asked, "Is somebody following you?"

"No one knows where I have come," she said, but with little conviction.

"Who would be searching for you?"

She glanced away from his face then back to it. "I believe Rolf is looking for me."

"Who's Rolf?"

"Rolf is my brother," she said, with a slight trill to the "R" and a distinct warmth that hadn't appeared when she spoke her sister Lupe's name. Also, Alvaro thought he detected a note of defiance, for which he could guess no reason.

"Maybe somebody got a look at your gold. Who sat next to you on the plane?"

"A very heavy woman."

"Well, either somebody's following us or I'm *loco*, like Augie Quartilho says." He described the man to her. Short, medium-dark, haircut like a monk's tonsure, and a stiff walk.

"I don't know him," she said. She wasn't much of a liar. Her eyes, otherwise steady and fixed on Alvaro's, had again flicked away for a millisecond. He might've missed noticing if he hadn't studied Tae Kwon Do and practiced Master Oh's theory that a fighter should always focus on the opponent's eyes.

The library was just up the street, then the police station. He thought of entering through the front of one of those places and exiting through the back. But, rather than lose the tail, he wanted to lead them somewhere the lady could get a clear look.

He spotted a cab and waved it down. The cabbie double-parked. Alvaro opened the rear door, shoved the suitcase across the seat, ushered the lady to the middle, and seated himself on the outside. "Hotel Del," he said.

Orange Avenue was a ghost town polished by the rain. Except for a handful of folks in each of the cafés and dessert shops, even the tourists were holed up. Probably thinking that if they wanted summer storms, they could've gone to New Orleans.

Alvaro's hips and legs were snug against the lady's. He wondered if she had a fever or if the heat came from him. He leaned as close as her wide brimmed hat allowed, and whispered. "Who else thinks the photo you showed me is of your sister?"

"No one," she said in a voice Alvaro heard as sorrowful. She felt alone, he thought. A feeling he understood. He'd often wondered if he had inherited from his *Indio* papa the sense of separation from others, of being an outsider, no matter how hard he tried to connect. He'd read that conquerors value themselves but conquered people don't. They often feel incomplete, like Alvaro often did. Which now and then laid him low. Only two weeks ago, during a spell of deep gloom, he squandered a month's grocery allowance money on cheap Scotch.

He stared at the lady. His logical faculties knew well enough that looking for a woman who could save him from gloom and liquor was foolish. Still, he couldn't help wishing.

◇◇◇

The Hotel Del Coronado was part beach resort, part relic, built over six years during the 1890s. Its steep red roofs were topped with cupolas above which flags waved in the sea breeze. California's answer to Victorian elegance, its balconies covered more square feet than did the rooms of most grand hotels. The Del had sheltered U.S. presidents and Marilyn Monroe when she and it starred in *Some Like It Hot.*

The cabbie dropped Alvaro and the lady at the crest of the circular drive, at the base of the steps leading to the porch and lobby. Alvaro waved off the bellhops, ignored the wink he got from the doorman and the sneer the blond desk clerk gave him. Her name was Joanne. No doubt she was steamed to see a guy who'd never dealt her a straight answer about why he'd stopped asking her out carrying another female's luggage into a hotel only blocks from his home.

In the lobby, whose stairways and paneling might've required an entire mahogany forest, couples in tuxedos and evening gowns paraded, going from the Crown Ballroom toward the elevators. The women, who would've looked better in bathrobes or mumus, either attempted or were forced by their spiked heels to walk like runway models. The men snuck glances at Alvaro and his companion. Probably thinking, For that babe I'd gladly blow a grand in one night, but for Eleanor here, phooey.

Alvaro led her through the lobby to a lounge where a pianist in tails played Vivaldi. He nodded to Alvaro. On Sunday evenings, the two of them often sat in and transformed Joe Morello's jazz trio of bass, drums and alto sax, to a quintet. Alvaro played guitar. The pianist scrutinized the lady and dropped a few notes.

Alvaro showed her to a stool at the end of the bar. They could see, and be seen from, the lobby. The bartender called him by name, ogled Lourdes, and asked in Spanish what they were drinking. Alvaro held up a finger. He was watching the small fellow who had entered the lobby, preceded by a doorman.

The pianist concluded his set, and the small man gazed around. Alvaro touched the lady's arm. "Here we go. Be cool, you're a tourist. Don't look back."

They crossed the lobby, his right hand at her elbow, his left arm straining with the suitcase. He leaned close and whispered, "Take a quick look at the guy by the door. Little fellow. Wearing black and white."

Off the lobby, opposite the ballrooms, a hallway of gift shops and boutiques began. It would lead them past another ballroom and an arcade of hotel memorabilia. As they entered the hall, he asked, "Did you see him?"

"I did not see his face."

That's not an answer, he thought.

The shops were closed but lighted. Alvaro stopped at a gallery, switched hands on the suitcase and stepped around, putting her on his left. For a minute he stared straight ahead at a painting, a modernist seascape in florid shades of purple and blue. "You like it?" he asked, turning her way, which gave him a view up the hall to the lobby. A fat boy tugged his mama toward them while she held her ground and stared into a gallery.

Alvaro motioned with his head and set the pace,

the slowest stroll he could manage without pretending to be lame. They passed photos of Teddy Roosevelt. Of Dwight Eisenhower. Of the Duke of Windsor who gave up the throne of England to marry Wallis Simpson, a commoner, whom rumors claimed he met at the Del. Farther along were shots of Marilyn in white sundresses and flesh tone bathing suits. They prompted Alvaro to note that the lady was built more like Marilyn than the twiggy style women struggled to maintain these days. He pointed at a photo. "She looks like Feliz, my brother's little girl. Her face, I mean."

The lady smiled.

At the end of the hallway, a door opened onto the pool deck with the beach beyond. A flurry of rain hit them. The lady hustled around a large agave and squatted under the scant cover a rubber tree offered. Only Mexicans were out working in the rain. They trimmed hedges, skimmed leaves out of a pool, even painted under eaves.

The air had chilled. The raindrops that whapped their heads and shoulders felt crueler than before. Alvaro wished he had devised a drier scheme to intercept the monk. This way, the lady could get pneumonia and die, he thought, and just maybe he would rot in hell for killing the Holy Virgin.

He was about to stand and lead her back inside when a tonsured head appeared, peeking out of the door they had come through. The small man stepped out and turned right, toward the beach.

Alvaro leaped up and ran after him but slipped on the pavement. The man heard him and wheeled around. When Alvaro dove and hooked an arm around his neck, the man spun and yanked himself free. He bolted for the trellised gateway in a hedge of bougainvillea.

Alvaro chased him as far as the hedge then stopped. He watched the man slog across a lawn toward the hotel's beach cabañas. Alvaro might've caught up, but he wasn't going to leave the lady. For all he knew, the man had partners. If others besides her believed the Virgin was Lupe Shuler, or Lourdes Shuler, the man could be an agent of the PRI.

Whatever happened, the workmen would ignore, having no doubt learned what can happen to poor folks who intrude. Alvaro ran back to Lourdes, wrapped an arm around her waist, and led her to beneath an awning. He went for the suitcase and returned. "Now you saw him better, did you recognize him?"

"No." Her eyes darted off for an instant. An auburn hue tinted her face. Next best to an honest person was a novice liar, Alvaro thought.

He considered finding a maid's cart and borrowing towels. But they would soon get drenched again, unless they took a room in the Del, which he couldn't afford and wouldn't ask the lady to pay for.

They re-entered the hotel by a rear doorway into a banquet hall where housekeepers bussed tables and vacuumed. He stopped one and told her in Spanish that a stalker was chasing his friend. He described the small man. "If he shows, tell him we went that way." He pointed across the hall, toward the front lobby. "Tell him you think we got on an elevator."

Alvaro and the lady crossed the ballroom and used the exit through French doors that led to a patio. He bent forward and slung the heavy suitcase onto his back like the opponent in a judo match. He wondered how much a single gold bar could weigh.

He pointed the way and tried to keep up with Lourdes, squishing across the lawn from hedge to hedge and remembering Vietnam and the pack he carried, which he believed was lighter than this suitcase. The lady's feet dug into the lawn and slurped out. Still, she ran with big, loping strides, her pleated skirt flying up so instinct urged him to stop running and focus on her shapely legs.

He tailed her through a gate to Richard Henry Dana Place and across, and into the dark corner of a driveway. He rolled out from under the suitcase, attempting to let it down gently. It crashed with a thud.

"Sorry," he said.

"I have dropped it many times."

As they crept out of the driveway, a cat sprang

from behind a bush and hissed. Alvaro led the way to Ocean Boulevard with its Tudor, colonial, Frank Lloyd Wright modern and eclectic styled mansions that exhibited California disdain for traditions except the one requiring the wealthy to show off their wealth. Some of the mansions required whole squads of Mexicans to scrub, detail, repair, and landscape.

Across the boulevard was the sea wall of piled granite bounders and steps that led them down to white sand, near where commoners of the tent city pictured on the Hickey and Sons office wall used to share the beach with the royalty staying at the Del.

On the widest of San Diego's beaches, they rested at the base of the sea wall, a hundred yards from the tide line. The boom of each wave echoed off the wall.

Again, Alvaro hoisted the suitcase onto his back. They hugged close enough to the wall so they couldn't be seen from the road. After a quarter mile, Alvaro dropped to his knees, eased the pack off his back and rolled and stretched his shoulders. "Not much farther."

She was leaning against the wall, half sheltered from the rain. Her hat was gone, probably back on the grounds of the Del. She combed her drenched, honey brown hair with her fingers, and watched him with bright, expectant eyes, as though she had asked a deep question and was waiting for a brilliant answer. He saw pinpoints of amber-tinted light glance off her eyes. Like the ones the newspaper had quoted a *campesino* describing. The feature that above all else had convinced at least some of the believers, as well as the children who saw her, that the one who visited them was the queen of heaven. He wondered if this lady staring at him truly had a sister.

He trudged ahead. At the last steps before his street, he climbed and peered both ways. They jogged across Ocean Boulevard and along the winding sidewalk of G Avenue, under a canopy of dripping elms and acacias.

◇◇◇

As they entered his duplex, Alvaro told himself, Okay, here are the rules. One, don't let your mind get hot and bothered. She's not a woman. She's a mystery to solve. Two, make her talk, give her a chance to slip up. And whatever else you do, don't agree to help her. Sleep on the idea.

His duplex was World War II vintage, slammed together over a few days during the housing boom when San Diego was the world's most populous and active military-industrial city. Alvaro had bought the place when he'd lately returned from Vietnam and decided to invest his savings before it got him into trouble.

The duplex was a flat-top hardly more sturdy than a mobile home. Each unit was two-bedroom one-bath. Each had a carport on the outside, which made no sense considering the place was framed with two-by-threes covered in 1/4 inch drywall, as Alvaro had discovered when he leaned an elbow against the dining nook wall.

If the carports were in the middle, between the units, occupants might've gotten some privacy. But if the layout had made sense, Alvaro couldn't have afforded the place.

His renters were brother and sister. Chief, a retired and widowed sailor, and Winona, whom Alvaro thought of as an aging hippie cowgirl, who waited tables at the House of Chang. On her nights off, until the late movies on TV concluded, Chief drank bourbon and Winona smoked weed. Whenever Alvaro brought home a woman, they put music they considered appropriate on the stereo, romantic stuff like Mario Lanza, Billie Holiday, or Otis Redding. Alvaro suspected they sat close to the wall, maybe with ears against it, and shared the scenarios they dreamed up about the goings on next door. At those times he often heard Chief's raspy laugh and Winona's cackle.

Tonight they played Sinatra. "Someone to Watch Over Me" serenaded Alvaro and the lady while he showed her his spare room. The bed sat wedged between congas, a keyboard on a stand, his Fender amplifiers, large, medium and small, and his guitars in their cases. A banged up classical from the Mexican town of Paracho, which he'd bought because it was a ringer for one that belonged to his long-dead papa, a mariachi. A Stratocaster he'd used with the Scorpions, a Tijuana night club cover band that for a couple months featured an under-aged Carlos Santana. A Martin D-18 acoustic his brother gave him after Pop bought Clifford a Gibson Hummingbird for his college graduation. And a Les Paul jazz guitar. The photos and posters on the walls were memoirs of bands he'd played with, including an action shot of The Blue Flames, rock, rockabilly and blues, a group fans expected to go big time. But the drummer insisted on drunk driving once too often, went for his last ride, and took the lead singer with him.

Alvaro moved an amp away from the closet doorway, opened the closet for the lady, and showed her the free space and extra hangers. He said, "Toss me out your wet clothes, I'll put them into the dryer. If the suitcase leaked and the stuff inside got sopped, give me a yell. I'll toss in a pair of sweats for you."

From the look she gave, he wondered if she feared that after she had stripped he would charge in and rape her. Or the look could mean she hoped he would do so. Or, he thought, maybe such impure thoughts never crossed her mind.

In the bathroom, Alvaro cleared the sink board of cough syrup, aspirins, and shaving gear. Then he called through the spare room door, "If you have other stuff that needs washing, we might as well throw it all in at once."

She didn't answer. He left her alone and went to his bedroom, opened the top dresser drawer and unwrapped the Smith and Wesson .22 pistol he had bought after some bikers who used to ride with the Cossacks came looking for his brother, following his parole. Clifford had served twenty-two months for manslaughter. The victim was a Cossack.

Alvaro's pistol was small enough to carry concealed. While he held it, he heard a floorboard creak. He wheeled and found the lady only inches away. Still in her wet clothes, she stood with hands on her hips and frowned at the gun.

"I'll bet the little man hasn't given up on us," Alvaro said. "How many gold bars do you have?"

"Eight of them."

"*Díos mio.*" He shook his head, and wedged the gun barrel into his back pocket. "Anyway, it's a toy, not going to kill anybody unless I stick it in his ear. Sit down." He pointed at the only chair, an Adirondack Pop had built long ago.

He drew a slow breath, rubbed the bridge of his nose, and attempted to think like a trial lawyer rather than like a guy suffering from infatuation. "Are you going to tell me who that fellow is?"

She only cocked her head.

"Or," he said, "should I, first thing tomorrow, take you back to Augie Quartilho and ask him to recommend somebody for you who doesn't give a damn about the truth?"

Alvaro's second mama used to sit in that same Adirondack chair on their deck overlooking Lake Tahoe, and he thought of her as he watched the lady fold her hands and lay them on her lap. For a minute or two, she only stared at his chest. Either trying to avoid his eyes, he thought, or peering into his heart. Then she said, "His name is Benito. My father's personal assistant."

"Bodyguard?"

"Yes. You see, my father was killed."

"Go on. When?"

"Tomorrow will be four weeks, I believe." She looked up.

"And what's Benito want with you?"

"He hopes I will lead him to Lupe. He believes she killed my father."

Alvaro leaned back, folded his arms and tried to imagine the Virgin of the sketch killing someone. It didn't work. "And you? Do you think Lupe killed your father?"

Her folded hands had risen to beneath her chin. They appeared to keep her head from falling. "I do."

He stood a moment trying to imagine the impact

to a family of the murder of one by another. He couldn't. He walked past her, through the front room and into the dining nook, to the wall phone. The lady had followed him. She watched him and ran a comb through the glossy hair that hung in loose waves to her waist.

"I'm calling my brother," he said.

Chapter Four

At two years and ten months, Feliz most resembled her dad. She was big-boned and blond like Clifford. But her hair was thicker and wavier like her mom's and with hints of Ava's auburn. She had Ava's shiny green eyes.

Clifford was reading to her. Her head lay on top of two pillows, which felt softer than one. Tears pooled on her cheeks. At least she wasn't moaning anymore.

Ava came in, arms clasped around the belly that made people ask if she was expecting twins. "Your brother's on the phone." She gave him a mildly sour look.

He handed *The Giving Tree* to his wife and went to the phone in the dining nook that served as his office when he needed to work at home. He wrote feature stories for the *Epitaph,* San Diego's major weekly.

"Yeah, X, what's up."

"Sorry to disturb your family time, *hermano,* but I've got a couple questions."

"Shoot."

"This Virgin that's in the news. I'm wondering, from

what I've seen, the PRI hasn't even tried to discredit her. What's with that?"

"It's strange."

"You bet. Any ideas about their motives?"

"Not offhand. What's up?"

"Aw, it's just this *hombre* with one of the fringe parties. His cousin's a honcho at the U.S. consulate in TJ. A guy who can help our clients with visas and such. Anything I can give to the *hombre* to pass along to his cousin is another favor they'll owe us. And you know what favors can mean to the shady characters at Garfield et al, LLD."

Clifford reached for a pencil and notepad. "You want me to snoop around?"

"Uh huh."

"Will first thing tomorrow work?"

"Yep. If I'm not here in the morning, I'll try to call you by noon. I might be in Baja, out in the wilds. You'll be home?"

"I can be."

After the call, Clifford stood a moment puzzling. Alvaro hadn't sounded right.

He returned to his little girl and took over reading. Feliz kept her eyes closed through *Goodnight Moon*. By the end she had nearly dozed off. He leaned and kissed his precious three-year-old's cheek. "Night-night, my love."

"Night-night, Big Daddy," she mumbled. In the past couple weeks, he and Ava had become Big Mama and Big Daddy, which always made him smile. It sounded like dialogue out of Tennessee Williams.

He remained sitting on the edge of her bed. Every half-minute or so her head tossed or she winced and her puffy cheeks rose up toward her brow.

Since the phone call, his thoughts were divided between his little girl and his brother. He didn't believe Alvaro's story about some client's cousin. He hadn't told it smoothly enough. He'd used clipped sentences and stuck too closely to the point. His usual style was given to rambles and digressions, the artist speaking.

When Feliz dozed, he went to the other bedroom. Ava was in bed, making notes on sheet music. Clifford said, "I need to make a run down to Alvaro's place. Something's fishy."

His wife brushed back a swatch of thick auburn hair. "Fishy?" She sounded like an interrogator.

He told her all about Alvaro's request. Still, he read in her eyes that she failed to see why he needed to go to his brother, except insofar as she believed that the Hickey men thrived on melodrama and intrigue.

He fetched his gun, the old .45 automatic Pop had given him last year when a neighbor got raped and murdered. Ava had followed him into their bedroom. She said, "Oh, well if you're planning on going to prison again, I should probably get an abortion. Will they give me one this far along?"

"Babe, that law firm X clerks for, amongst their clients are *coyotes* and such." He patted the gun. "It's just a precaution, just for show."

She made a poof sound. "Go on, then. Do what your hormones dictate."

"You don't mind my waking you up when I get home?"

"Funny." She gave him a sour look, the sourest all day.

◇◇◇

"Why did you lie to your brother?" the lady asked.

"Clifford's got problems," Alvaro said. "Their second baby's due in a couple weeks. His wife's acting crazy, like she thinks he's a bum because he doesn't make enough money. He's a writer. And he's *loco* like me. What'll happen, if I tell him we're going to hunt for the Virgin, he'll insist on going to Baja with us. And when he comes home, Ava and Feliz might be long gone."

"And your father? Tom Hickey. Will you call him?"

"Pop's almost seventy-three. His heart doesn't tick like it ought to."

He imagined she gave him a skeptical look, as though wondering if he was capable of helping her on his own. "Maybe tomorrow I'll call him," he said. "We'll see."

The lady turned and walked into the spare room. Alvaro changed to jeans and a T-shirt with a faded line-drawing of Django Reinhardt. He boiled water to the tune of "You Go To My Head," with which Frank, by way of Chief and Lola, was currently serenading them. He plopped bags of peppermint tea into the mugs. The lady had already taken so long changing, he wondered if she was looking at the posters.

She came out in a yellow dress, loose fitting, with a collared neckline and elbow length sleeves. It cinched at the waist with a yellow rope and was hemmed below her knees. The outfit pleased Alvaro. It didn't reveal much, and he preferred not to get any more titillated than he already was over a woman who might be running a scam on him. And who, at the least, was asking him to abet the escape of a murderess who killed her own father. Though, if the old man was a Nazi, Alvaro wasn't about to condemn her.

Lourdes carried an armload of dresses, skirts and blouses, and a towel stuffed with underwear. Alvaro took the armload from her. He laid it on the counter and invited her to sit and drink her tea, which he delivered before he took the wash out to the carport. He sorted the white blouses, white socks, and white panties from the bright dresses and skirts, none of which matched the brown muslin smock the Virgin in the sketch wore.

He found her perched on the edge of the old wooden desk chair that faced the sofa. He wondered if she had chosen that seat to assure that he wouldn't plop down beside her and gradually ease closer and closer. From beyond the paper walls, Frank crooned "Stormy Weather."

"Do you play all those instruments?"

"Mostly guitar."

"You will play for me?"

"Okay."

Her eyes flicked toward the side window, which opened onto the carport, and stayed there.

Alvaro looked that way. "Did you see something?"

"I thought I saw a face."

He slipped the little gun out of his pocket and held it beside his cheek. "Stay here."

He crept through the dining nook and flicked on the carport light. He opened the door a crack and peeked out for half a minute before he stepped outside. He rounded the '55 Chevy wagon that belonged to him and Clifford, walked into his meager back yard and peered into the shadows. A neighbor's dog yapped. Alvaro crept back through the carport to the front yard, gazed up and down the street.

When he spotted his brother's family car, an old gray-blue Volvo, he laughed. Clifford had busted him. The Volvo was at the end of the block toward the beach, pulling away from the curb.

He went inside and found the lady still on the edge of her chair. He shrugged his hands. "Nobody."

"*Señor* Hickey," she said, "if someone knows I am with you, can he find out where you live?"

"Call me Alvaro. Or X, like my family does."

"*Equis?*"

"Short for Xavier, my middle name."

She leaned toward him. "Alvaro, can anyone find your home?"

"Who is anyone?"

"Benito, or perhaps someone who talks to *Señor* Quartilho."

"What did you tell Quartilho?"

"Only that I am looking for my sister."

"But he got a good look at you, right? And no doubt he's seen the sketch of the Virgin. He could've made the connection. You're thinking he might sell you out?"

"Do you think so?"

"He might. But I've got no reason to believe he knows where I live, and I don't broadcast my whereabouts. The phone's unlisted." In case she was the kind to lie awake worrying, he didn't mention that any experienced crook or persistent nitwit, let alone a government agent, could find most anybody. "Why would somebody besides Benito come looking for you?"

"To find my sister. To arrest her?"

"No other reason you know of?"

Her eyes narrowed. "I don't know any other reason."

"Gold, maybe?"

"Yes," she said, with a trace of impatience.

Alvaro offered a conciliatory smile, though he hadn't meant to. He wanted to act tough, stick to business and take his mind off the lady's charms. But when he looked at her face, he got struck by the way she appeared so attentive to him, and when his gaze fell anywhere below her face, he felt something like awe. If she had come out wearing a nightgown, he thought, his willpower might've suffered a lethal blow.

"*Señor* Alvaro, you will help me find my sister?"

"What makes you think she killed your father?"

"Our *criada*, Doña Flor, came home from shopping. She saw my sister, in a car, going away from our home. When she looked for my father, he was dead. On the floor of his study.

"I had gone riding, alone. Rolf and I had argued the night before. I had not seen him all morning. I was tethering Negrito, my horse, and I heard Doña Flor's screams. I ran into the house, to my father's study. My father's blood was black and it ran away from him like water. His teeth looked like fangs. I thought this was a dream, in which my father became a monster. In this dream, I was both thrilled and terrified, because I had slain the monster. I knelt beside him and placed my hands into a pool of his black blood."

She closed her eyes and gulped as though to help herself through a spell of nausea. "Doña Flor told me she saw Lupe. Then Doña Flor ran out of the room. That is when I opened the safe and took the eight bars of gold."

"Opened it?"

"Yes. He had given me the combination. He was old and forgot things yet he would not write the combination. He believed I was too cowardly to steal from him."

"Did the police charge Lupe with the murder?"

"No, you see, no one else knows Lupe is alive, only me and Doña Flor. Doña Flor would never tell them she saw Lupe. She loves Lupe. She hated my father."

"Maybe she killed him."

"No." As though she were pondering the suggestion, her brow furled and she looked down. But she looked up too soon to make the gesture convincing. "Doña Flor would not have used a gun. She would have poisoned him."

"Did they find the gun that killed him?"

"I don't know. I was gone. In addition to the gold, I stole my father's car. I drove to the Capital and parked the car in front of my brother's mansion in Colonia Roma. It is a very fine Jaguar I knew he would recognize. On the seat I left a note, explaining that the sight of my dead father troubled me in so many ways, I needed to go far away until I could have clear thoughts. I promised to contact him, from another country. Mexico is no longer my home."

While watching her, Alvaro stood no chance of thinking straight. Yet he couldn't altogether avoid looking at her without appearing so rude she might quit talking. He tried staring at her feet. He forced himself to imagine telling her no. Even though she admitted to crimes, the thought of refusing to help her made him feel like a weasel. "Does Benito know the gold is missing?"

"Perhaps he does."

"Did you leave the safe open, or close it?"

"I don't remember."

"Okay. So Benito could be after the gold. Or he might've seen Lupe and pieced together some observations and reasoned that she killed your father. Maybe somebody offered a reward for your father's killer."

The lady shrugged. "Perhaps."

"Or Benito could be working for somebody who wants to stop the Virgin, no matter if he thinks the Virgin is Lupe or Lupe's ghost."

"Ghost?"

"It could be. Or they might think you are the Virgin." Or the murderer, or both, he thought. "No matter, the Virgin is gunning for the PRI, so the PRI must be gunning for her. If we're going to find her first, we'd better move out at first light."

"Then you are helping me?"

"I'll give it a day," he said, and felt a wave of remorse, as if he'd just mortgaged his home to bet on a long shot. "Tomorrow I'll either sign on for keeps or fix you up with somebody more capable."

She rewarded him with a smile. "Perhaps no one is more capable."

He considered how many people had a stake in dethroning this Virgin. The PRI, if you included all the cops and bureaucrats on their payroll, had to be at least a million strong. And foreigners, whoever was invested in Mexico and depending upon deals made with the PRI. So the Virgin's potential enemies included vast corporations and half the world's governments, besides drug cartels, and maybe the Catholic church.

The lady rose from the chair. For an instant he thought she would offer him a grateful kiss. But she only asked permission to use the bathroom. He pointed.

Of all the pits Alvaro had stepped into, including the Vietnam war, he imagined this one as the deepest.

After she shut the bathroom door, he muttered, "Sucker." He wondered if he might die like his first mama had—killed by the PRI.

Chapter Five

When Clifford returned home from snooping on his brother, he found Ava at the kitchen table, reading a book on parenting by a Christian talk show host. Clifford had thumbed through the book that morning and considered tossing it out. But he and Ava disagreed about too much already.

She gave him the wry half-sneer, a recent addition to her arsenal. "How many people did you shoot?"

"I peeked in the window, that's all. False alarm."

"What'd you see?"

"Only X and a pretty woman."

"As usual." She turned back to her book.

Thinking he hadn't seen her smile in a week, he figured it was time to get honest. "Babe, if you imagine sour looks, and loaded remarks, and criticism about the choices I make are eventually going to get to me, they aren't. I mean, if you think I'll ever get bummed enough to leave you and Feliz and the baby, forget it."

She heaved to her feet. The look she'd turned on him could mean she intended to chomp his nose. She leaned in as close as she could without toppling forward. "What are you talking about?"

"I'm saying, if you want out, or want me out, you'd better just go. Because I won't."

"Oh, and you're saying I'm manipulating you into leaving me. And just why would I do that? To make you into the bad guy?"

"Beats me."

"Clifford, I'm not like that." She fell on him, wrapped her arms around his waist. He pulled her tight as the belly allowed. She wept.

Between sobs, she said, "I'm just sad. Awfully sad and confused. Maybe we'll be okay, once Tommy's here." Boy or girl, the baby would be Tommy. Or Tommi.

"Yeah. We will."

◇◇◇

The lady went to bed. In the carport, Alvaro moved her white clothes to the dryer and put the colors in to wash. He scooped the newspapers out of the bin where he kept them for a recycler, an ancient black fellow who made a weekly pass through the neighborhood in his old Dodge pickup. Alvaro carried the newspapers inside to the kitchen table. He lifted the pistol out of his pocket and laid it on the table, peeled off his sweat shirt, went to a drawer for scissors, and sat over the last ten issues of the *Sentinel*. Sorting through, he found nine pertinent articles and clipped them.

Before they ran off searching, he wanted to draw conclusions about the reality of this Virgin. If he knew for a fact that she was from earth, not heaven, he might know where to start looking.

He fetched a steno pad. As he read the articles, he jotted notes: The writer of all but the first two, which came from a wire service, was a *Sentinel* reporter named Roxie Hewitt. She observed that the Virgin had appeared only to children, and had met them at rocky places where they went to climb or to slide down hills of tule weeds on cardboard mats. Most of the children were Kumeyaay Indians.

She always appeared about a mile from a village. She descended from the sky and rose into the sky. Although, like all reporters, Roxie Hewitt attempted to appear objective, Alvaro gleaned from her choices of words and the sources she chose to quote that she grew ever less skeptical as the details from different visitations matched. The colors the Virgin wore, the low-pitched, velvet tones of her voice, her blue-gray eyes and golden brown hair.

The Virgin had cured one child of a burn scar, another of a high fever. A family claimed their baby died and returned to life while, a mile away, the Virgin was admonishing the baby's six-year-old sister to expect a miracle.

Most of the Virgin's advice was about how to live: Love even the cruel; Be diligent with confessions; Fast all morning at least one day a week; Pray through the rosary before taking communion. And, every appearance concluded with a warning that Mexico must rid itself of the PRI.

"*Ándale*," Alvaro muttered. "Go get 'em, Lupe." Since the first report, he had fervently hoped that no matter the truth about this Virgin, she would succeed in overthrowing the PRI. He saw them as bandits who had betrayed the revolution and the people of Mexico. For the past thirty years, and under different names for twenty years before that, the PRI maintained power through every crooked means. Their stooges, as well as the kingpins, did little without the payoff, *la mordida*. They bought votes, voter registrars, and vote counters. They ransacked whatever opposition newspapers the laws they enacted couldn't silence. They massacred *Indios* when expedient. They co-opted the Catholic Church and partnered with drug cartels. And they murdered Alvaro's first mamá.

She was an orphan of mostly Spanish descent, who fell for and married an *Indio*, a mix of Huichol and Yaqui. He was a player of the violin and *guitarrón*. She was a dreamer who shared her dreams of social justice out loud, in public. Once too often she roused anger against local kingpins. When a strike turned into a battle, the battle into a small war, and Alvaro's mama disappeared, a rumor got spread that she ran off with a *federale*. Alvaro's papá knew better.

Still, it wasn't only politics or the notion of revenge that made Alvaro pull for this Virgin. It was also on account of Pop. Only two weeks ago Alvaro had gone to visit Pop at his shack on Lake Tahoe. This was shortly after the Virgin first appeared. Pop, who rarely missed a day's news, had remarked, "Who knows, maybe she's for real." Alvaro detected a glimpse of hope in the old wise man.

Whatever faith Pop had grown up with had gotten wrung out of him by a vicious world. Then he met Wendy, Alvaro's second mamá, who had suffered more at the hands of wicked men than most anybody. First, with the crimes of her wicked father. Then a man she trusted sold her to a gang of German and Mexican Nazis, who gave her a trip through hell. Still her faith endured, and she resurrected Pop's hope, at least a smidgen of it. But she died. And the world had gotten no less vicious. By now, Pop needed a booster.

The way Alvaro read him, Pop didn't exactly fear death, but the thought of eternal separation from the people he loved was so bitter, he wouldn't accept it without a fight.

Alvaro continued reading, about Baja California's Catholic Bishop going to Agua Dulce to see the girl's sketch of the Virgin. Several of the local priests had judged her to be genuine, thanks particularly to the amber flecks that issued from her eyes. One of them called the flecks "pearls from heaven" and claimed they were seen by many of the blessed who had witnessed true manifestations of the Holy Mother. But the Bishop contended she might be some trick of man or Satan. Alvaro suspected this Bishop was a PRI stooge. Even though the party affected an atheist stance, it had long ago made a devil's pact with the church.

What Alvaro found most puzzling was the PRI's apparent neutrality. No official, not even Tijuana's voluble municipal governor, had declared her a fraud.

He went to a shelf in his bedroom where he kept a box of maps. He found one of Baja California, returned to the table in the dining nook and marked the sightings by date.

She had first shown up on a rocky hillside near Dos Lobos, about fifteen kilometers southeast of La Rumorosa on the eastern rim of the Sierra de Juarez. Three days later, she appeared about eighty kilometers due south, near Las Cuevitas, at an Indian burial ground below what Roxie Hewitt called "a labyrinth of caves." Next she visited the children of La Rosa de Castilla halfway between the village and the Agua Dulce mine, where Yolanda Elena Morales sketched her image. Eight days later, she blessed the children of

Rillito, a hundred kilometers south of Agua Dulce, in the shadow of Cerro San Matias in the Sierra San Pedro Martir. Last Thursday, she visited Porvenir, an hour southeast of Ensenada. And Sunday, the day before yesterday, she had revisited Rillito.

Nothing he read convinced him that the Virgin was or wasn't the lady's sister. He stood and stacked the clipped articles. Before he returned the rest of the newspapers to the recycling bin, he found today's financial section and looked up the current price of gold. $368 per ounce.

He stood shaking his head for a minute. Then he crept to the wall near the door to the bedroom, pressed his ear to the wall and listened. All he heard was a faint gnawing he supposed was a mouse feeding on the newsprint the builders had used as insulation. He stepped back and rapped his head with his knuckles. Somehow, he needed to kick his nagging suspicion that Lourdes might be something more divine than simple flesh. A good start might be to catch the men who were tailing her.

He tapped lightly on the spare room door. The lady didn't answer. He silently opened the door and tiptoed through to the window that looked onto the back yard. He rolled the window shut, set the hook in place.

In his room, he slipped into moccasins and a black hooded windbreaker with big pockets. His .22 fit into one of them.

Chapter Six

He flicked off the bedroom light, turned the dimmers in the living room and kitchen, and rapped on the kitchen wall near the front door, opposite the other unit's kitchen where Winona and Chief would most likely be sucking Camels, their ears to the wall. "Hey, *amigos*, shut Frank up. It's lullaby time."

He secured the other windows. Then he turned out the lights and went through the dark living room to the front door, and locked it. He left the house through the back door, locked and dead-bolted it using his key and crept between his carport and the next house, which served as base for a half dozen flight attendants, two of whom Alvaro had dated. Aside from that house and his duplex, the neighborhood was mostly single family detached homes occupied by retired military or families with kids.

On the sidewalk, he told himself, Okay, cool down, she's probably just a woman like any other, with admirable traits and a bunch of hang ups that would send you packing in a month or so, even if you can keep her from getting robbed and murdered or snatched by the *federales*. You're not her soldier or anybody's. All you're doing is working as a gumshoe one more time.

The rain had lightened to warmish spurts like a shower in a budget motel. He peered both ways. All but a few of the neighborhood's house lights were out. He noticed one unfamiliar vehicle curbside, a white Pacific Bell van across the street at the west end of the block. He ducked back into his carport, squished across his back lawn to the alley, jogged up the alley to the end of the block and turned right on 9th. He crossed G Avenue swinging his arms like a power walker. When he passed in front of the van, he shot a long glance through the windshield. Nobody in the seats. The rear was all cabinets and tool boxes.

He continued two blocks west and crossed back to his side of G Avenue. He walked the alley past his duplex and two blocks farther then came around front and returned home thinking, if the PRI was after the lady, say using her to get to her sister, they would have almost as many resources as the CIA. They might be watching the house using some gadget that sees through walls, or tailing Lourdes with cameras mounted on a satellite.

He had seen nothing notable except a boy sneaking into a house through a window and a fat woman dancing alone behind a gauze curtain. But, as he dug in a pocket for his keys, he noticed something new. On the other side of his street and across 9th, three car lengths past the intersection, beyond a fire hydrant, a red Buick was parked where one hadn't been ten minutes ago. He leaned on a porch rail, watching the Buick until he thought he saw either a head or headrest move.

He was half way across his street when thunder cracked. As he reached the far curb, a wicked volley of rain fell. The driver of the Buick flicked a cigarette out the window, fired the motor, and stomped the gas. At the intersection, he skidded a three-quarter turn, straightened the car, and zoomed away, spraying up a tail of water.

Though Alvaro had failed to get any letters or numbers, he recognized the license plate as one from Baja California. And he decided that whoever they were, they were no amateurs. And they would no doubt return.

◇◇◇

Back home, he dug through a closet for the shotgun Pop had sawed off years ago and given to Clifford when the Cossacks came looking for him. They thought twenty-two months in road camp was too light a sentence for killing one of them. But possession of the shotgun gave Ava night terrors. So it came to Alvaro, who kept it loaded with birdshot. Non-lethal but able to inflict nasty wounds. Tonight he would keep it beside his bed.

Holding the gun, he stood by the door to the spare room and wished he could dream up sufficient justification to go in and watch the lady sleep for a minute. Maybe he should open her window, he thought. But he preferred to keep it locked. Maybe he should just go in for a look. If she woke and caught him, he could explain that he considered women the most splendid and mysterious creations. And, this lady that Augie Quartilho, a crook and reprobate, had sent him, might be the deepest mystery of all.

◇◇◇

He awoke at five wondering where to stash the lady's eight bars of gold. His clock radio played a Mozart sonata. Though classical piano didn't jolt him awake like Hendrix would, it helped him approach the day more optimistically, with hope that beneath all the crises and chaos, life was scored in harmonies. Which helped him stave off the gloom that too often led to his excesses.

He started coffee, rapped on the bedroom door, slipped into a clean T-shirt and loose jeans with big pockets, and moccasins. When he heard the door to the bathroom shut, he went out to stash the pistol in the '55 Chevy station wagon he and Clifford had beefed up and restored. They kept it at Alvaro's because Ava wanted her husband to put the past behind him, which included giving up the car his mother died in. Besides, Alvaro wouldn't be able to afford another car until he became a real lawyer, and his job with Garfield et al called for frequent trips into Mexico. In Mexico, on city streets or country roads, the sturdier the vehicle the better.

The storm had blown away, leaving the air steamy and the sky, already brightening, flecked with stars. He caught the first whiff of a Santa Ana, the wind off the desert that charged the air with something that intensified every emotion, such as Alvaro's longing for whatever it was he couldn't name but which he caught himself imagining the lady could offer.

He walked out front and looked around for the Buick. He went to the ends of the block and peered both ways, around and through trees and hedges. No sign of anybody except a flight attendant who waved as she ran to her Dodge Dart convertible. Still, Alvaro couldn't get over feeling watched.

He gathered the lady's clothes from the dryer and carried them inside. He found her making coffee, her face bare, without powder or lipstick, in her yellow dress. He believed he would remember the sight. The Virgin homemaker. She relieved him of the laundry and delivered it to her room.

She took her coffee black, her toast with jam, her apple quartered and peeled. "What shall we do with your gold?" he asked.

"A bank? Perhaps a deposit box."

"By the time a bank's open," he said, "we'll be over the border. If you wanted the gold in a Mexican bank, it would already be there, no?"

"You are right."

"How'd you get it over the border, through customs?"

"Señor Quartilho drove me across, on his way to meet someone in Chula Vista. Customs asked us nothing."

"Augie's friends get rewarded," he said.

"There is a safe in your house?"

He remembered what the previous owner had called his strong box. A place to stash drugs, the man's wink had suggested when he showed the box to Alvaro, probably hoping it might clinch the sale to a guy who'd lately returned from a tour of duty in Vietnam, where soldiers found abundant drugs and plenty of reason to use them.

"I've got a place," Alvaro said. "Let's get busy while it's still pretty dark."

In the time it took him to open a drawer and take out a flashlight, she went to the spare room and returned carrying two bars. She handed them to Alvaro and went back for more. He estimated their weight at ten pounds each. He calculated 32 ounces at $368 per. Better than $100,000 each. Not quite a million in all, but close enough.

As she delivered the bars two by two, he packed

them into two canvas tote bags he used to carry groceries. When he'd finished and went to lift them, he wrapped the straps around his wrists and still felt as if each hand carried a body builder's dumbbell.

Lourdes followed him out through the carport. The wood-fenced backyard was smaller than the carport, and darker as the glow from the street lamp didn't reach it. He set down the bags and peered in every direction. His mind declared nobody was watching, but his instincts felt otherwise. He knelt at the door to the crawl space under the back porch. The lady knelt beside him. He lifted the door, peered in, raked his hand through a curtain of spider webs and squeezed through the opening. Leading with his flashlight, he crawled to a corner eight feet away, where he scraped in the dirt until he located a handle and pulled. The wooden box, except its cover, was buried. Rot had eaten holes big enough for rats or gophers. The floor of the box was caked in mud. Wishing he had thought to bring a trash bag, rather than go back inside for one, he stripped off his T-shirt and laid it on the floor of the box. He crawled back to the entrance and reached out. Lourdes passed him the gold bars, two at a time. He carried them to the box, laid them in a stack, four abreast, on top of his T-shirt. He folded the T-shirt over the gold, closed the box and spread a layer of dirt over it.

Even after he crawled out and gazed all around and saw nothing suspicious, he couldn't quit feeling uneasy about leaving a million dollars in that place. Still, he gave the lady a confident nod.

He followed her inside. While she filled her big purse with clothes and toiletries, Alvaro changed the message on his answer phone. "Today's Wednesday, June 27. I'm in Baja. Back no later than Friday, I hope."

◇◇◇

At Orange Avenue, he turned right toward the business district and drove to a newsstand beside Lucy's All-Nite Cafe. This morning's *Diario*, Tijuana's daily news, hadn't arrived. He settled for yesterday's edition.

He asked the lady if she had much cash. Less than $50, she said. He ran into Lucy's. The only waitress was a shy girl named Tita whose student visa had expired long ago. Either because he had offered to help her get legal, or because she had a crush on him, she let him cash a check for $200. He walked out musing over the irony that he would be paying expenses when the lady had a million in gold.

Mexico was only a few minutes down the Silver Strand, the land bridge that kept Coronado from being an island, then through Imperial Beach and down I-5 through San Ysidro. But Alvaro preferred to drive on the north side of the border and cross in Tecate, forty-some miles east. The shorter their stay in Mexico, the less chance the lady would get recognized.

He made a U-turn. "Look, I'm trusting your papers are all in order. What kind of visa did Augie get you?"

"*Señor* Quartilho arranged for my tourist visa."

"I mean is the visa legit?"

"I don't know 'legit.'"

"Legal. I don't suppose Augie would've told you, but he arranges both kinds."

In the pause before she said, "It is legal," from her eyes, Alvaro knew better. At least her third lie, he thought, and told himself the Holy Virgin wouldn't lie. He had barely entertained, even as whimsy, the notion that Lourdes might be the honest-to-God Holy Virgin. Still, he felt a portion of disappointment. But after a moment he realized that he probably had no idea what a Holy Virgin would or wouldn't do.

"So," he said, "what's your real name?"

Her eyes drilled his. "Maria de Lourdes."

"Maria de Lourdes what?"

"Garcia."

"No it's not."

After at least a minute of silence during which he glanced over twice and saw her staring at him, she said, "My name was Shuler. No more. My father is dead."

Alvaro drummed his fingers on the dash. "Okay, so how about you tell me why Lupe killed him?"

They were crossing the bridge into San Diego just

as the sun tipped over the mountains and flashed the harbor and downtown skyscrapers a dozen shades of golden. The lady leaned heavily into her seat and cast her eyes down, as if gazing at the yellow of her skirt would keep her from distraction. "Lupe was eighteen. Our rancho is twelve kilometers of perilous road from the town. My father prized his seclusion…"

◇◇◇

Alvaro didn't quite hear the story. He saw it. All the while he attended to the road, he also entered the Shuler house.

It was built from stone, on the side of a hill overlooking a wooded valley. A narrow road wound up to it. The spacious parlor was furnished with heavy mahogany chairs and tables, all except the one with padding and soft leather where Hans Shuler sat. Lupe was on her knees in front of her father. She wore a modest party dress, yellow with white birds and butterflies. Her golden hair was pinned up and adorned with a yellow rose. The skin of her bare arms and face appeared to glow from an inner light. She held her father's hand with both hers and kissed it. Between kisses, she pleaded, "Papá, you must trust me."

Hans Shuler was slender and looked strong and younger than his sixty-some years. His hair was dark brown. He had a sharp face and crafty, wandering eyes. His voice was a long-time smoker's rasp. "I will trust Doña Flor," he said.

After Lupe and Doña Flor left in a pickup driven by a ranch hand, wind came in gusts that gave way to a steady howl through the walnut and almond trees. Branches cracked. Limbs slapped against the house and scratched at the windows. Dark came, then rain. Even before it turned to hail, it sounded like machine gun fire.

In the parlor, the mother perched on a sofa bench gazing out the window toward the road. She was a copper-skinned mestizo less than half Hans Shuler's age. Her face looked chiseled, then bent and broken from years of abuse and neglect. Near her, Lourdes and Rolf sat beside a game table with a chess board set up. Rolf was fourteen, gangly and possessed by indignation. He kept shooting fierce glances at his father. Lourdes wouldn't look at the old man. She hated his lascivious eyes and feared he would call her over, insist she sit on his lap, and fondle her hair.

Nobody except Lourdes knew that Lupe intended to dance with a boy named Pepe who came to the Shuler *hacienda* every week delivering feed for the cattle and horses. Lourdes had warned her sister that their father would surely pay someone to watch her, and that he would punish her for dancing with a common boy. Hans raised and educated his daughters to marry powerful men, so these men could install his sons into high positions.

In the corner of the parlor farthest from the

window was an antique clock from which cuckoo birds used to mark the hours. The cuckoo mechanism broke, but the clock still told time. At ten minutes before ten, the hour Lupe was due home from the Christmas party, Hans turned his chair toward the clock and set on the floor the book he'd been reading, a volume of the collected works of Johann Ficthe.

While the hail became sleet and the wind uprooted trees, Lourdes, Rolf, and their mother listened to the radio. They heard a forecast that this would be the cruelest storm in decades, that the winds could reach gale force and the temperature might fall low enough to bring snow, which Lourdes had never seen.

At nine-thirty, Hans ordered Lourdes to turn off the radio. The mother began praying the rosary. As the hour approached, Lourdes and Rolf went to sit on the sofa bench beside their mother, one on each side.

At five minutes before ten, they saw the truck. The mother leaped up and flew to the front door, which opened onto a porch that ran along the north and east sides of the house.

Doña Flor came running through the sleet from the truck and onto the porch. She was alone. At the doorway she met and embraced the mother. Through her sobs she reported that Lupe had slipped away, and that someone saw her with Pepe Velasquez in his uncle's old Chevrolet.

Hans had come to stand behind the mother. He shoved her aside and lifted a fist above Doña Flor. She didn't move or wince. But when Hans pointed to the kitchen, she slinked away, weeping.

After Hans slammed the door and shoved the safety bolt into place, he went through the kitchen to the pantry, to the back door. Even with the storm blowing, from two rooms away, Lourdes heard the lock click and the bolt scrape.

Before Hans returned to the parlor, he went to his office, opened his gun cabinet, and took an old pistol from its rack. He shut and locked the cabinet, walked back to the parlor, and sat in his leather chair, staring at the door.

The mother sat facing him, relentlessly shaking her head. Lourdes and Rolf stood beside her, each holding one of her hands while Lourdes demanded, "No, Papá. Please put your gun away," and Rolf kept asking, "Who are you going to shoot?"

They heard a motor. Lourdes and Rolf were first at the door. But their father gripped the scruffs of their necks and flung them away. He posted himself at the door. A car door slammed. An old car pulled away. Lupe ran out of the storm, onto the porch. She clutched at the doorknob. When it refused to turn, she pulled and pushed. "Please, Papá," she shouted. "I am freezing, please, please!'"

Lourdes was on her knees hanging onto her

father's leg. Lupe cried out, "I only went with Pepe to pick up his sister from the movie and take her home, but the car skidded off the road."

Hans raised his gun. "I do not know you," he rasped. "You are trespassing." He aimed the gun.

Lourdes screamed. The mother wailed. Rolf attempted to bellow "No!" but his voice cracked.

With her party dress and shawl lashing in the wind, Lupe disappeared into the sleet. Rolf dashed through the kitchen to the back door and outside with Lourdes and their mother close behind. They ran different ways, Lourdes through the almond and walnut groves toward the barn. But Hans stalked and caught them, one by one. In place of the pistol, he carried his favorite toy, a bull whip. He used it to herd them inside.

◇◇◇

Alvaro swerved to miss a box in the road. "He whipped you?"

"I could show you a scar. He was a terrible man." She bit her lower lip until Alvaro thought it might bleed. "He sent our ranch hand to search the barn and, if he found her, to chase her away."

Though her tale sounded more like a *telenovela* than reality, Alvaro believed it. "And your brother who lives in the Capital, he was already grown up and gone?"

"Yes. He is my father's eldest son. He is an advisor to the *presidente*."

"President of what?"

"Mexico."

Alvaro gulped. "He's PRI?"

"Yes."

"Does he know about the gold bars?"

"I think he does not."

He shook his head, rubbed his neck and thought, if he'd chosen to take on this job for the money, a million in gold wouldn't be one-tenth enough.

Chapter Seven

Alvaro told the lady, "When we cross the border, we're behind enemy lines. You're going to need to stick close to me. Have you got makeup?"

"I have only lipstick."

"We'll stop then, and you can paint up like a floozy. You know 'floozy'?"

"I know."

He tapped the *Diario* on the seat between them. "Look through it, would you? See what you find on the Virgin."

Alvaro rolled down his window. The sky was cloudless. The heat promised to become lethal. As they entered the eastbound ramp onto Highway 94, she found a story. She read it and summarized. "Oh, thousands of pilgrims, some from far away in Europe and Australia, are devoting their vacations to roaming the mountains of Baja California. They hope to be at the place where the Virgin comes.

"Some of these pilgrims are crippled. Or they are dying of cancer or other maladies and seeking the Virgin's power to heal. Priests and nuns are among them, and protestant missionaries. And all over Mexico, crazy prophets are warning the people to trust Our Lady's message and expel the PRI with their votes. Many of the crazy prophets are in jail because some of the crowds who listened to them attacked the police as they tried to keep order. You see, this reporter praises the PRI, because none of the party's candidates for national or state offices have called the Virgin a fraud."

Because somebody at the top was stepping on them, Alvaro believed. Somebody was writing their lines. "Your brother Andres, he's an advisor to the *presidente?* That's no lie?"

Her dark golden eyebrows drew closer together. "It is no lie."

"But Doña Flor wouldn't have told him about seeing Lupe?"

"No," she said with conviction. "Andres is not our ally. He is my father's son, and is not to be trusted."

A mile after the freeway ended and Route 94 became a four lane, Alvaro pulled into a strip mall and parked in front of a Thrifty Drug. The lady followed him past puddles left by the storm and into the store. In the cosmetics aisle, he helped pick out scarlet lipstick, eye-liner, powder, mascara, and a small case with a mirror.

Back in the car, while the lady blotched powder on, he said, "Looks like you haven't used that stuff very often."

She nodded and scratched powder from her cheeks.

"I know your father was a…"

She stopped him with a frown, as if she'd heard the epithet before he let it out. He softened his voice. "I know your father was strict. But, smart as you are, you must've gone away to school or university."

"I have only lived with my family."

He turned to pondering what her circumscribed life could mean. Either the Nazi had kept her home by coercion, or she was a weakling who feared the big world. But weaklings don't often steal gold and smuggle it out of a country. As he watched her fuss with eyeliner, she looked no weaker than a grizzly.

"So, tell me if I've got this straight. We're going to Baja not only to find your sister, but once we find her, we need to get her somewhere safe, where the *federales,* or any other of the PRI stooges, or God knows who all, can't get to her."

The lady gave a sharp nod.

◇◇◇

Clifford had been up since dawn, skimming through his files of clippings on crime and corruption in Mexico, particularly Baja California. He kept the files because his only regular source of income was the feature articles he wrote for the *Epitaph,* and by all indications the *Epitaph's* readers loved to wallow in crime and corruption.

The clippings were replete with intrigue, murders, twists, and scandals. But Clifford found nothing that seemed what his brother wanted. Besides, he wasn't at all sure what Alvaro wanted.

Over two cups of coffee, he tried to remember the face of the woman he had spied in Alvaro's front room, and wondered why she looked familiar.

At seven, he made a phone call.

As soon as Tom Hickey heard his son's voice, he asked, "How's Feliz?"

"Still got the headache. Her temp's about one-oh-two. I'm going to take her to the doctor this morning. Listen, have you talked to X recently?"

"About a week ago," Tom said.

"Well, last night he called and asked me to get the scoop on the PRI and this vagabond Virgin. He'd like to know why the PRI isn't smearing her and what their plans are regarding her these last few days before the election."

"Sunday," Tom said.

"The election. Yeah, four days is all."

"Could be just nerves. If your brother met a genie and got one wish, I'll bet he'd ask the genie to bring down the PRI."

"That's not the whole of it," Clifford said. "I didn't quite buy what he told me, so I went down to his place and snooped, peeked in and saw him with this woman. A knockout."

"And?"

"And I figured you'd want to know Alvaro's acting peculiar. I mean, why would he break from a hot date to call me unless it was for something more urgent than what he said, which was about racking up a favor for the bandits of Garfield et al?"

"I'm with you," Tom said.

"And he's already gone. To Baja, from what he told me last night. I'll bet he's looking for the Virgin. Do you think Harry might know somebody deep in the PRI?"

Tom was living in the four-room cabin he had built long ago on the Incline Village shore of Lake Tahoe. His closest neighbor, Harry Poverman, whose mansion featured bathrooms as big as the Hickeys' cabin, had founded casinos and invested in Mexican racetracks. And though Tom had scruples Harry didn't subscribe to, they were *compadres*.

"I'll wander over and ask," Tom said. "If I wake Harry up before nine, he might have his boys crucify me, to set an example. I'll give him a couple hours. When you talk to your brother, ask him to break away from the gal long enough to call me. And you, give me a ring as soon as you get Feliz home from the doctor. Could be the wonder girl needs her grandpa."

"Maybe so."

As he hung up, Clifford heard his wife whisper to Feliz, "It tastes like cherries, I promise. Don't hold it in your mouth, just swallow."

Clifford thought: Mexico, politics. He found himself looking for the phone number of Pete Carrillo, an *amigo* from college who had gone with the FBI. Last Clifford knew, Pete was in Phoenix. He found Pete's work number, called it, and reached a machine.

After Pete's greeting, Clifford's brief lament that they hadn't talked lately, and his suggestion they meet next time Pete came to the coast, he said, "Alvaro's in Baja, looking for the Holy Virgin. I've got to know if he's in any danger, because he wants to know things like who's behind her. Say, if it's one of the opposition parties, which one is it? If it's the church, is a schism happening or what? Any facts or rumors will help. How hot an issue is she? And I want to know, should I worry about my brother? *Mil gracias, amigo.*"

Feliz screamed.

Chapter Eight

The old highway that paralleled the border climbed into woodlands of oak and sage and grazing cattle. Alvaro shot glances at the lady, who appeared to turn ever more gloomy. He might've tried to cheer her with conversation, but he needed to concentrate on forming some tentative plan and on watching out for Benito or any other of their potential foes.

The name Shuler kept resonating in his mind, but it didn't connect with anything. Which was no reason to question her. The way he understood Mexican politics, the wheels whose squeaking the *presidente* heeded would kill to remain anonymous.

He watched two vehicles that reappeared on every long straightaway. One of them continued on the highway when Alvaro turned south on Route 188. The other, a Chevy pickup with Baja plates, continued following them. Shortly after 7:30, they crossed the border with only a nod from a weary Mexican guard.

Alvaro sighed his relief, though he had no reason to worry about a search, which wouldn't likely expose the small .22 in the socket wrench case in his tool box.

Tecate had a reputation as the cleanest of border towns. A few tourists came to visit the brewery or the organic, holistic meditation and health spa. San Diegans came for cheap bricks and hand painted tiles. But the town mostly catered to the surrounding farms. The altitude, about 3000 feet, and the distance from cities, left the air fresher, crisper than in the coastal lowlands, even as today's hot and dry Santa Ana wind whooshed through.

But Tecate was Mexico, which meant the only way people could avoid the sight of misery was by refusing to look. This morning, Alvaro saw a screaming, staggering woman topple off a sidewalk into a muddy gutter. He saw two boys thrashing a smaller boy, then running off with something they had stolen from him. The little boy kept slinging rocks in the direction they ran even after they had disappeared down a side street.

The Chevy pickup followed Alvaro's station wagon into central Tecate and pulled to the curb in front of a hardware store. The driver climbed out, went to the shop's entrance, knocked a few times and got let inside.

Alvaro continued on Calle Cárdenas to Parque Hidalgo and stopped beside the grassy plaza where the dozen laborers who hadn't already gotten hired stood waiting for another farmer to appear. Several of them approached Alvaro's window. He dismissed them and asked the lady if she wanted anything, like food or a wash room. She didn't.

He rooted in the glove box for the Baja map he kept there and handed it to her. "Can you remember the names of the villages?"

"I remember them all."

"Circle them, please," he said. "There's a pen in the glove box."

He left her in the wagon and walked into a corner *tienda*. One step inside, he turned and watched out the door. Nobody had approached his wagon. While he shopped, he kept passing the door and glancing outside. He selected a pair of bat wing sunglasses and a brown floppy hat for the lady. At the counter he stood sideways, one eye on his wagon. After he paid, he asked the clerk, "If you were hoping to see the Virgin, which village would you go to?"

"*Pues*, Dos Lobos?"

Back in the wagon, he told Lourdes the village name. She held out the map with the villages circled and the dates noted beside them. Dos Lobos, Tuesday June 5, three weeks ago yesterday. Los Cuevitas, three days later. Agua Dulce, Sunday June 10. Then Rillito on Monday, June 18. Porvenir, Thursday, June 21, six days ago. And back to Rillito just last Sunday.

Along the road east of Tecate, old tractors poofed columns of smoke. A gang heaved shovels of black dirt out of a trench, hand-digging what *gringos* wouldn't have touched without a backhoe. The wind had turned gusty. A dust devil hopped and swiveled through a grape arbor. The Mexicali bus roared up from behind, its cowcatcher like a locomotive's, as though it meant to knock Alvaro's wagon from the mountains all the way to the desert floor. But it swerved and flashed by, running a westbound flatbed carrying hay bales over the shoulder. The flatbed clipped a fence and ripped out some lengths of barbed wire. The bus two-wheeled the turn. It vanished behind a rocky mound.

The farther east, the rockier the land became. Granite boulders appeared to have grown out of the soil like mammoth melons, too big and too many to clear. Farmers had cultivated around them and planted tomato, corn, apple trees, and bush beans.

At El Condor, a village a few miles short of La Rumorosa, Alvaro turned south onto a graded dirt road. They rattled past structures fashioned from old trailer and car parts, or from rusted buses, or from jagged rocks that appeared fitted together without mortar, or from stacked hay bales roofed with patched canvas. Alvaro couldn't tell if some of them were homes or goat pens.

He said, "Prosperity, thanks to the PRI."

The lady smiled. "You don't approve of the PRI."

"You could say that. So tell me, when we find your sister in Dos Lobos or wherever, are we supposed to try and stop her from posing as the Virgin?"

She watched his face for a half-minute before she answered. "The more times she poses, the more she is in danger."

"So we're going to take her out of the game."

"Now you tell me this, please," the lady said. "Would you rather help me find my sister, or help my sister hurt the PRI?"

"You want an honest answer, right?"

"I want to believe you."

"Then I'll have to think about it."

He did, and his thoughts became ugly. He wondered if the lady could be in cahoots with her brother Andres and through him with the PRI. That would make Alvaro a pigeon working for his life-long enemy.

He wondered if Lourdes might've invented the tale about Lupe's disappearance, when truly the girl had lived at home until she went mad and shot her abusive father. Or Lupe might be a spoiled debutante who got enraged because daddy wouldn't buy her a Jaguar of her own. Say she'd run to her friends, one of whom was a student radical contemplating the overthrow of the PRI, and he had seen her Virgin potential and enlisted her.

Farther down the dirt road, the cattle were skinnier, the sheep grayer, and the goats abundant and curious. They ran and leaped toward Alvaro's wagon as if they planned to eat it.

As the Chevy passed through a village called Piedras Gordas, children swarmed to the roadside waving bandanas and sombreros and shouting. When Alvaro heard shouts that sounded like, "*Viva la Virgen*," he braked.

He asked the lady to tip her floppy hat forward. Then he jumped out and held up a hand to quiet the kids' requests for candy, dollars, and the Padres cap he wore. He asked if any of them had seen the Virgin. They shouted and pointed down the road toward Dos Lobos, calling out the names of the blessed children, which Alvaro already had gotten from the *Sentinel* and jotted into his steno pad.

They passed through more villages, Cisneros and Jacaranda, quizzed more children and got the same answers. Go to Dos Lobos. *Derecho, derecho.* While leaving Jacaranda, Alvaro leaned out the window and looked back the way they had come. He saw no rooster tails of dust. Which meant anybody who might be tailing them was at least a mile behind.

Far from the nearest village, they passed a trio of men beside the road. They looked wild, as if they hadn't washed in a year. They were squatting in a semicircle around something furry and dead, and watching Alvaro's wagon pass as if they feared he might be a *ladrón* come to steal their prize.

As the wagon rounded a hillock, the village of Dos Lobos appeared on a rise a mile ahead. To their left was what looked like the site of a deserted mine, a cutaway hillside of reddish brown dirt. A new trail, sided in tall grass and weeds and deeply rutted from tires, led to a makeshift campground at the base of the hill. Motor homes, tents, pickups with shells, vans, at least twenty in all. Plus a few cars of day visitors already arrived from Tijuana, about sixty miles west, or Mexicali in the desert nearly as far east.

Alvaro groaned and rubbed his forehead. The lady said, "Too many people."

"Yeah. And at least one of them is in a red Buick." He pointed.

Chapter Nine

Alvaro turned off the road onto the trail toward the campground. He eased the Chevy over the ruts, though he trusted his driving skill to take them where novices in four-by-fours shouldn't go.

He parked at the end of the row of day visitors, six cars from the Buick and about fifty yards of meadow from the motor home-and-tent campground. He asked the lady to stay in the wagon. Then he crept around the rear of the line of cars to the red Buick. Its plates were from Baja, like those of the Buick that tailed them in Coronado.

For the next ten minutes he and the lady wandered through the campground scrutinizing *campesinos,* society matrons, priests and nuns, newshounds, shutterbugs. Since Benito might be wearing a cap, boots with high heels, and overalls in place of his black waiter's outfit, Alvaro studied faces. None looked even vaguely like Benito's bland mug. And, Alvaro comforted himself by noting, no one appeared to suspect that the painted lady in a floppy hat and bat wing sunglasses might be their Virgin in disguise.

They tramped through knee-high weeds to the west side of the hill and climbed to where they could look down at the spot where the Virgin had appeared, in a cutaway at the base of the hill that might once have been a sand or granite quarry. Several dozen folks clustered around the three children who sat on lawn chairs next to a motor home. Alvaro studied each of them. On the way back to the wagon, he said, "Either Benito isn't around, we're blind, he's hiding in a tent or motor home, or he got replaced by somebody we wouldn't recognize. Which is it?"

Without hesitation, she said, "I think we must not let such thoughts concern us."

"Okay, suppose we find Lupe, only Benito snatches her from us and kills her, or turns her in to the *federales*. That's not our concern?"

"Not yet," the lady said, which prompted more of Alvaro's suspicions, the darkest ones so far. That Lupe wasn't a murderer, but Lourdes was. That the lady meant to frame her sister for the crime.

The vehicle next to his wagon was a Dodge van with the logo of *Noticias Uno*, a Tijuana news station. A cameraman with bushy hair fringing his cap sat in the van's open side doorway and poked a toothpick into the machinery of a shoulder-mount video camera. He looked up and nodded.

"*¿Que pasa?*" Alvaro asked. "Why all the people?"

"Waiting for the Virgin, *hombre*. What else? She returned to Rillito, is what they are saying. Why not here too?"

"What do you think? Is she for real?"

"Don't ask me, *hombre*. Go ask the *niños*."

Alvaro ushered the lady into the wagon, closed the doors and rolled up the windows. Sunlight through the windshield threatened to ignite his jeans. The lady gave him a puzzled look.

"Maybe I'm paranoid," he said, "but the bad guys might have equipment so they can sit on top of a hill, point some gadget and hear us whisper. Inside the car is the most privacy we can get. So, are you ready and willing to go talk to these kids, take a chance on them recognizing you? Or should I go alone?"

"I want to go." She glanced at the mirror and grimaced. "I look so awful they will never think I am this Virgin."

"Nowhere near awful," Alvaro said. "Maybe not quite as classy as usual. Anyway, don't get too close. If they stare, you search for a cloud or an airplane. When you look down, if they're still staring, back off and lose them in the crowd."

They locked the wagon and tromped through red-brown sandy mud, both of them peering ahead and glancing side to side. Alvaro still watched for Benito. He wondered who Lourdes was looking for, if she might be part of a team of conspirators. He led her toward the base of the hill and the cluster of tourists outside a Greyhound-sized motor home lettered Golden West Vacation Rentals.

A plump blonde grandma in tight shorts waylaid them. "*Buenos días,*" she said in a Texas drawl. "*Me llamo* Nancy."

"We're *gringos*, Nancy," Alvaro said.

"Aw, sorry then. Look here though." She handed them each a matted copy of the savant girl's sketch of the Virgin. "And look on the back."

On the back of each was a hand-lettered verse of scripture. Nancy said, "This here's somethin' she told the kids down in Porvenir. 'Course they only remembered snatches, but the priest, he knew where it's written down. I made a deal with little Yolanda, ain't she some artist. I borrowed one of her drawings, ran into Ensenada and made copies. But I done the lettering myself. You can have one for only ten bucks. Two for eighteen."

Alvaro held the poster where he and Lourdes could both read: "Saint James prophesied, 'Now listen, you rich people, weep and wail because of the misery that is coming upon you. Your wealth has rotted, and moths have eaten your clothes. Your gold and silver are corroded. Their corrosion will testify against you and eat your flesh like fire. You have hoarded wealth in the last days. Look! The wages you failed to pay the workmen who mowed your fields are crying out against you. The cries of the harvesters have reached the ears of the Lord Almighty. You have lived on earth in luxury and self-indulgence. You have fattened yourselves in the day of slaughter. You have condemned and murdered innocent men who were not opposing you.'"

"And all that's right out of the Bible," Nancy said. "Sounds more like some Russian commie wrote it."

Alvaro reached for his wallet and handed the woman a ten. Lourdes slid the poster into her purse. The Texan said, "I got plenty more. You won't find a better gift to give your rich uncle. Ha ha!"

As they continued toward the crowd around the children, Alvaro stopped to watch men, women, girls, and boys carrying large stones along a path around the hill and laying them at the feet of masons who appeared half finished with the rear wall of a shrine. Three-sided. Six feet high. Several women were thatching a roof from saplings.

A whirling gust of reddish wind plucked off Lourdes' floppy hat. Campers laughed excessively to witness the painted lady and her escort scurrying after the hat like farm kids chasing chickens. Alvaro supposed they needed comic relief from the heat and the waiting.

The crowd around the children didn't all appear to be seekers of holiness, prophecy, or miracles. The notepads and tape recorders of a few revealed their motives. But five or six others, Alvaro sensed from their postures and their less-than-ardent expressions, could be somebody's agents.

He needed to figure out who they belonged to. If he had some conception of what kind of forces he would be called upon to outwit or outmaneuver, he might reasonably hope they had a chance in a million or so. Otherwise, clueless as he was, he couldn't keep stringing the lady along. Soon, unless he learned or decided she was conning and playing him for a sucker, he would be obliged to confess the truth. That his motive was more to stick with her than to accomplish the impossible by finding the Virgin.

Or else he'd need to find some angle that made possible the impossible, like Pop had sometimes done. But Alvaro, though he still carried a private investigator's license, felt like a semi-pro at best. The apprenticeship he and Clifford had served under Pop only taught them about libraries and basic surveillance. The three years he practiced the trade, he'd spent mostly on trickery such as tossing quarters on the sidewalk in front of an insurance crook's home and catching him on film when he threw down his crutches and scooped up the coins.

He saw nearby a tall, rosy-cheeked fellow who looked square enough to be an FBI rookie. Alvaro whispered to Lourdes, "Stay close to me." He went to stand beside the man, who noticed his approach and offered a polite smile.

Alvaro smiled back. "Let me guess. You're a priest."

The man chuckled. "A graphic designer, working my way through Baptist seminary. You?"

"Tourist. I had a week off, watched a news special and figured this was the happening place."

"Apparently it is."

"A lot's at stake here," Alvaro said.

"Excuse me?"

"Money. Power."

The man knitted his brow as though reflecting upon an issue he hadn't considered before. Then he nodded and drifted away.

Alvaro motioned to the lady, asking her to follow. He rounded the crowd to a fortyish man in a golf shirt and slacks. He had a yachtsman's tan. His mouth formed such an inverted U, Alvaro guessed his best smile would only turn it into a straight line. In all ways he looked as if he wouldn't be grubbing around this mud-hole if not for the salary and benefits.

The man glanced over, and Alvaro said, "Now, why couldn't the Virgin show up at Puerto Nuevo or someplace else with a paved road and a lobster restaurant?"

The man pointed at Alvaro's steno pad. "Are you a reporter?" His voice was peculiar, duck-like.

"My brother is. He's doing a piece for the *San Diego Epitaph*. I'm helping out."

"Well, then, what've you got so far?"

"Classified." He nodded and moved on, hoping that if this fellow was an agent, now that Alvaro had planted a bug, the man would soon enough give himself away.

Lourdes had gone ahead on her own. He caught up at the end of the semi-circle where the crowd was only two deep and from where she could see the children. They were sitting in the shade of the motor home, beneath the Golden West Vacation Rentals sunset logo, in folding camp chairs. The two boys sat to the right of their translator, a priest clothed in gray like a machinist. The girl was on his left. The boys could be brothers. The girl was skinnier, smaller. She looked starved, yet she wore the broadest grin. All three appeared between five and nine years old.

A voice from a woman Alvaro couldn't see hollered in Spanish, "You, *niño*." She must've pointed, as the smaller boy leaned forward. The voice demanded, "You said she promised to return?"

The boy gave a confident nod, but the girl called out, "No she didn't."

"We didn't hear her say that," the older boy added.

Still the voice persisted. "Did she say when? Or where?"

The little boy shook his head. The voice made a groan then fell silent. Alvaro turned to a nun beside him. "I wonder what makes these people think she's going to show up when adults are around? So far, she only trusts kids, no?"

Hushed as though passing along a secret, the nun said, "Our Lady often appears first to children and subsequently, in the same location, to a wider audience."

An older man in a Panama hat called out in English, "You kids all agree she came from the clouds and rose into the clouds before she vanished?"

After the priest translated, the two boys shouted yes, but the girl said, "Not the clouds, the sky."

A young woman in a wheelchair waved her bony arm. The priest placed a finger to his lips and gazed around to silence the crowd. The cripple cupped her hands around her mouth. "Did you touch her?" she stammered in Spanish.

The girl and littlest boy said they tried to touch her, but she was like a ghost they could see through. The older boy nodded with conviction. At the priest's encouragement, he said, "*La Señora* held my hand." The priest translated. Sighs and moans rose out of the crowd.

The nun leaned close to Alvaro. "Believe that one," she advised. "The others, surely they were too frightened to come close."

The girl who sat beside the priest was staring at Lourdes. Alvaro watched her eyes widen. Her hand groped toward the older boy.

Alvaro sidestepped in front of the lady, clutched her arm and hustled her away, toward and through the campground, listening for commotion from behind them. He didn't look back until they were seated in the wagon and he had fired the motor.

Then he saw that only a few of the crowd had followed them. A nun, or someone disguised as one. Not the nun he'd talked to, but a younger, prettier one. And an older man, at least sixty, probably a *gringo*, who looked dressed for a soccer game. And the fellow with brush cut hair and a duck's voice.

Alvaro didn't bid them goodbye.

Chapter Ten

Feliz was in Mission Bay hospital, sedated so she wouldn't freak about the IV or the tubes they had stuck up her nose to drain her sinuses. Without them, according to the doctor, the sinus infection could break through the sinus wall and enter her brain.

Clifford sat almost three hours with her. When Ava returned from an errand, he went to the lobby and used the pay phone to call home. He tried to access messages. They only sputtered and hissed at him. Back in Feliz's room, he paced and fidgeted until Ava said, "For God's sake, go home and make your calls."

The hospital was five minutes from their house. He promised to return in an hour.

At home, after trying the answering machine in person, he unplugged it, slammed it into the nearby trash can, and vowed to subscribe to a human answering service. Then he made a call. When Pop came on, Clifford said, "My machine is junk. Did you leave me a message?"

"Yep, one at your home and one at the office."

"What was the message?"

"Get your brother out of Mexico," Tom said.

"Oh boy, that might not be so easy." Clifford wasn't going to trouble Pop with news about his granddaughter in the hospital.

Tom said, "Tell him I went over and asked Harry if he could tap into the PRI, let us know why they're not trying to squash or even smear this militant Virgin. Well, Harry's always keen to do us a favor. He said no problem. But when I go back there in an hour, he's wearing his grim reaper look. And he says, 'Get your kid the hell out of Mexico. If he already found this Virgin, don't even let him stop to kiss her goodbye.' So I push him a little, and all I get is that certain nongovernmental big shots are not in accord with the PRI's strategy, and they've got employees posted all over Baja waiting for the Virgin to show up, so they can determine if she'll survive a bullet between the eyes. If she does, they'll repent in sackcloth and ashes.

"But she's not our problem, Clifford. Your brother is. And if he's standing next to her when the shooting starts, you know. You can't tell me Alvaro's stake in this game?"

"I wish I knew. Did Harry let on what exactly is the PRI's strategy?"

"He didn't say. If I were a guesser, I might suppose they want to discredit her before they get rid of her. Otherwise, she becomes a martyr. A cross between Joan of Arc and Che Guevara. A rallying cry. That way, even if she doesn't get the job done this election, there's another in three years. Time for the legend to grow."

Clifford was processing that notion when Tom added, "Do you recognize the name Andres Shuler?"

"Not offhand."

"Well, Harry's man mentioned this Shuler was lobbying for the lay-off-the Virgin-until-we-nab-her policy. So, I go to the library in South Lake. Not much of a library, but I did find enough on Andres Shuler to make him look like he could be one of the puppeteers that pick the *presidente* and then pull his strings. And, I can't say this means anything to us, but I stumbled on a murder. Andres Shuler's father, name of Hans. A big shot financier."

"Hmmm," Clifford said, only half attentive, because out of nowhere a picture from last night had come to him. "Crap."

"Excuse me?"

"That girl in Alvaro's house last night, I thought she looked familiar. Just now I figured out why."

◇◇◇

Alvaro drove fast, four miles back toward the Tecate highway, past the villages of Jacaranda and Cisneros, before he noticed a late model pickup a mile behind and closing the distance. It flashed silver beams as though shooting back at the sun.

While Alvaro kept one eye on the mirror, the other on ruts and potholes, Lourdes reached into her purse for the poster they had bought from the Texan. She stared for a minute then quoted. "You have hoarded wealth. You have failed to pay the workmen. You have lived in self-indulgence." She turned to Alvaro. "I am not a reader of the Bible. Do you know this part?"

"James something," Alvaro said. "My second mamá's favorite book."

The lady rolled the poster and put it away. "Will you tell me about your two mamás?"

Alvaro felt a twinge of guilt for not counting the prostitutes who took him in when at seven years old he otherwise would've slept in Tijuana alleys. "The first, my birth mamá, disappeared when I was four. She wasn't much past twenty. She'd been on her own for quite a few years, since her mother got taken away to some asylum in Europe. I never got the whole story. But what she told my papá was, her father died fighting in Spain, in the civil war. He was a painter and some breed of anarchist.

"My Mexican mamá lived for a while with an aunt whose husband couldn't keep his hands off girls. Then she ran off and somehow got enough education to be a teacher. She came to Pajarito, a village in Nayarit.

"My papá was a *mariachi*. After they married, he

tried to persuade my mamá to quit speaking her mind. But she was a crusader. She gave one too many speeches like your sister's, only without the God element. She took on the PRI. They won, and she disappeared.

"Then my papá drank a lot, you know how it goes when men lose their dreams. We moved to Mazatlán where a player of violin and *guitarrón* could make enough to pay for his liquor. Then, you know, a bar fight. My papá got accused of stabbing a guy. And the guy had cousins in the Sinaloa State Penitentiary. One of them killed my papá."

Alvaro glanced over, met the lady's eyes. They appeared to give him all her attention and exhibit a sympathetic heart. He thought, either she was a consummate grifter or, whoever she was, she was a grand prize. Nobody else could have left troubles big as hers behind for a minute.

The pickup roared up behind them. It honked. Its lights flashed on and off. Then it zoomed around them, spewing a rust-colored dust cloud.

"So," Alvaro said, "what do we Mexicans do when we're in a fix? We go north. I caught a ride out of Mazatlán with a family of *gringo* tourists. They dropped me in Nogales, where they crossed the line. I hustled for bus fare to Tijuana, went looking for a friend, a woman I knew from Mazatlán. I'd heard she was in Tijuana, but I couldn't find her. So, I hung around downtown Tijuana." He preferred to keep the lady ignorant about the various tactics he had used to survive in that city. "I got lucky. Tom Hickey came along. He and Wendy adopted me. Wendy, my second mamá, was as sweet as…" As you seem to be, he thought but didn't say. "She didn't know how to be mean. All she could do was love."

Alvaro glanced over and saw a bead of something glisten under the rim of the lady's bat wing sunglasses. Not as big as a tear. Maybe one of those flecks that seemed to issue from her gray-blue eyes.

◇◇◇

At the curb beside Tecate's Parque Hidalgo, Alvaro said, "I need to make a call or two. Do you want to listen in?"

"I am trusting you," she said, in a manner so sincere he felt ashamed that he still hadn't acquitted her of conning him or committed to stick with her. Maybe as soon as he returned to the car, he thought as he entered Lonchería Vesuvio. He ordered a small pizza with chorizo, and slipped the proprietor $10 for the use of his phone.

Clifford didn't answer, nor did his machine. Alvaro dialed the ten numbers that connected him to San Diego information, requested the number for the *Sentinel* and dialed those fourteen numbers. When at last he connected with the newsroom and asked for Roxie Hewitt, the reporter who took his call said Hewitt was out and currently unreachable.

"In Mexico?"

"I couldn't tell you."

"Couldn't or won't?"

"Both."

"Then would you please have her call my office?"

"I could do that."

He gave her the number of Garfield et al. "Ask Hewitt to tell the receptionist where and when we can talk, if she wants an exclusive scoop on the Virgin. I'll check in later today."

Between calls, he looked across the sidewalk at Lourdes. She was on a bench, the yellow dress tucked around her knees. He admired the broad shoulders and light brown arms, her face turned down in a thinker's pose. Her posture, her folded hands, and the recollection of her strong but mild voice that seemed to match her character, kept touching ever deeper places in his heart.

He slapped his cheek and turned back to the phone. After a call to Tijuana information, he dialed the *Diario* number and asked for Ruben Silvera, whose by-line had appeared on this morning's article about the Virgin. The operator connected him to an editor. He asked for Silvera. The editor hissed. Alvaro said, "*Perdón?*"

"Silvera I haven't seen for many days."

"He's out looking for *la Virgen*, right?"

"Sure he is, same as everybody."

"Who's everybody?"

"First, who are you?"

"Juan Gomez, a guy with a lead for Silvera. Have him leave a message, where and when we can talk, with the secretary at the law office of Augustín Quartilho."

The editor made a cluck, which clued Alvaro he was familiar with Quartilho's shady reputation.

In the plaza, a tall man stood over Lourdes. He was Spanish, dressed in a beige linen suit. A doctor, attorney, or the son of a politico. Hitting on her, Alvaro thought, and told himself he'd better snatch her away before the man got a close enough look at her face to see the Virgin in it. But he recognized another, more primitive motive for snatching her away.

As he crossed the street, he noticed her glance up at the man and give him a brief smile. Then she saw Alvaro. She sat taller and watched him as though she sensed a confrontation brewing.

The man turned and held out a hand to Alvaro. While they shook, he gave his name. Rigo something. Alvaro didn't reciprocate, only nodded then touched Lourdes' shoulder. She rose. He hustled her across the park to his wagon. He opened her door. She climbed in and stared at him.

He settled into the driver's seat, fired the engine. "Maybe you think I should've let you spend a few minutes with that *hombre* before we go on?"

"I know, you believe he will mistake me for my sister."

"Look, everybody who gets a close look at you is putting us in danger. Besides, you can't trust an *hombre* who chases painted women." He hoped that joke would win him a smile. It didn't. He pulled away from the curb, circled the plaza, and turned south on Calle Ortiz Rubio, which would become the Ensenada highway. A few blocks along, as they neared the outskirts where smoke poured from tile kilns, he noticed she hadn't quit staring at him. "Okay," he confessed, "maybe I got a little jealous."

She took off her sunglasses and squinted at him. "Jealous."

"Never mind," he said.

The sunglasses leaped to cover her eyes. She nodded and faced forward. Something like a whimper came out of her. Seconds later, a tear slid out from under the glasses. Alvaro reached for her hand. She shook her head. He leaned back over the wheel and drove south.

From Ensenada, if they hurried and didn't encounter washed-out back roads, before dark they might get to snoop around the sites at Porvenir and the Agua Dulce mine.

Chapter Eleven

Feliz was sleeping, the tubes still up her nose. When a nurse came in, Clifford asked, "Could you please sit with my baby while I make a quick phone call?" He promised to return in five minutes, no more.

Ava answered his call. She said, "I just got off the phone with a man named Pete, some old friend of yours? He left this number." She gave it. "Why's the phone machine in the trash?"

"It failed me," Clifford said.

"Should I take that as a warning?"

"Nope."

She sighed. "I'll go buy a new one."

"Thanks. Feliz is sleeping."

She had already hung up. He dialed O, gave the operator Pete Carrillo's number, and asked her to bill the call to his home phone.

Carrillo answered.

"Look, *amigo*," Clifford said, "I've got to be brief.

I'm at the hospital, my little girl's got a bitch of a sinus infection."

"Hey, that's tough. Poor thing. One piece of advice. Get her out of the hospital as fast as they'll let you. Those places give more infections than they cure."

"Thanks." Clifford rubbed his temples.

"Yeah. Hey, so here's what I got for you. But you didn't get it from me, unless you're willing to pay my widow and kids fat retirement checks."

"Deal."

"Then, sure enough, the Bureau's in on the hunt for your Virgin, and so is DEA. The whys, like why we're working south of the border, are not for grunts like me to know. But it's got to come from the top."

Clifford said, "Okay. One more thing—if you can get word to any of the hunters, tell them an old friend of yours might be down there with a girl who's a ringer for this Virgin, who maybe *is* this Virgin, and he's *not* in on the act. He's just along for the ride, unarmed, with no agenda besides romance." Clifford hoped all he'd just said was true. "Tell them please—"

"I hear you. Tell them don't shoot Alvaro."

◇◇◇

While driving, Alvaro tried to make up his mind how much of the lady's life story to believe. Although he'd long ago lost his patience with women who talked incessantly about whatever came to mind, if Lourdes were a bit more like that his task might get easier.

He had found no evidence to discredit her, unless he counted the outrageousness of the story she'd told about her sister being locked out to die in a ice-storm. But the way she'd told it, the detail and feeling in her delivery, had left him unwilling to doubt. And, given his own life, he was nobody to question the truth of anyone else's family history. Besides, the lady had come with a million in gold, which lowered the odds that she was a grifter. Unless the gold was phony. But Alvaro had spent most of a summer prospecting. He believed he could detect any less than an expert forgery.

If she were in cahoots with the PRI or with anyone out to discredit the Virgin, he could see no reason why she would've settled on a law clerk as her Galahad.

From all that reasoning, he concluded she must be what she claimed. Or, if she was lying, she was the one playing the Virgin.

Or, she *was* the Holy Virgin. And, he decided, for even considering that option he ought to go straight home and commit himself to an asylum, like the one where his second mamá did time.

He wondered if, whoever the lady might be, she was leading him into a trap. If so, what kind of trap? And why lead him into it? He couldn't imagine a single reason.

Their stop at Porvenir proved a replay of that morning at the Dos Lobos site. Last Thursday, the

Virgin had touched down, spoken, and lifted off at
the foot of a small hill, only a little farther off the road
than at Dos Lobos. The dirt there was also reddish-
brown. The pilgrims and snoops were a similar crowd,
from whom he gathered as little knowledge as he had
gained that morning, or as he could've gotten from a
newspaper.

A pair of matrons whose jeweled crucifixes gave
them away as society Catholics passed along the children's report of the Virgin's Porvenir message.

She had counseled the children to warn the
campesinos that all who voted for the PRI risked link-
ing their eternal destinies to the fate of their wicked
governors. Then she recited Psalm 52. The heavier
matron read aloud from her Bible.

"Why do you boast of evil, you mighty man? Why
do you boast all day long, you who are a disgrace in the
eyes of God? Your tongue plots destruction; it is like
a sharpened razor, you who practice deceit. You love
evil rather than good, falsehood rather than speaking
the truth. You love every harmful word, you deceitful
tongue. Surely God will bring you down to everlasting
ruin: He will snatch you up and tear you from your
tent; He will uproot you from the land of the living.
The righteous will see you and fear; they will laugh at
you, saying, 'Here now is the man who did not make
God his stronghold but trusted in his great wealth and

grew strong by destroying others.'"

Through the reading, Alvaro watched Lourdes' face, which held its tranquil pose. But as they walked toward the car, her mouth crimped as if to hold inside something that fought to get out. Alvaro stopped and faced her. She walked on, a few steps, then turned and whispered, "Every accusation she speaks is about my father."

A memory visited Alvaro. He said, "In college, a professor assigned *The Treasure of the Sierra Madre*. Do you know the story?"

"I do," she said. "The writer, B. Traven, is German like my father."

"Well, this professor claimed Traven was the bastard son of some Kaiser who never recognized him, and that was what made Traven an anarchist. I argued that whatever made him believe something didn't make what he believed any less true. The professor dropped my grade. Authorities like to do that, push the truth aside and talk about the truth-teller's motives. It's one of their ways of keeping the truth under wraps, where it won't make trouble.

"What I mean is, Lupe's right about the PRI. Her reasons for speaking don't matter."

On the road that carried them out of the mountains, he got her to talk about her favorite pastimes. She loved horses, long rides through *montañas* with Rolf, picnics and swimming with Rolf and their trips to see great murals such as Diego Rivera's. She adored the novels of Jane Austen and the poetry of Christina Rosetti and Sor Juana de la Cruz. When he passed his box of cassette tapes and asked her to choose some, out of the assortment of blues, jazz, and classical, she chose the Segovia, classical guitar. "Rolf learned Bach études in the manner of Segovia so he could play them for me."

The way she said "Rolf" reminded him of the way some preachers said "Jesus." Alvaro wished he'd brought a guitar along. He could play a Segovia piece or two. "Tell me your dreams?"

"Only to be with…" She stopped and stared out the window. "My sister. And your dreams?"

He wasn't ready to come clean and admit what he wanted most. The only person he'd told was Clifford, and to spill it, he'd needed for them to split a bottle of mescal. His fondest, most enduring dream was of a woman with a heart big enough to share with more than her own. Someone who could also help him adopt and raise at least a few *niños* from a Tijuana orphanage.

He knew falling for the lady might prove to be his last, fatal error in judgment. Yet, besides the physical magnetism and the strange harmony he felt issuing from her, he admired everything she was, or appeared to be. Refined yet courageous, and athletic, he could tell by her muscled arms and legs and the mention of her love for swimming. He viewed her as sensitive to feelings and a pursuer of beauty. He could imagine her surrounded by a mob of happy kids. And he thought getting to know her would be like watching her wipe off her tramp face. The more she wiped away, the more lovely she would become, especially in her heart and spirit.

No doubt his vision of the lady was too much like his dream of what a perfect life partner would be. Too much like what Lela, a psychologist he'd dated, would call his anima. But who could reject somebody for being too perfect? Maybe somebody who valued the mind over the heart. But that wasn't Alvaro.

They stopped for tacos and a phone call at one of the tourist snack and plaster-of-Paris statuary emporiums on the outskirts of Ensenada.

◇◇◇

Clifford had just unpacked the new answering machine when the phone rang. He caught his breath when he heard his brother's voice.

"Where are you?"

"Hey, I'm the one who called, so I get to ask the questions."

"Okay, then, but first—if you're in Baja with anybody who looks like this Virgin, get yourself back here today, and as far as you can put yourself from her, immediately."

"Hmm," Alvaro said, with what Clifford guessed was a muted chuckle. "Where'd you get the idea I'm with anybody, especially some Virgin look-alike?"

Rather than confess to spying, at least for now, Clifford said, "That's not what matters at the moment, *hermano*."

"Okay, mystery man, what matters?"

"The word is, the PRI wants to catch her first, prove to the world she's a phony instead of just calling her one without any proof. Meantime, some *drogas* are watching for her through rifle scopes. They need the PRI to stay in power, to cover for them and all, but I guess they disagree on tactics."

"And this news came from who?"

"Pop. He got it from Harry, who got it from some fly on the wall in the office of the *presidente*. And, you remember Pete Carrillo? Well, he says, in addition to his own FBI, the DEA's on the case. Which means what?"

"I get the message."

"And, *hermano*, this isn't about your first mamá."

"I hear that too, Doc."

"So we'll expect you home when?"

"Fast as I can get there. After I take care of a couple matters. How's Feliz?"

"She's great," Clifford said, because if Alvaro knew Feliz's condition, he wouldn't ask for his brother to come to Baja and help, no matter if he were surrounded by enemy infantry and outnumbered like the *gringos* at the Alamo.

Not that Clifford was anxious to run to his brother's side. On the contrary, he hoped to God Alvaro wouldn't ask, at least until Feliz was out of danger.

◇◇◇

Alvaro couldn't imagine why his brother hadn't offered to come help him out, when Clifford and Pop knew him better than to think he would turn tail and leave a lady without an ally. Maybe Pop was on his way to San Diego and Clifford promised to wait for him. But then why didn't Clifford arrange for another phone rendezvous, instead of pretending he expected Alvaro to come home?

Not that he wanted either Pop or Clifford to join him in Mexico. Not when Pop had to gulp nitroglycerine tabs to keep his heart pumping. Not when Clifford's marriage was foundering, and Ava was so big people asked how many babies she was expecting. Or when Ava was spending hours every week with the slick brother of James Valenciana, one of Garfield et al's stable of ethics-free attorneys. According to Ava, she and this brother were working on arrangements for the church choir. According to James, they were at least playing footsy. And all the while, Ava continued to look for occasions to slip in digs at Clifford's failure to hold a "real" job.

Alvaro would've asked Clifford to research the murder of Hans Shuler, except the lady had stood beside him during the phone call. She remained at his side after the call, while he pondered. She didn't speak or even ask questions with her expression. He wondered if she was sticking so close to him because closeness to him comforted her, or to limit what he would say on the phone.

He motioned toward the wagon. "My brother says we better find Lupe in a hurry, and the second we find her, we better get her out of sight."

"He knows about Lupe."

"I'll tell you on the way. I'll tell you everything. No more secrets. Right?"

She didn't answer fast enough.

◇◇◇

Tom had packed his medicine kit and a few day's clothes, just in case. Armed with the latest clue Clifford had provided, the resemblance of Alvaro's mystery woman to sketches of the vagabond Virgin, he had sped off the mountain to Reno and the university, to the closest serious library to his home on the lake in Incline.

The research librarian he consulted was a dusky beauty who reminded him of someone he shouldn't have fallen for, a jazz singer long deceased. The librarian must've liked Tom's looks. With the fedora in place of the missing hair, and his mustache still more blond than gray, and his sharp blue eyes, he looked fiftyish and virile.

She consulted a magazine index for articles mentioning the Virgin. Then he asked her to look up Hans and Andres Shuler. The Mexican oligarchy had long been an interest of his. And even after almost forty years, he hadn't managed to extinguish the fire that filled his gut whenever something sparked a remembrance of the German and Mexican Nazis who held Wendy as their slave in Tijuana.

The Virgin material offered nothing new. But among the latest articles on the Shulers, near the top of the pile, in a follow up story to the Hans Shuler murder, he came upon a photo.

The librarian helped him translate the article. He proceeded to the nearest payphone, outside the library. Standing in a hot wind that made him hold his hat and think about the Chubasco a TV weatherman had predicted could affect the Californias from L.A. south, he reached Clifford.

"You're in contact with X?"

"Only when he calls. Why?"

"I found an article, in a newspaper out of Durango. About the murder of Hans Shuler, a man of influence, it appears from the way the reporter calls his unknown killer every derogatory adjective in Spanish I know and then some. The photo that goes with the article is of a daughter, Lourdes Shuler. Guess who she's a ringer for?"

"The Virgin."

"Yes sir. And here's the punch line. She's wanted for questioning in regards to the murder. If you can tell me what that means besides the obvious, I'd be deeply obliged."

"Have they got proof?"

"Hans gets shot with his own gun. Lourdes disappears, and when the law shows up, the safe's wide open. The old man was too senile to remember the combination, says Hans Shuler's bodyguard. The only person who knows it is this daughter."

"So," Clifford said, "it looks like Alvaro's probably done it again. Signed on to help a killer."

"This is turning into something I can't bear to watch from a distance," Tom said. "I'm on my way. I'll see you in about five hours."

"At four-fifty miles, that's averaging ninety-something."

"I already came fifty miles. I'm in Reno. Make it four hours."

◇◇◇

Some minutes passed while Clifford recovered from the news and began to sort out what it meant. Then, as he sat brooding, for the first time ever he thought he shouldn't have fathered a child. Not because he didn't love Feliz. He loved her with a passion he hadn't known was possible before she arrived. But in his fewer than thirty years he had already killed a man and gone to prison camp, then married, and failed to prove worthy of his wife's expectations. Now his brother was running around Baja with a fugitive who probably had killed her own father. He couldn't stay home with Alvaro in danger. But he couldn't leave Feliz, though he doubted he was wise enough to protect her, or anybody.

Chapter Twelve

As evening approached, the fast falling sun turned bright orange through the dust the Santa Ana wind had raised. Alvaro sat on the roof of the wagon, which was parked in a meadow along with at least three dozen other vehicles. He gazed around, looking in the meadow for Benito and up hillsides for any sign of a sniper.

Pilgrims had transformed the meadow into a campground a half mile west of the site of the Virgin's third appearance and a quarter mile from the village of El Tule. As in other places, she had shown herself at the base of a hill.

A loudspeaker van blared propaganda for *el Partido de la Gente*. Alvaro didn't know much about that group. Only that it began with remnants of the *Septiembristas* the student uprising of 1968 had radicalized. And only this year, for this election, had it gained recognition as a political party and placed candidates on the ballot in a few locales.

Between its slogans and campaign promises of food subsidies, public health programs and the end of government and police corruption, the loudspeaker advertised an Ensenada restaurant, a bakery, and a discount tire store. No doubt the ads paid for gas and a driver. Alvaro jotted the advertisers' names. If he survived long enough, he would patronize the business of anyone bold or foolish enough to align himself against the PRI.

Through twilight and into dusk, pilgrims watched the sky. Alvaro watched the pilgrims. Mexicans and *gringos* of all sorts, shapes and ages. A few European *turistas*. A Japanese couple. Nuns and priests in uniform, others in slacks or jeans. A Hollywood-looking fellow with a parrot on his shoulder. Huddles of mostly women who gossiped, sang, or prayed while they monkeyed with rosary beads. And a few men young enough, sufficiently uninvolved, and appearing estranged enough from the others so that Alvaro thought they could be plainclothes feds or cartel shooters. But as he watched those men at length, he decided they were more likely the husbands of women who had come to worship or get healed. They acted like guys who slouch around the mall while the wife shops.

Alvaro had reached the state of mind where part of him craved action. He was bored and more jumpy than alert, the state he'd learned to try to avoid while in Vietnam, since the Viet Cong often seemed to wait for those times before they attacked.

Even the lady, serene as she could be, acted on edge. All the while Alvaro sat on the wagon roof, she sat below on the tailgate, except when she stood to buy them each a torta and a bottle of orange juice from a passing vendor. Though her eyes remained calm, she steepled her fingers and gnawed pretty lips with her teeth. She darted glances here and there, and up at him, as though she expected someone to arrive for a meeting. Or she might be waiting for a chance to slip away.

Between sunset and dark, the size of the crowd doubled. Alvaro wondered if some news outlet had prophesied, or a rumor had circulated, that the lady would show tonight. When a heat flash whitened the eastern horizon above Cohabuso Peak, a hundred people leaped to their feet or rose on tiptoes. No doubt they hoped or expected to witness the Virgin descending from the sky.

As full dark arrived, the crowd began thinning. Cars rattled away down the rutted and rocky road that led to Baja Highway 3, a route from Ensenada across the Sierra to the Sea of Cortez.

Alvaro climbed from the roof of his wagon and into the driver's seat and tuned the radio to XRRR, a Tijuana news station. He only had to listen for a couple minutes before the newscaster segued from a report about plans to upgrade Tijuana's sewage processing to the story of the Virgin. When he said she hadn't appeared that day, Alvaro thought he detected a note of bitter suspicion in the man's voice. The newscaster might wonder, like Alvaro did, if the PRI had silenced the Virgin for good.

He climbed out of the wagon and asked the lady, "How about a bonfire? Maybe it'll cheer us up."

"I am not yet discouraged," she said. "Only I am tired."

He insisted she tag along when he wandered outside the camp to collect fallen sticks of mesquite and dogwood. He told her it was only for her protection. But her expression, stony as the face of a drill instructor or karate master if you tried to make excuses, told him she knew better. Besides, he supposed she believed he didn't trust her not to splash the makeup off her face, slip into a muslin outfit, find some kids and start prophesying.

When they returned to camp, he used one of the sticks to dig a small pit. He built a meager fire for them to stare at while they waited for inspiration or for their weariness to deepen so they could sleep.

"What did we learn today?" he asked.

"I think not much."

Four days from now, he thought, the election would be history. He couldn't wait any longer before signing on for keeps or helping her find somebody more capable. He said, "The way I see it, we can keep bungling along on our own or we can go look for a guy named Hector. He used to be a private investigator in Mexico City. But he was too good, caused too much trouble for the big shots. The last I heard he was retired, or hiding out, in a trailer up the highway in Angel's Camp. What do you say to that?"

"Do you mean you are giving up?"

"I'm rarely smart enough to give up on anything. But, if you asked for my recommendation, I'd go with Hector." He hoped she would ignore his recommendation. "We could leave right now, maybe have a real P.I. on the job first thing tomorrow."

"Alvaro," she said, "you are wise and you are honest. Most men are not."

"Meaning you'd rather stick with me, forget about Hector?"

She nodded, and he let out the breath he'd been holding. "Only four days, and it takes about a day for word to get around. So whatever she does on Saturday won't matter as much. I'm betting the Virgin will show up somewhere tomorrow. If not, then what?"

"Tomorrow, we will decide about tomorrow."

"Was there anything you saw today but didn't tell me about?"

"You think I would not tell you something?"

Alvaro shrugged. "Maybe you forgot, or saw something that didn't seem important, but maybe it is."

"Nothing," she said.

"No sign of your brother?"

The look she gave him could have meant that a cramp had just struck her. It so broke the harmony that up to now defined her, he had to stifle a nervous laugh. Then he wondered if the tension of knowing they might any second get set upon, or shot, was making him giddy. While he watched her face recover, he recalled that once before when he asked about Rolf, she had begun to lose her composure.

She reached into her large purse, brought out a package of tissues, held them up and said, "I must go somewhere. Can I do this without a chaperone?"

"I'll walk you part way."

The latrine zone was across a dry streambed, behind a row of cottonwood. Alvaro let her go alone the last fifty yards, but he squatted and peered through the dark. Just before she disappeared, her hand reached into the pocket on the right side of her yellow dress. When it came out, it went straight to the side of her face, like somebody putting the receiver of a two-way radio to her ear.

A minute passed, then another, before she came out of the dark. They returned to the wagon. The lady climbed in and lay down on the mattress. Alvaro brushed his teeth. Then he climbed in beside her. "Do you mind?"

"It is your car." She squirmed herself up against the side. Still, he caught the scent of sage her hair had attracted and held. He listened to her soft breathing and thought he felt magnetism drawing them closer.

After many long minutes, realizing he wasn't yet tired enough to fall asleep beside her, he climbed out, sat on a large stone and stared at the coals in the pit. He wished his brother were along. Not only could he use Clifford's logic and insight in this Virgin business, but he wanted somebody to talk to about the lady. Never before had he felt that his heart was quite so vulnerable or in such danger of breaking.

A clunk sounded. Lourdes had probably rapped the wall of the wagon with an elbow or heel. He imagined her thrashing from a nightmare. What kind of nightmares visited the daughter of a Nazi, he wondered. Or, maybe she had kicked the wall in a restless fit her conscience inspired because the whole story of her sister killing their father was lies. Because she was a thief, a murderer, and an incomparable actress and liar.

Still, from some opposite deep and illogical part of his mind came the thought that had recurred a dozen times that day, that just maybe Lourdes Shuler was in truth the Holy Virgin.

He mumbled, "Then why the hell would she drag a reprobate like me around?"

◇◇◇

Neither Clifford nor Tom Hickey slept much that night. Tom had arrived at nine, spoken to Ava for a few minutes, then gone to join Clifford at the hospital.

The swelling in Feliz's cheeks had receded some. Her temp was back down to 102. She'd gotten used to the tubes in her nose enough so that the doctor cut back on the sedative. Her head only ached rather than pounded. But she couldn't find the energy to speak except to ask every few minutes, "Can we go home?" After Clifford told her they couldn't go home until daytime, she changed her recurring question to, "Is it daytime yet?"

By two a.m., Feliz looked sound asleep. Tom was dozing in a chair. But Clifford's eyes wouldn't even stay closed. When Tom woke to massage an aching neck, Clifford said, "I can't sit here anymore. I'm going to Baja. If Alvaro calls, tell him to meet me at Hussong's."

Tom sat up straight. "No good. X might be just outside Tecate, farther from Ensenada than from here."

Clifford said, "I guess I can try to wait. But soon I'll start tearing my hair and rending my garment."

"Been reading the Bible, have you?"

"Not lately."

Alvaro woke alone in the wagon. The tailgate was down. He slithered out. The lady came walking toward him from the campground. She wore a green dress with sleeves to the elbows, a modest V-neck and a tie-belted waist. She was holding her pack of tissues, so that Alvaro could believe she had only gone to do her personal business among the cottonwoods. She had washed off the powder and rouge, only worn her floppy hat and sunglasses for disguise. Her face seemed to glow. And she didn't look straight at him.

Before, whenever they spoke or in any way attended to one another, she gazed at the sides of Alvaro's eyes, as if she found the whites more intriguing than the pupils. He had noted this habit because it made him feel cared about yet in no way challenged or imposed upon.

But this morning, her gaze was on his chin, his shoulder, or just wide of his ear. He also noted that her dress was loose enough to hide a peasant smock underneath.

Dusty wind swept down from the Sierra, already hot at just past six o'clock. The sky looked blanketed with silt. Alvaro boiled water and sipped instant coffee. Along with his other preoccupations, he contemplated the weather. Day before yesterday, thunderstorms. Yesterday broiling but calm except for occasional gusts and swirls. Today, the Santa Ana. In this part of the world, such swift and radical change felt ominous.

Alvaro tuned his car radio to XOCA, Ensenada's best station for news. He listened for word about the

Virgin while he munched a roll with raspberry jam and watched the lady touching up her hair while she looked up at a hawk that circled, dipping, rising and gliding on the wind.

The news came as a special bulletin. The Virgin had appeared not thirty minutes ago, on the outskirts of El Rayo, near the road to Laguna Hanson in the Parque Nacional. She had appeared to a boy who was all alone rounding up goats. She arrived shortly after first light and stayed only about five minutes.

The lady quit brushing her hair. She clenched her fists and stared at them. The broadcaster promised to deliver more detail and the themes of her message as soon as the report came in.

At the end of the bulletin, the lady rushed to his side. "El Rayo," she said. "How soon can we be there?"

He watched her face for a blush or twitch that might give her away. It didn't come. She brushed her hair back with her hand, pulled on her floppy hat and batwing sunglasses, and began stuffing makeup, tissues, and all else into her big yellow purse.

Along the rutted dirt road, Alvaro decided to phone Clifford and ask him to research small two-way radios. And while researching, he might read up on devices, if any existed, that could transport an image from a remote camera to some kind of gadget that could project the image onto the side of a hill in some version of 3-D that didn't require special glasses. Maybe something like the holograms the crew of Star Trek used actually existed.

The Chevy wagon fell into a line of vehicles bunched behind a rattling pickup with a homemade cab-over camper that rocked and swayed and wouldn't budge from the center of the dirt road. Whenever someone behind honked, the pickup driver's arm appeared shooting the finger.

The lady's hand lay on the seat between them. Her fingers were spread and clutching the seat. He tapped the back of her hand with one finger. "We've been doing this all wrong."

"What do you mean?"

"We wasted a day hunting for her. We need to make her find us. Do you think she would, if she knew you were here?"

"I don't know," she said. "Perhaps."

"Let's send a message. Something like, Lupe, meet your sister at so and so place and time."

"But Benito. He will come there, and the *policia*. Lupe will know this. She will not come."

"Not to the exact place," Alvaro said, "but she's a bold one. She might come near to take a look, see who shows. And we might get a glimpse of her from where we'll be stationed, on top of a hill with field glasses. At least, from who does show up, we'll get a better idea what we're up against."

"Who delivers this message?" she asked.

"We could start with one of those loudspeaker trucks, as soon as we get to El Rayo."

"Lupe won't be there to hear the loudspeaker."

"I doubt she's working alone," Alvaro said. "She's bound to have scouts. Or disciples."

The lady's cocked head and slightly pursed lips made him wonder if she thought his idea was useless or if it could be part of a scheme that might expose her.

Chapter Thirteen

Clifford was supposed to attend a trial for an *Epitaph* article. The accused was his friend Dr. Fred. The charge was attempted murder.

Fred had shot his wife's lover when he caught them in his bed. Ever since Clifford had accepted the assignment to write an article about the case, he'd wished he hadn't. The way Ava had been treating him, too many issues the story touched upon gave Clifford suspicions that not only troubled him, they made treating Ava with love and respect while she goaded him all the more difficult. But Dr. Fred, a knuckleball pitcher for the adult league Saturday ball team Clifford and Alvaro played on, deserved a sympathetic treatment of his story. He only had bought the gun after threats from his wife's ex. And the only reason he came home, dug out the gun, and loaded it before going to the bedroom, was that a neighbor had called him to say he'd seen a dangerous looking man enter Fred's house.

Then, when the wife's lover rose up, all 250 tattooed pounds of him, it wasn't murderous intent but instinct that made Fred pull the trigger.

Besides, the *Epitaph* paid Clifford $2000 for cover stories, and he needed the money, especially since money was an issue that stood between him and Ava.

They had married less than a year after his release from the road camp where he'd served twenty two months. Feliz was conceived on their honeymoon. Now Feliz was almost three, and another child was on the way. Ava's first pregnancy had lifted her spirits. But with this one, they came crashing down. Because, he thought, her husband had become what she considered a loser. When she met him, he was on his way to law school. Seven years had passed. Now, he was an ex-con with no career except his writing, which she thought of as unemployment.

He wrote enough feature stories for the *Epitaph* to keep them out of debt, except the up-and-down balance on a few credit cards. His writing could support them as long as they stayed in the cottage on Mission Bay, where Clifford and Alvaro had spent most of their childhood years. But, as Ava pointed out every week or so, the cottage was only two bedrooms, about 900 square feet. She wanted a place she could call their own, and where she wouldn't feel as if they had driven Pop out of his home and forced him to live in the other family residence, the cabin on the shore of Lake Tahoe.

Yet neither Ava's consternation, nor an *Epitaph* deadline, nor Dr. Fred's reputation mattered to Clifford today, when Feliz was this sick and Alvaro was in mortal danger. Clifford would miss at least a day of the Dr. Fred trial.

◇◇◇

Ava had gone to pick up a sheaf of song lyrics her music pastor friend wanted her to copy in calligraphy, one of her several artistic skills, so they'd look good on the overhead. Tom had gone out to buy newspapers. Clifford was sitting with Feliz and taking her temperature. The thermometer registered 104 degrees. Clifford hoped the rise was all from the exertion of leaving the hospital and coming home.

The phone rang. He kissed his baby's steaming forehead and went to the phone.

The voice on the other end sounded like a boy imitating a man. "Am I speaking to Clifford Hickey."

"That depends who you are."

"Special Agent Kevin Pratt here. FBI."

"Okay, I'm Clifford Hickey. I'll bet Pete Carrillo asked you to call me."

The agent cleared his throat. "Mister Hickey, what can you tell me about this Virgin?"

"The one in the news?"

"Yes."

"All I know is what's in the news."

From the crackle on the line, Clifford guessed the call was from Mexico. The agent paused long enough to write Clifford's response on a note. "And what's your connection with *Partido de la Gente*."

"None."

"But you know of them?"

"I read the paper."

"And, you're employed as a private investigator, correct?"

"Not currently."

Clifford imagined the agent scribbling *Respondent (a smart aleck) CLAIMS he is not a private investigator.* The agent said, "And you *are* employed as?"

Clifford supposed that to get any information out of this irritating fellow, he needed to sound as polite as he could manage. "A journalist."

"What's your relation to Alvaro Hickey?"

"Brother."

"And he is the private investigator? Or is he a lawyer?"

"Law student. Law clerk."

"He is employed by the firm of Garfield, Robles, Patterson, Finney, and Torres, LLD?"

"Yeah." Clifford waited for the agent to mention that Garfield et al had been charged with conspiring to forge and sell green cards and tourist visas.

But the agent asked, "Your brother is a member of *Partido de la Gente?*"

The front door swung open and Ava came in. On any normal day, Clifford would've wondered why it had taken her almost an hour to pick up something from her music pastor friend who lived about three minutes away. He watched her go to the kitchen, lay the sheaf of song lyrics on the counter and open the fridge.

"Mister Hickey," the agent said, "I need your cooperation."

Between worries about Feliz, Ava, and Alvaro, and this fellow's playing cop with him, Clifford lost his patience. "Look, Mister Pratt, I'll tell you everything I know about Alvaro and the Virgin as soon as you tell me you know what cooperate means, that it starts with 'co.' Which means, in this case, both ways."

The agent didn't answer for so long Clifford wondered if he was consulting a dictionary. Then Pratt said, "I can tell you this much. *Partido de la Gente* has released a video cassette in which this Virgin, while levitating, brings a message. We have pinpointed the locale where the video was shot as a public beach north of Malibu."

"Hmmm," Clifford said.

"My partner and I were assigned to a stakeout at a known residence of members of *Partido de la Gente.* Yesterday, we were called away for a meeting. Our replacements got detained. When we returned from the meeting, neighbors were looting the house in question. We entered the house and found two men recently shot to death, as well as boxes of blank video cassettes and rather sophisticated equipment for copying them. The dead men were known members of *Partido de la Gente*."

"Whew," Clifford said. "And you're in Mexico because?"

"Did I say I was in Mexico."

"Yeah."

"Well, I don't believe I said that."

"But you're looking for the Virgin, right? And you're down there because you think she might lead you to the shooters of these guys in—where did you say the killing happened?"

"Long Beach."

"So you get to cross the border for something like hot pursuit, right?"

"Hey," Pratt said, "don't even think about putting this in one of your *Epitaph* stories."

"Did I say I wrote for the *Epitaph*?"

"How else would I know it?"

Clifford let the agent win that round. "Okay, go on then."

"That's all."

"All you're going to tell me?" Clifford asked. "Or all you know?"

"Whichever answer you prefer, go with that. Now, you tell me everything *you* know."

Clifford could either keep his brother's confidence or spill what Alvaro might not want the FBI to know but which might save his skin. He said, "Okay. My brother calls me, asks me to find out why the PRI isn't railing against this Virgin, making her look like a phony. And Alvaro would like to know who all is looking for her. That's all he asked. But I sense he's not giving me the whole story. So I go to his house, peek in a window, and see him in there with a girl who's not only a ringer for this Virgin, but it turns out she's a ringer for one Lourdes Shuler. The Shuler who's wanted for questioning in regard to the murder of her father, deep in Mexico. Which Alvaro surely hasn't a clue about. He doesn't pay that much attention to Mexican news."

The agent muttered indecipherable stuff, no doubt while madly scribbling. "That's all?"

"Yep."

"And what do you make of it?"

"Not much. You're the pro. What do *you* make of it?

Pratt said, "When you talk to your brother, tell him if he's smart, he'll phone me right away. You have a pencil and paper."

"Always."

"Give him this number, they'll patch him through."

◇◇◇

As Alvaro pulled up alongside the ranger station at the entrance to the Laguna Hansen recreation area, he was thinking about a motor home they had passed at the junction where the convoy they had followed turned toward El Rayo. An early Winnebago, the vehicle was so caked in mud it looked deserted, except the windshield was clean, and the tall antenna that poked out of the roof indicated it hadn't been scavenged.

What caught Alvaro's attention was the rear bumper. Alongside the California plate in a holder that advertised a Santa Monica dealership was a lineup of stickers. "*Viva la Raza*." "MECHA," a student association whose members had attempted to enlist Alvaro. "Boycott California Produce." "*Partido de la Gente* rules."

From all the folks he'd witnessed seeking the Virgin, student radicals had been conspicuously lacking. And, Alvaro thought, they might be folks worth talking to. Radicals traded in big ideas, such as conspiracy theories. But by the time he'd processed the sight of the motor home, he and the lady were a quarter mile up the road and on their way to the ranger station from which he intended to phone Clifford.

At the ranger station, he advised the lady to stay in the car, since the rangers would surely have a copy of the Virgin sketch. The ranger on duty was young, part Asian. In English, to find out whether the fellow could eavesdrop, Alvaro offered $10 for a phone call. The ranger held out one hand while the other pointed at the phone.

Clifford's number got him a busy signal. He dialed Quartilho's office. Neither Augie nor his receptionist were known as morning people, and nine o'clock was still a few minutes away. He left a message, saying he would call back and that he had asked a reporter to leave a message for Juan Gomez at their office. He hung up and once again called his brother. Still busy. Since he figured it could well be Ava on a lengthy call with some confidante or her slick music pastor, he decided to drive to the El Rayo site. If he couldn't find a phone in El Rayo, he could drive back here in an hour.

Back down the road, he would've stopped and knocked on the door of the motor home. But it was gone.

Chapter Fourteen

He veered off the paved road onto the gravel that led them past El Rayo to the turnoff to the site. From the crest of a hill, the site looked like a refuge for survivors of a bombed city fleeing to the wilderness. Cars, trucks, busses, and motorcycles clogged the dirt road and pieced themselves into an artless mosaic against the red and black soil at the base of yet another hill. The site was already inhabited by vendors of sweets and tortas.

The loudspeaker van had arrived. It circled the periphery, and as it neared the hill, the praise of *Partido de la Gente* candidates echoed off the hill, which was volcanic and jagged with outcroppings like the bows of ships. A solitary cloud perched above it. The cloud appeared to lean eastward, as though challenging to a duel the black thunderheads that were clotting together along the crest of the Sierra.

Alvaro parked near the vendors. Around the carts offering tortas and *refrescos*, a gypsy girl wandered, selling earrings and medallions she had carved from ironwood and decorated with tiny photos of the sketched Virgin. While she sold one to Alvaro, she stared at Lourdes too long with narrowed eyes and lips that moved like a ventriloquist's. She knew. She recognized the Virgin's face. The rapture in her eyes spooked Alvaro. Any second the girl would run and snitch, he thought. But then she turned to him and grinned, and gave a conspirator's nod that let him hope she would keep the secret.

A few yards along the quarter mile walk to the site, Alvaro caught the first mention of the Virgin's latest promise. Because he knew how fast rumors distorted, he didn't stop to ask anybody until he and Lourdes encountered a quartet of nuns at the edge of the crowd. Lourdes stayed back from the nuns. She checked her face in a compact mirror and lit one of the Delicado cigarettes Alvaro had bought to complete her disguise.

The nuns were huddled together and gazing down as though to compare toenail polish. When Alvaro tapped the shoulder of one, all four turned as if they all had felt the tap. He begged pardon for the intrusion. He claimed to be a maker of film documentaries and asked if they might acquaint him with the Virgin's latest missive.

The eldest nun spoke for them. "Oh, *Señor*, last evening Our Lady didn't come with a message, but with a promise. Disbelief has grieved her innocent heart. With hope of vanquishing doubt, and to bless those who have come to her, she has promised to meet us at Playa Sin

Olas this evening, and to make herself visible to us all."
The nun and her sisters quivered in delight.

The lady had come just near enough to hear the
news. She dropped the cigarette she'd been holding in her
right hand that dangled at her side. Though it bounced
off her foot and left ashes there, she didn't appear to
notice. She looked pale, carved out of marble.

Alvaro touched her arm. She twitched then
breathed. He told the nuns goodbye. Then he and
the lady weaved and nudged their way through the
crowd, closing on the holy ground, where the Virgin
had touched down. Nearly all the chatter Alvaro heard
concerned the promised visit. What message would she
bring? What miracles might she perform? This time,
would she walk among the crowd?

Kids competed to sell the maps to Playa Sin Olas
their mothers or big brothers were busy tracing. The
kids shouted and undercut each others' prices. Alvaro
bought two, one from a girl with a hornet-orange face,
another from a boy with a rope-like scar from his ear
to his nose who stood weeping at his failures to sell.
All the poor children of Mexico touched sore places in
Alvaro's heart, but most of all the orphaned, displaced,
or disfigured. Whenever a gang of beggars approached,
since he couldn't help them all, he tried to single out
the saddest, the ugliest, and the most despised.

Near the front, the crowd guarded its territory.

Alvaro grasped the lady's hand and bullied through until he was close enough to see, from tiptoes, the action that drew them. People were soliciting blessings from the boy to whom the Virgin had appeared. This time, she had chosen a single child, a stubby little fellow who still had his baby cheeks. A woman reached out to him with the stump where her hand used to be. The boy recoiled and bared his teeth. His hand trembled even while it reached toward the bony stump.

Alvaro watched the boy pat ancient heads, grip tight onto crippled arms and legs, run his forefinger around oozing sores, and poke it into goiters.

Alvaro noticed the lady was gone. He didn't recall letting go of her arm. He weaved through the crowd, often walking on his toes to peer over people, in search of her brown floppy hat. When he reached the campground, he looked through windows into vans, and through netting into tents. He started believing she might've vanished, gone back to heaven.

But he found her where he should've guessed he would, talking to the driver of the loudspeaker van. He was a sleepy young fellow with a patch on one eye. She had convinced him to broadcast the message she and Alvaro had composed, which she had jotted onto the back of a map to the Virgin's promised appearance.

"And you will contact others like yourself, at other sites?" she asked.

"Fifty pesos each," the driver said.

Alvaro pulled out his wallet and paid the fellow in dollars, slipping him an extra twenty. "Right now. *Este minuto.*"

The fellow smiled and clicked the On switch of his CB radio. While they were still walking toward Alvaro's car, the van resumed it's circling the campground, and the loudspeaker's first words were Spanish for, "Lulu, meet Rollo at the Santa Inez Mission, at five p.m. today."

"Lulu? Rollo?" Alvaro asked. "I thought the message was to meet your sister?"

"They are nicknames we used long ago. For Lupe and Rolf."

"Rolf? Since when is he part of the deal?"

She gave a defiant glance then looked away.

"Okay," he conceded, "Rolf's fine. But will you promise me something?"

"What will you ask me?"

"Don't go off anywhere without me again."

"Did you worry I would be captured?"

"That's not all."

She watched him, waiting for more. He thought of several phrases such as, I just didn't want to lose you, but they all sounded phony or trite. He shook his head.

◇◇◇

Back at the Laguna Hansen ranger station, after paying

the ranger another $10 for the use of his phone, Alvaro tried his brother's number first.

Sheet lightning flashed along the crest of the Sierra. Alvaro guessed the storm was still over the Sea of Cortez, a hundred and some kilometers across the peninsula. Unless a high pressure system came off the Pacific and deflected the front north or south, the storm might arrive at the Pacific coast about the same time the Virgin was due to appear. He wondered if the storm could be one of the rare and violent Chubascos that came off the Caribbean.

Clifford answered. He sounded relieved, as if Dr. Fred had just struck out their opponents cleanup slugger. But his voice sobered. "Sit down, *hermano.*"

Alvaro leaned on the ranger booth counter. "Okay, I'm sitting."

"You know one Lourdes Shuler, right?"

Alvaro hoped the ranger either hadn't heard him gasp or wasn't the suspicious kind. "Yeah."

"Did she tell you her father got shot in the head on May twenty-ninth of this year?"

After a long look over his shoulder at the lady, who was checking her makeup in the visor mirror, he said, "Yeah, she did."

"The way it looks," Clifford said, "She's the murderer."

Chapter Fifteen

Without a word to the ranger or the lady, Alvaro returned to his seat in the wagon, rested his head on the steering wheel and tried to think. He recalled Lourdes saying that while looking at her dead father, she felt as if she had killed him.

Clearly, he needed to reevaluate everything, including the propensities of his heart. To reel in and wonder if all his powers of intuition and judgment were useless or worse, at least when the subject was women. Though he heard the lady climb in and shut her door, he didn't move until a horn beeped at him. Alvaro despised car horns. He might've flipped off the honker, but his arm felt as if it weighed a hundred pounds. He managed to sit, start the engine, pull a few yards ahead and to the edge of the road.

The lady still hadn't spoken. She was watching him as though with pity. He snapped, "Look, you give me the whole truth, or we go straight to the police."

"The police?" she said, as though innocent of any wrongdoing, lies included.

He led off with the easy question. "Clifford says a couple guys got killed in Santa Monica, the day before yesterday. They belonged to *El Partido de la Gente*, and they were sitting on a bunch of blank video tapes."

"I am sorry."

"Why sorry?"

She darkened her gaze. "Because people are dead."

"Happens all the time," he said. "Somebody was making tapes of Lupe, to spread the word around. That's my guess. Am I right?"

"You are treating me like a criminal."

"Which you are. Remember the gold? And you're wanted for murder."

"I know."

"You didn't tell me."

"You are not my attorney."

"Right. So what am I?"

"That is for you to say."

Her last comment left him speechless. Besides the words, he thought her look might imply she was offering whatever he had the will to take.

"Did you kill your father?"

She scowled in a way less angry than frustrated. "Why do you ask me after I told you Lupe killed our father?"

"Because I'm almost convinced you have a sister, but not quite."

Now Lourdes' face expressed nothing but calm. "Then you believe I am this Virgin."

Alvaro shook his head and wheeled a U turn. "I don't believe anything."

◇◇◇

While Alvaro wondered if he was serving as the pawn of a killer, they drove in silence, all the way from El Rayo to the location where the Virgin had promised to appear, on the north shore of Playa Sin Olas.

The place was less than twenty kilometers south of the resort at the Blowhole, a tourist attraction, yet five kilometers of the twenty was gravel and five more was rocky sand. Passage to the site required a four-wheel drive vehicle, a horse, mountain bike, motorcycle with knobby tires, good shoes or callused feet, or a '55 Chevy wagon with the positraction rear end and a driver as crafty as Alvaro.

Entrepreneurs shuttled back and forth to parking lots they had established near Punta Banda. Before two p.m, hundreds of pilgrims had arrived. So far, Alvaro hadn't seen any army or federal or state *policia*. He kept watch for Benito, for the dour fellow with a duck voice who had followed him toward the car yesterday, for cartel thugs, and *gringo* G-men. Most of the pilgrims appeared to be Mexican and innocent enough. Half of them limped or stooped with disease, or stared around with hands out, begging, or walked like broken people do, with downcast eyes.

Among the few *gringos* were two blond fellows in button down sport shirts and dark slacks. He would've guessed they were Mormon missionaries come for a look at the competition, except they looked a few years too old.

The beach ran about a hundred meters from the tide line to the low mesa that bordered it. The sand was white with streaks of steely gray. The ocean's tangy fragrance was laced with something acrid, maybe dead and grounded seals or dolphins. From the water, the beach sloped gradually up to the base of the low mesa, which could've been a meadow in some other land where rain came more than a few times annually. Here, instead of grass and wildflowers, sage, agave, jumping cholla, and stunted mesquite grew out of the sandy dirt. East of the mesa, the hills looked like the humps of a half dozen seated camels. The Virgin might appear at the base of one of them, if she only meant the appearance as an extravaganza, her image afloat in the distant sky. But Alvaro, and no doubt most of the pilgrims, expected she would come to the hill that rose from the north end of the beach.

That hill drew the pilgrims' attention because it looked most like the others at which she had appeared. Similar height, a similar rise, about 60 degrees. Besides, a boojum tree, like a five-meter-high bent pitchfork, added drama to the spot, and to its potential of distracting from the mechanics of whatever illusion the Virgin might have planned, to dupe thousands of believers.

Alvaro and the lady sat on the tailgate of his wagon. He caught her glancing up at him and tried to read her face. She ducked behind her newspaper. He wondered, if he asked her to wash off the makeup and then stared at her, if soon enough he might lose all these doubts that bedeviled his concentration. The sight of great beauty always inspired him with a vague and mysterious peace of mind. One reason Clifford held to his Christian faith regardless of the behavior of too many Christians was, he believed John Keats' line, "Beauty is truth, truth beauty." And Clifford considered Christ's life and message the supreme masterpiece.

But, Alvaro thought, beauty was also a trickster.

The lady read today's *Diario*, Tijuana edition, while Alvaro browsed the *San Diego Sentinel*. They were seeking insights. Most every *Sentinel* piece that mentioned Mexico concerned the election. Only three days.

The PRI candidate for Tijuana Municipal Governor promised a living wage to the police. Candidates for the Chamber of Deputies vowed to bring federal money to develop the Zona Rio. The *Sentinel's* Roxie Hewitt's article about last night's promise and this evening's scheduled visit speculated that the Virgin might, this evening, to a rock festival-sized crowd, endorse specific opposition party candidates.

"She'd better show up at the mission," Alvaro said. "By the time we get back from there this place will look like Woodstock or Altamont. Rock festivals," he said, in case the stories about them hadn't reached rural Durango. "Maybe we shouldn't have asked her to meet us before the gig. If she doesn't show, we'll come back here and find the road stacked like an L.A. rush hour, with us at the end of the line a half mile back. We'd have to use binoculars just to see her."

He was looking her way, waiting to catch her eye as soon as she lowered the newspaper, when cool metal pressed into his neck at the base of his skull. A voice said in Spanish, "Fold your arms and stand up."

If he'd been alone, Alvaro just might've tried to duck, spin, and flip the man head first into the sand. But the lady was beside him. As he stood, he crooked his eyes far enough left to see the *Indio* in khakis who held a serrated fishing knife to her throat.

A second man in khakis appeared. He had bug eyes and a flat nose in a face lined with cracks, like sun-scorched clay. He wore a badge, a sidearm, and a khaki trooper hat.

"Give me your hands."

Alvaro presented them. The policeman wrenched his arms back and cuffed him.

The gun barrel pulled away from Alvaro's neck. The gunman backed two giant steps away. Benito, with his bland lipless face and tonsure. He lowered the gun until it hung at his side. From the looks the *policia* and the *Indio* gave him, they were on his payroll.

The lady didn't act panicked or fearful. Instead, with teeth bared and eyes flashing white fire, she glared at Benito.

"*Digame*," Alvaro said. "What's the crime?"

"Crime?" Benito asked. "Not you, mister. You are only doing your job, I think." He hitched a thumb toward the lady. "Here is the killer."

"*Mentiroso.*" Her voice seemed to originate in her bowels.

Benito responded with a sneer and waved his free hand toward the *policia*. "Maybe I will let you go, Mister Hickey, if you tell me a couple things."

Though dozens of pilgrims had viewed parts of this scene, few even slowed their progress toward claiming places on the beach. The policeman went to the lady and clutched her free arm, so he and the knife man flanked her like twin suitors as they marched her, kicking and writhing, toward an olive drab Chevy Blazer. When they were several meters ahead, Benito motioned for Alvaro to follow them.

He walked slowly, a meter or two in front of Benito, reminding himself that he had trained for this moment, both as a soldier and as a student of Tae Kwon Do. The first dozen steps, he matched his breathing to the beats of his heart. One breath to every seven heartbeats. Then he looked and analyzed. The enemy had made two mistakes. They hadn't cuffed the lady or bound Alvaro's feet, his best weapons. He walked on, listening to Benito's footsteps, calculating his distance, remembering he held the pistol in his right hand.

As they neared the Blazer, Alvaro quickened his step, dreaming they might bunch close enough so he could hit the *Indio*, the policeman, and Benito with a single spin kick. But as he came within reach he changed his mind. Martial arts were about precision. He needed to aim for a single target, the gun. And he couldn't aim unless he saw it. He stopped, two meters from the Blazer, just as the policeman opened the rear side door.

"*Una pregunta,*" he said in his most innocent voice, as though on his first date with a church-going woman. He cocked his head left, peered from the corner of his left eye and spotted the gun. It looked to Alvaro like an antique. WW II vintage. A Luger.

In one fluid move, he bent his left knee, pivoted his left foot, spun, and kicked with his right foot. Benito yipped. But Alvaro had missed the gun by inches, hit Benito's arm too high, near the elbow. The pistol didn't fly, only lofted and dropped a meter or two away. If Alvaro had chosen to complete the spin, he might've caught the *policia* in the face. But he needed to shorten the kick and finish disabling Benito, who dove after his gun.

Just as Benito reached for it, Alvaro landed a front kick to his forehead. Benito flipped backward like a dying gymnast.

Alvaro dipped and picked up the Luger, holding it between his cuffed hands. A door of the Blazer slammed. While he found a grip on the pistol with his cuffed right hand, he wheeled and saw that the lady, from inside the Blazer, had slammed the rear door between herself and the enemy. The *Indio* fumbled for his sidearm as though half-afraid to touch it after witnessing Alvaro's moves. The policeman flung open the front door and plunged into the Blazer, seeking cover, chasing the lady, or both.

Alvaro pointed the pistol at the *Indio's* midsection. The *Indio* whipped both hands up as though to snag a pass.

"*Tire abajo la pistola*," Alvaro commanded. "Kick it under the car."

"*Si, patrón.*" The *Indio* dropped his short-barreled Colt and kicked it out of sight under the Blazer.

The lady had crawled over the rear seat into the luggage space and found a tire iron. She flailed it. The policeman howled. She whacked him again while he groped for the door. After it flew open, as he stumbled out, Alvaro dropped him with an elbow to the back of his neck.

Benito was on the ground beside the rear wheel. He had lifted a hand to his head, but hadn't yet started to rise. The *Indio* stood with hands out, proclaiming his neutrality.

"*Las llaves*," Alvaro said.

The *Indio* fished out his keyring.

"Give it to the lady," Alvaro said.

The *Indio* nodded, stiff and polite as a butler. He waited for Lourdes who was climbing out of the Blazer. He showed her the key to the cuffs. She freed Alvaro. Her cold fingers worked without trembling.

"I'll watch these guys," he said. "You collect the weapons, please. One's under the truck."

She plucked the pistol out of the fallen policeman's holster. Then she dropped to her knees, pressed her skirt around her legs, and tunneled under the Blazer. On the way out, she bumped her head, yet she hardly winced. She handed him the Luger carefully as though it were a bomb. Then she dropped the keys on the sand beside him and hustled to the front seat of the Blazer. She lifted a shotgun off the rack on the dash.

He knelt beside Benito, rolled him over and gouged a knee into his back while he yanked the man's arms together and cuffed them. He picked up the key ring, found a Chevrolet key next to a Guadalupe medallion. He tried the key in the Blazer's passenger door. It worked. He pocketed the key ring.

The *Indio* was nodding and presenting the face of somebody waiting to be clued if smiling is allowed, and as if he'd all along been an ally of Alvaro and the lady. Though Alvaro wouldn't have trusted the man to direct them from the beach to the ocean, he played along and nudged the fellow's arm in a playful way. Then he walked to Benito, who sat on the dirt. "So, either I kick you in the face, or you tell me exactly what you want with us."

But the lady had rushed to Alvaro's side and grasped his arm. She leaned over Benito, her hands out like claws, her face contorted so savagely, Alvaro thought she might grab the man's head and start ripping. She demanded, "Where is Rolf?"

Benito shrugged his hands, looking stupefied enough to convince her. She groped for Alvaro's hand without looking. "We must go now, quickly."

"You're the boss. Give me a minute, though." He gently released his hand from the lady's grip, then reached around to his back and retrieved the Luger from where he had stuck it under the waist of his jeans. He stood over Benito and passed the gun back and forth between his hands. "Tell me something. Why'd you kill those guys in Long Beach?"

Again, Benito looked stupefied. He knew nothing about Long Beach. Or else the Shuler household was a troupe of consummate actors. "Look here, Benito," he said. "Next time we meet, you get to be a punching bag. Or a target." He raised and aimed the gun. "Whichever Lourdes prefers."

He used his Swiss Army knife to slash the sidewalls of the Blazer's front tires.

Chapter Sixteen

Alvaro fired the motor of his Chevy, rammed the gear-shift into low, worked the clutch and punched the gas so rapidly all those moves seemed to happen at once. They bulleted off, slinging gravel and dirt behind. The wagon fishtailed onto the one-and-a-half-lane trail. They were the only outbound traffic. A column of inbound trucks, SUVs and dune-buggies swerved onto the soft roadside.

"You are a warrior," the lady said, but rather than sounding complimentary she appeared concerned, as if the title wasn't all honor.

"Before the army, I was in some karate tournaments. I didn't know if I could still aim a spin kick, especially without warming up. We're lucky I didn't just pinwheel into the ground. Rolf," he said. "Why did you ask Benito about him?"

"He is…my brother." She grabbed the fingers of her left hand with her right hand.

Alvaro let his question and her response and gesture wander his mind and lodge in the place where dilemmas got stored. After a few minutes' silence, during which he imagined her heart slowing down and her adrenaline subsiding, like his was, he said, "I'm feeling okay about that little scuffle. Look what it got us. Three guns."

Without looking over, she said, "I suppose one never knows when she may need a gun."

Alvaro thought, anyone who speaks so casually about deadly weapons could probably commit murder.

◇◇◇

From the coast to Highway 1, Alvaro flew over gulleys, skimmed over deep, fine sand and watched ahead for *policia*, while Lourdes used the side mirror to scout the road behind. During moments when the road didn't require his concentration, Alvaro worried that he and the lady were driving into a trap they set for themselves with the broadcasted message.

On the highway he kept to the speed limit. They arrived at the turnoff to the Mission Santa Inez at 3:40. A hundred meters short of the mission, he veered off and climbed his wagon along a goat trail up a hill. The back and sides of the hill was a lemon orchard. On top was the ruins of a shack. He parked behind it, out of sight from the roads.

Ripe and fallen lemons scented the air. What

remained of the shack were two full walls and a half wall and several long branches that used to serve as roof beams. The floor was dirt with a fire pit in the middle. Alvaro had to pause a minute and convince his unconscious this was not Vietnam. He couldn't quite erase from his memory all the patrols into villages when they ran, shouting and with weapons raised or ablaze, into hootches too much like this hovel.

From evidence such as candy wrappers, fruit skins and burnt cans that might've held condensed milk and nectar, he guessed the shack served as a way station for *pollos* trekking north to the border.

He fetched the beach chairs out of his wagon. He and Lourdes stationed themselves in the shadows a couple meters back from the doorway. While they watched and waited, to keep his mind off the dangers that might be speeding their way, he reminded himself of all that could be at stake. First, the future and maybe the life of a woman of great spirit and beauty—which she was whether or not she had murdered her Nazi father. And the fate of her sister who could be as remarkable. Also, the future of Mexico might depend on them, outrageous as that sounded.

He tried to imagine a Mexico whose people didn't have to trek thousands of miles and live in squatters' camps, or hovels, or apartments with six to a bedroom. He attempted to picture a Mexico with few beggars, where the sick and the orphans got cared for. But a question kept interrupting.

"How does Rolf fit in?" he said.

She looked as if he had asked something slightly out of line, like whether she preferred tampons to napkins. "Fit in?" she asked, her bottom lip trembling.

"Into the reason we're down here?"

She caught her trembling lip with her teeth. Then all appearance of harmony deserted her. She wept with pure abandon.

Alvaro reached for her hand. Her grip was strong but shaky. "Rolf is my best friend," she said in a voice so passionate Alvaro wondered if she could be more than a little crazy. Maybe, he thought, what he'd mistaken for serenity was only a manifestation of something dead inside her. Maybe she was the opposite of a Holy Virgin. Maybe the lady was a psychopath.

A small station wagon, green except for a blue front left fender, had turned off the highway and was creeping toward the mission. Alvaro backed away from Lourdes, reached for his binoculars, jumped up, and peered through them. He saw a Subaru emblem and California plates. He grabbed for the notepad and stubby pen in his breast pocket and handed them to Lourdes. He dictated the license number.

The men sat in front. The driver had a goatee and a ponytail. The fellow riding shotgun was clean shaven with a mop of kinky black hair. In the back seat, slumped so low Alvaro hadn't readily noticed, someone with lighter hair sat. The head was smaller and the shoulders sloped more than the men's did. "Lupe?" He gave the lady the binoculars.

The Subaru swung a turn and pulled in sideways to the building, as though preparing for a getaway. The driver left the motor running, Alvaro saw from the wisps of exhaust out the tail pipe and because the wagon occasionally quivered.

The man riding shotgun jumped out. He looked both ways, opened the rear door on his side, and spoke to the woman. She looked up. Lourdes gasped.

"Your sister?"

The lady didn't answer. The binoculars fell onto her breasts.

Alvaro jumped the half wall, dashed to the wagon, and fetched all three guns he'd taken from Benito and his posse. He hustled back to the lady's side. "The guy with the Afro, I saw him before, along the road." He had stood outside a junky motor home on the road to El Rayo, this morning, wearing the same T-shirt from Gorky's Hollywood Café.

Alvaro had just returned to Lourdes in the doorway and was handing the lady the Colt revolver when three men in khakis raced out of the mission, their weapons up and ready. The man with an Afro bolted around the Subaru. The shotgun door flew open, and he tried to leap in but the wagon was already pulling away. He clutched the door and got dragged along. The three *policia* knelt to fire.

But Alvaro fired first, with Benito's Luger. He yelped to Lourdes, "Don't hit anybody. Shoot air or dirt." Bullets lofted over the mission, into a wheat-brown meadow. The *policia* scampered back into the mission. The Subaru skidded a turn over the gravel road and slowed just enough so the man clutching the door could dive in.

Alvaro and the lady dashed to the Chevy. While they bounded and crashed down the hillside, the Subaru reached Highway 1 and turned north. It had about a kilometer head start, but Alvaro's Chevy was rigged with a 427 cubic inch V-8. He punched the gas and flew along the mission road and onto the highway, over a hill, around switchbacks, and up a long straightaway. He passed a bus, three farm pickups and a sputtering tractor without catching sight of the Subaru. After ten kilometers, he knew it must've turned onto one of the farm roads or goat trails. Or vanished into the sky.

The lady said, "When we were little, Rolf made up stories for me and Lupe. He told us of a fairy land where grown ups could not go. If we ate enough of the mangoes, we disappeared. Rolf wore a purple cape. Even when he was invisible, we could see his cape. That way, we knew he was always near and would not let the giants or the ogres devour us."

She was smiling and looked light years away.

◇◇◇

Tom Hickey preferred sunlight to indoors. The cord of Clifford and Ava's phone reached the patio, where Tom sat in one of the Adirondack chairs he had built long ago. Out on the bay past the mud flats, water skiers slalomed around the buoys.

Tom had asked Clifford how his brother met the Shuler woman. Clifford phoned Garfield et al and quizzed the receptionist, who remembered a woman who had called for Alvaro and said Augustín Quartilho referred her.

Clifford reported to Tom, who phoned Quartilho. "I am pleased all you Hickeys are working for her," the *abogado* said. "This is what I recommended. She, and her problems, may be too much for one man."

"So, you knew she was mixed up with this Virgin when you sent her to Alvaro?"

"Yes, I noticed a resemblance to the sketch."

"And you knew her real name was Lourdes Shuler?"

"Garcia, she told me. I took her at her word. Shuler, you say?"

"Shuler," Tom said. "Like Andres, a big shot in the Capital. And like Hans, a financier, murdered last month in Durango."

"Ahh."

"But you didn't know this Lourdes was wanted for the murder."

"For murder. No, Tom, I swear."

"Listen, *Señor*, my boy's going to be an attorney next year. My other boy's a writer."

"I know this. We talk, Alvaro and I."

"You got kids?"

"Six," Quartliho said.

"You raise kids, one of the points is, make them better than you, so they can change the world a bit, you know what I mean. See, lawyers can change things, sometimes for the better. Writers too. P.I.s, we just clean up messes. What I'm saying, you want a P.I., you don't even think about going to one of my boys. Next time, you call me. I'm not up to it, I refer you to somebody."

"Agreed. Tom, you tell *Equis*, stay far away from Paco Monreal."

"Who's that?"

"A *comandante* of the federal judicial police. He has come to Baja on a special assignment, which I believe is to stop this Virgin."

Tom finished the call and went into the house to sit with Feliz. She gave him a smile that appeared to exhaust all her energy. Since he'd arrived, her face had brightened then darkened again. Her temperature had fallen, then risen, as if antibodies fought and whipped the enemy but the enemy came pounding back with reinforcements.

The phone rang. Tom carried it out to the patio.

"Special Agent Kevin Pratt. You called."

"I did," Tom said. "Thanks for getting back to me."

"You have information?"

"About what?"

"Why, your son and the Virgin. Isn't that what you called about?"

"Actually I called to make you a deal. I'm willing to keep you posted about Alvaro, in exchange for what all the FBI can tell me about this Virgin. Like, have you found any pattern in her movements, made any guesses about where she'll next appear. Like, who's behind her, and how big an effort is being made to hunt her down."

"Sir, I told your son Clifford to ask Alvaro to call me directly. I may be able to give him some of this information. But none to you. No offense."

"The thing is, Alvaro's busy enough, and dealing with enough complications, so the odds of him contacting the FBI are about one to infinity."

"Well, he should reconsider. Okay, one thing I can tell you. There appears to be a connection to *el Partido de la Gente* and to a Mexican student who may have been involved in the theft of sophisticated projection equipment from the UCLA film school. And there is little question but that the image of the Virgin is being projected into these remote villages, using some kind of hologram. You've heard of them."

"I saw Mister Spock use one. Try this: are you in contact with a *federale* named Paco Monreal?"

"That I can't say."

"Well, look him up. Tell him I'm one mean, resourceful old sonofabitch whose connections reach his side of the border. And I'm holding him personally responsible for anything that might happen to Alvaro."

◇◇◇

Alvaro sped to the coast. On the way, he itemized what he knew. One: either Lourdes truly had a sister, or she and some co-conspirators were treating him to the most convincing performance since Bogart played a tough guy.

Two: the state police, local police, *federales*, FBI, drug cartel gunmen, and municipal *policia* from every city and *pueblo*, and the Catholic church, the CIA, and for all he knew the Danish and Ukrainian and every other secret service worldwide, could by now be alerted to watch out for him and Lourdes.

"Here's an alternative," he said. "We could leave your sister to her work, trade my car for some horses or donkeys, hike the *montañas,* and jump the border. That's the only way I figure we've got a decent chance of being alive and free tomorrow. Then, after the election, when the newshounds get off your sister's back and the police are once again preoccupied with collecting *mordida* from lawbreakers and other suckers, we'll find Lupe, no matter which side of the border she's on."

The lady had her eyes closed, her head sideways on the top of the seat. "My friend, is this danger too much for you?"

"Whoa." He thought, this is it. No more waffling between she's a murderer and thief, she's the Virgin, she's a psycho. Right now, he needed to choose, then drop her at a bus stop or take a pledge to play for her team, whatever the hell she was. He felt like a guy at the altar asking himself, Till death, you say?

He said, "We need to ditch my car."

Chapter Seventeen

After stashing the stolen guns under bushes in an arroyo, they left the Chevy in a dirt lot between a storefront evangelical church and a corner grocery on the outskirts of Playa Estero. A quarter mile back, they had passed a field overrun with vehicles. Alvaro suspected every taxi driver and unemployed man with a car or pickup was down here shuttling pilgrims to Playa Sin Olas.

Alvaro and the lady wore matching baseball caps with a cockroach logo, from The Pests of the National Adult Baseball Association. The caps were tugged low, their heads hung like *penitentes*. They rode with twelve others in an ancient DeSoto. The sun had dipped into the Pacific. Above the sunset that looked like a distant forest fire, the sky had shaded to purplish gray. The outside air smelled of creosote, the inside reeked from sweat and sour breath.

At the speed this overloaded wreck of a sand taxi was traveling, he calculated they should arrive just after the Virgin had blown a farewell kiss and vanished into the sky. Only the fact that Lourdes was perched on his lap kept his spirits from plummeting. Straddling his right thigh, she was lighter than he'd imagined. Every few seconds, her left cheek, snug between his legs, twitched and then he felt her stomach tighten. He was holding her around the waist, hands folded on her belly. His nose was nestled in her sage-scented hair. He felt at peace.

◇◇◇

While the eastern sky with its tumbling black clouds closed in on Playa Sin Olas, the taxi delivered them as close as anyone could in traffic like rush hour on the 101 through Hollywood. The pilgrims spilled out of the taxi. The lady and Alvaro tromped over packed sand along the inland side of the crowd. The seaward edge of the crowd was knee-deep in the rising tide. Bold pilgrims who ventured into the middle of the crowd appeared to get swallowed. From the edges of the beach along the low mesa to the east, where the crowd was mostly engaged in picnicking, came whiffs of burning mesquite and hot grease.

Alvaro thought of the Bible, the book that more than any had taught him English. He suspected nobody here could ever again read about the Sermon on the Mount or Jesus feeding the multitude without picturing this place today.

None of these folks were going to move until the

Virgin showed or failed to, unless they found a better vista point than they had already staked out. In fact, the crowd was shrinking, inward and toward the front, like crowds he remembered from rock festivals when the Stones, the Dead, or his old band-mate Carlos walked onto the stage. But the raggedy folks here were honestly poor without parents or prosperous brothers and sisters to mooch off, like hippies and Deadheads usually had.

Alvaro held no grudge against hippies or Dead-heads, many of whom he counted as friends, but these Mexicans, not the *ricos* but *la gente,* were his people. No matter that he'd gotten rescued out of the fix they were in. And the *ricos,* at least the rulers and their sup-porters, were still his enemy. Not only the PRI but the whole setup. Police who needed *mordida* to supplement their puny wages, the ass-backward Napoleonic law that made poor folks guilty until they proved them-selves innocent, the jails and prisons where the wealthy got feather beds, lobster and whores, while the *pobres* lived like vermin. And where, if anyone wanted to kill somebody, such as Alvaro's papa, he only had to pay a guard a few pesos to look the other way.

Alvaro and the lady double-timed and caught up with a group of late arrivals who were rounding the southeast corner of the crowd, which by now climbed the low mesa. Crusty dirt broke away under their feet. At the lead end of the group were a prosperous Mexican, short with wavy salt and pepper hair, with woolen slacks and a silk shirt that made Alvaro guess he could be from the Capital. He could be a federal cop of some kind, Alvaro thought. But his companion was a *gringo*, and as civilian as anyone could be, with dusty, stringy hair and no more flesh on his bones than a twiggy model. He had a hook nose, baggy trousers and sandals, an old Levi jacket over a white T-shirt gone gray. He carried a guitar in a cloth case slung over his back. A small gray terrier walked at his heels. If this fellow was a cop, he was in mighty deep cover.

The crowd kept squirming closer together. It looked like trout in a hatchery. The front edge of that mob, at the base of the hill, was still a hundred and fifty meters ahead. Alvaro and Lourdes had already come halfway from the rear. He guessed around 4000 souls were there.

A pudgy fellow with a shaggy Afro and a faded green T-shirt, which Alvaro knew advertised Gorky's Hollywood Cafe, was going the wrong way, against the flow. He was a captive, Alvaro saw, sandwiched between the two *gringos* Alvaro had noticed that afternoon, young, stocky blond men in button down shirts and slacks. The fellows he'd taken for Mormon missionaries. One of them was holding the captive's hands behind his back and steadying him so he didn't tip and roll down the slope. He walked with a pause between each step as though he needed the pauses to gather strength or willpower. The blond guys could be taking him to a medic or hospital, he reasoned, but after they passed, he caught a glimpse of the cuffs on the fellow's wrists.

Alvaro didn't know whether to follow them, or continue pushing on to a better position for seeing the Virgin. If the Virgin would appear now that one of her companions was in custody.

He was nudging the lady, to tell her what he had seen and ask her advice, when he noticed the guitarist peering all around. He looked spooked, like a kid lost in Disneyland. "Carlos," he muttered, then shouted, then muttered again. Alvaro thought the guitarist's *amigo*, the prosperous Mexican with salt and pepper hair, must've ditched him.

The blond men and their captive had vanished into the crowd. Alvaro gave up on them, for now. A few steps farther along, the group got stalled behind a weary Mexican husband and wife escorting a feeble grandmother. Nobody could pass them without bowling over, on one side, a pack of women who looked like schoolteachers or, on the other side, a band of short Indians herding their bony children. Every few seconds a man yelped with delight as if he'd seen Her, or a woman sprang up yowling and pointing. Others whirled arms above their heads. The crowd got wilder by the second. When lightning flashed on top of the mountains, some people must've thought it was She. A few yards from Alvaro, a woman fainted. Others shoved, groped, even clawed their way toward the front. Pilgrims got knocked down or tripped and men driven to anger began defending their territory or battling forward with fists and elbows. Grownups hoisted children into the air and tried to push ahead with the kids held high, attempting to wedge through spaces they couldn't have pushed a sheet of paper through. And still Alvaro saw nothing in the clearing at the base of the hill, except the air looked darker and redder than a minute ago.

The guitarist was still peering around when he stopped still in front of and facing the lady. His baffled face broke into a wide smile. "Lupe," he said. "Don't you remember me?"

Lourdes grabbed him by a shoulder. "You know Lupe?"

He held still as though petrified except his squint kept narrowing.

She squeezed his arm. "Lupe is my sister. Where is she?"

"Everywhere," the guitarist mumbled.

◇◇◇

When she appeared, she came out of the storm clouds

over the mountains. No flash or thunder, just a white speck that grew as she flew closer. Kids, with their sharp eyes, saw her first, when she was still tiny, miles away. And as she neared, all the commotion stopped. In the minute it took her to fly the twenty or thirty kilometers from the mountains to the beach, the pilgrims had finished their cheers and gasps and hallelujahs. So, by the time she arrived, everybody had frozen to stare at Our Lady in her cream-white robe, with her bare feet and long brown hair cascading over her shoulder and breast. Her hands were folded and placed low on her belly.

She hovered about ten feet above ground, as if to protect the crowd from tragedy when they rushed to grasp her, which they surely would've. They might've tried running and leaping if at least a squad of *policia* hadn't dashed in and formed a line between the crowd and the apparition. Alvaro imagined pilgrims breaking through the police line, bounding into the air, ripping her naked and clawing her to shreds. But he knew that wouldn't happen. They would grab for her and catch nothing but air. She looked almost ghostlike, not quite solid, and slightly less than three-dimensional.

Only a few people shouted, and neighbors hushed them. They waited for her words. For a minute, she stood still. Only a slight turn of her shoulders and a lift of her chin assured them she was alive.

The guitarist said, "She listened to my songs. She

called one of them glorious. I can't remember which one it was."

Alvaro tried to stay close to the guitarist. Afterward, he would grill the fellow. The Virgin had begun to speak, in a voice clear and strong. "*Bienaventurados los humildes…*" She spoke Spanish, but translated often, short phrases like "Blessed are the meek." In a voice easily as serene and melodious as the lady's, she said, "The rulers of your country, having been born of a revolution that painted the land with blood, have ruled with bloody hands. The church has catered to the violent, to the oppressors, and in so doing has drawn as far from Christ as did the evil one. I beg you, my children, to flee from the evil ones, to ignore their threats, reject the lies and the bribes with which they buy your favor. And remember always, you are not of them, you are of the living God. Therefore, when you have overcome, when your land belongs to you, remember these words, and make them your theme—Blessed are the merciful, for they shall receive mercy.

"And you rulers, and you who stand beside the rulers and prosper as they do, search your hearts and see the misery that haunts you. These poor ones are happier than you. They know love. They serve God in their small ways. They share what little you allow them to have. Only in these ways is happiness gained. Only the givers are blessed with peace and happiness.

The takers know ever-deepening misery. They long to escape from themselves. Search your hearts, my children. Ask heaven to show you where happiness lies."

She held out her hand as though blowing kisses except she hadn't touched her lips. Thousand of hands reached out as if they could touch her white fingers. Alvaro wondered if they all felt a strange heat race up their arms and through their shoulders to their hearts, like he did.

Then she flew away, up and angling toward the ocean. The guitarist started to stagger away and wedge through the mob, going toward the hill. Alvaro followed him. They squeezed between pilgrims who remained staring into the night sky as if they awaited a second coming and dodged others who were already scampering to get out front of the traffic jam. In the center section of the crowd where the first dozen rows would've been, men shouted. Bottles shattered. Women screeched. Men shouted louder.

The guitarist ran that way, dodging, swivel-hipped, holding the little dog tight to his chest, the guitar to his side. He had almost reached the melee when he stopped and yelled, "Carlos?" He reached out for the man Alvaro had seen him walking with earlier.

But Carlos didn't answer or turn. He rushed out of the crowd, under the rope and into the clearing.

The guitarist lunged and slammed into a wall

of pilgrims. He back-stepped, ducked, and blasted through a crack in the human wall.

Then Alvaro saw the rifle. A uniformed cop passed the long rifle to a tall man in shiny jeans and boots and a cowboy hat.

Now Carlos was sprinting up the hillside. He had almost vanished in the dark when the cowboy raised the rifle and reached for something on the barrel. A reddish glow haloed the scope. When he pushed the stock into his shoulder and fixed the barrel steady, the guitarist yelled and dropped the dog. He charged toward the rifleman, broke through a pair of *policia* and dipped his shoulder like a blocking back. He threw a cross-body and crashed into the cowboy's spine.

The cowboy didn't fall, but he stumbled. The rifle boomed. On the hill, a woman screamed. Two *policia* and two other men hit the guitarist from all sides. He dropped from his knees straight to the ground, on top of the guitar he had wrenched around front. He ducked his head to protect the guitar, but he looked up in time to see the cowboy raise his rifle. He yowled, let go his guitar, and thrashed. His captors held him down.

The rifleman sighted, steadied himself, and fired. He lowered the gun to his side and peered through a set of red-haloed binoculars. After a minute, he turned toward the guitarist. He spat on the ground.

Alvaro had lost sight of the lady. He tried to find

her by peering over and through the crowd. He back-tracked to where he guessed they had stood when he last saw her, but everyone in the crowd had changed places. All he could imagine was that she might've gone toward the apparition. He headed back that way, bumping and weaving against the crowd.

A Red Cross helicopter landed in the clearing at the base of the hill. When Alvaro broke free from the crowd, he sprinted across the clearing through the dust and riot of noise the copter made. He started up the hill, but ran into a mob of reporters and camera crews, all of them held back by a line of *policia*.

Chapter Eighteen

As he backed out of the mob, Alvaro saw the lady. About twenty meters up the hillside from what had been the front edge of the crowd, she was hanging onto a man he recognized. He hadn't seen the man before, or seen a photo, or seen anyone who looked like him. He didn't even look much like his sisters. His hair was a lighter brown, rather short, and wavier than theirs. He was a head taller than the lady, and thinner. His face was striking, with prominent eyes and a square jaw. In Hollywood, he could've found a starring role in a remake of *The Three Musketeers* or *Wuthering Heights*. He looked deep, and noble.

He had Lourdes gripped tight to his side. He watched the pilgrims who knelt at the lady's feet and cried out, "*Bendigame, Santa Virgen!*" She clutched with both arms around Rolf's waist.

The sight so distracted Alvaro, he didn't see or hear the *policia* until they dashed by him. Before he could act, two of them had grabbed the lady. One by an arm, one around the neck. A third caught hold of Rolf. He tried to thrash away. The policeman cracked his head with a baton.

Alvaro rushed the lady's captors. With a guttural shout, he threw a flying side kick that caught one policeman in the cheek. But the side hand strike to the lady's other captor missed when the policeman ducked. Then the one who had knocked Rolf unconscious came from behind. He looped the circle his arms and baton made around Alvaro's neck. He was strong. The baton cut into Alvaro's windpipe. His hand had found his pocket and reached the small .22, when his legs buckled.

The policeman wrenched Alvaro's arms back and cuffed them, tore the .22 out of his pocket, bound his feet with a nylon rope, and hitched the rope to the cuffs so he couldn't flail around. When he managed to roll onto his side and look behind him, he found they had fixed the guitarist the same way. They were about two arm-lengths apart.

The guitarist gasped, "Gretchen? Where's my dog? Anybody seen my dog? Gretchen?"

They hadn't thrown the lady to the ground or bound her feet like they had with all three men. They had cuffed her and ordered her to sit on the dirt and keep her head down so the pilgrims couldn't see her face. Rolf had crawled to his sister and lay beside her. She caressed his back and shoulders with her cuffed hands. They talked, but Alvaro couldn't hear distinctly above the commotion of the pilgrims who still surrounded them, as well as the police and the guitarist calling for his dog. He only caught enough to know Rolf was gushing apologies, which the lady was gladly accepting.

They were only fifty meters from the base of the hill. Much of the crowd had dispersed toward the parking field and shuttles. The moon was near full and rising when Alvaro spotted the cowboy rifleman about thirty meters up the hillside. He was standing beside a fallen woman the medics hovered over. The woman bucked and yowled when a medic did some procedure. They were about to load her onto a stretcher when a man jumped out of a skiff grounded at the shoreline and came running across the beach. A woman climbed out of the skiff and stood in the shorebreak.

The man had a goatee and glossy black hair in a ponytail. Alvaro recognized him—the passenger in the Subaru at the mission. Now he carried a weapon that looked to Alvaro like his Vietnam M-16. The man zigged to the uphill side, clearly trying for an angle from which to shoot the cowboy while sparing the medics. But the medics were moving, blocking every angle. The man slowed and plodded straight toward the cowboy.

But the strong policeman who had used his baton on Rolf and Alvaro had seen the gunman. The policeman crept in a circle. Alvaro would've yelled to the gunman, except one of the *policia* saw his mouth open and hissed and turned a pistol on him. Then the strong policeman reached the gunman and chopped his baton so fiercely, Alvaro felt relieved when the gunman's head didn't fly off.

The woman at the shoreline wore an overcoat and a cap with her hair tucked into it. "Lupe," Alvaro muttered, too low for the lady or her brother to hear.

Lupe didn't move until the policeman knocked her companion down and stepped on his throat. Then she wailed and stalked across the beach toward the cowboy, screaming. "*Cochón! Cochón!*" She moved like a ghost, beyond any need to hurry, beyond time. Two *policia* rushed her. She clawed and kicked, even after they had cuffed her. She kicked and screamed for minutes, until a four-seat helicopter landed nearby.

The helicopter carried her, the gunman, and one *federale* away. The cowboy's victims, a young woman wounded by the errant shot, and the guitarist's dead *amigo*, got loaded into the Red Cross helicopter. A *federale* dismissed the various plain-clothed and uniformed cops a few at a time. They walked or rode away in trios or foursomes like ballplayers after the game arranging to meet for pizza and beer, until all that remained were two feds and four *policia*. The *policia* shooed pilgrims away from Lourdes. Alvaro believed neither she nor Rolf witnessed their sister get captured, because pilgrims surrounded them, still weeping for her and beseeching her favors.

As the last straggler joined the departing crowd, a six-wheel GMC pickup, each of its tires tall as a VW, came off the low mesa. It swung a U-turn and stopped between Alvaro and Lourdes and her brother. A Toyota Land Cruiser pulled in behind it.

The feds ushered Lourdes into the pickup bed. Then they heaved Rolf, Alvaro, and the guitarist onto the bed like bundles of laundry.

Once the prisoners had squirmed into place, Alvaro tried to catch the lady's eye. But she didn't look his way, she was so intent on comforting her brother. Her cuffed hands were on his knees.

The *policia* who climbed in with them was a surly *Indio.* Alvaro guessed he might be one of those tortured people who avenge themselves by torturing. He sat on a wheel well, gripped his M-16 in both hands and swept it back and forth between his prisoners.

The driver raced the motor in neutral then banged into gear. The truck lurched away, creeping through the sand. A siren from inside the cab and a portable flashing light on the roof sent pilgrims scampering out of its way. The Land Cruiser tailed, a few car-lengths behind.

If he'd had the slightest use of his legs, Alvaro thought, he could lunge head first, butt the surly *Indio* guard on the upper chest or shoulders and topple him out of the bed. But even if all the prisoners managed to dive out of the pickup, the escort in the Land Cruiser would catch or shoot at least some of them, and Alvaro wasn't willing to sacrifice anybody. Not even Rolf, he thought.

He tried to imagine a jailbreak, but couldn't. The best he could hope for, short of the more likely scenario involving months of lawyers and judges and a carload of *mordida*, was that a jailer might be willing to risk his occupation for a gold bar or two. If Clifford could deliver one. More likely, the lady, her brother, and Lupe if the cowboy didn't kill her first, would get sent back to Durango. And one or more of them would get charged with the murder of their father. Alvaro would land in Tijuana's La Mesa prison or an even deeper chamber of hell for whatever Mexican law called aiding and abetting. The lady's brother Andres would learn about the gold under Alvaro's duplex. Either Lourdes would volunteer the gold's whereabouts, or Andres would cajole, threaten, or beat it out of her. Pop would sell the bayside cottage and the Lake Tahoe shack for the *mordida* to free his adopted son, whether or not Alvaro wanted him to. Alvaro so hated the idea of Pop and Clifford losing heir homes, he decided that at some point he'd give the cops the opportunity to simplify matters, to apply *la ley de fuga,* the law of fire, by shooting him while he ran. Or hopped, if somebody hadn't yet unbound his feet.

An admonition from his Tae Kwon Do training came to mind. "Do you have indomitable spirit?" Master Oh used to ask them.

Alvaro muttered, "Yeah, right." He crooked his head for a glance at Lourdes, who was leaning against her brother. He tried castigating himself for allowing self-pity and remembered that the best way to lift oppression was to think about the welfare of someone else. Like the lady, the guitarist, or Mexico's poor.

Maybe, he thought, he could get a message to Clifford, who could go to Augie Quartilho, who could enlist an army of *coyotes* and other *banditos* if he chose to, and if he knew about the lady's gold. If Alvaro could pass Clifford's number and a message to somebody. Maybe this guard.

"Pssst."

The guard looked around, Alvaro said, "*Amigo,* I'll bet you could use some big money."

The guard stood just long enough to kick him in the side.

◇◇◇

From the east, a small pickup and a dune-buggy came racing lights out, side by side, straight at the Land Cruiser. Gunshots cracked. Bullets sparked off the roof of the pickup's cab. The guard jumped off the wheel well to the bed. The Land Cruiser behind them swerved right, off the trail. Then it cut back too fast, flipped onto its side and slid to a stop.

The driver of the pickup stomped the pedal. The pickup roared and shot ahead. It sailed over a gully and a dip and raced wildly up a flat straightaway and fishtailed a hundred meters on a slight upgrade. At the crest of the hill, the driver must've seen the blockade forming. He punched the brake. All the riders, even the guard, tumbled forward and crashed, some into the tool box behind the cab, some into each other.

The blockade was composed of old trucks and cars. Alvaro counted seven of them, not one that anybody except a *campesino* who had grown up driving such vehicles off road could pilot through the sandy dirt. The vehicles formed a semi-circle.

If Alvaro had been driving the pickup, he would've whipped a U, raced back toward Playa Sin Olas watching for a trail to take him east across the plain and into the foothills. On a trail, he could've easily outrun these vigilantes or Virgin worshippers or whoever they were. But this driver was too stupid, panicked, or macho to retreat. He yanked a turn straight left, into a wasteland of desert and darkness. The first gully, he jumped. The next, a wide arroyo, grabbed the nose of the truck and swallowed it.

The prisoners and guard careened, piled together, and again slammed into the metal tool box. After a stunned moment, Alvaro found Rolf tangled around him. With a mighty buck, Alvaro rolled to the side. The guard had dropped his weapon, he saw. Because Rolf was closer, he shouted, "Rolf, the gun!"

The guard was fast. He dove and caught the M-16 in one hand. Rolf lumbered to his knees. Hands cuffed in back, he appeared to throw himself at the gun. His belly muffled the noise of a single shot.

Alvaro waited for more. When none came, he wondered why the guard hadn't set the weapon on automatic.

Rolf toppled backward onto his sister's lap. Two vigilantes leaped into the arroyo. The guard spun to face them and froze, staring down the barrels of two long rifles.

Chapter Nineteen

Alvaro admired these vigilantes. They had mustered a squad of able vehicles and a platoon of armed men and coordinated an attack so that they suffered no casualties. The men had worn a variety of masks. Bandanas, ski masks, bean sacks with eye, nose and mouth holes, and drawstrings at the neck. A round-bellied man in a New York Yankees T-shirt produced bolt cutters and clipped the prisoners free. Five minutes after the escape, all their vehicles had vanished except the aged Chevy panel truck, into which they hoisted the fugitives.

The lady sat against the driver's side wall, cradling the head and shoulders of her brother, her right hand in a rag pressing on the wound. The bullet had struck him at an angle and torn a gash out of the side of his belly, just above the hip. She must have slowed the bleeding. The stain on his shirt, the size of a gallon paint can lid, didn't spread anymore, and it appeared to be drying.

Alvaro leaned against the opposite wall. The guitarist

rode up front with the driver, a kid about sixteen who only used one speed, top end. The panel truck skimmed over the sand like a hover-craft over water.

The guitarist asked, "Where are we going?"

"*Yo no sé nada*," the kid said.

Alvaro wanted to question Rolf about the murder of Hans Shuler. But if he disturbed her brother, the lady would no doubt fix on him a look he didn't care to see. He leaned and tapped her shoulder. "No offense," he said, "but are you sure Rolf's on our side."

For just an instant, she looked like an angel imitating a gargoyle. Alvaro said, "I get the message." Yet he felt no more confident about this brother. For all Alvaro knew, he could be his Nazi father's son in more ways than blood.

The guitarist leaned over the back of his seat. "Tomorrow, will you guys go back to the beach with me, so we can find my dog?"

Alvaro laughed. "We'll try to work that out," he said, glad to have this fellow's company.

◇◇◇

As they neared the paved road from Punta Banda, the kid pulled alongside a Ford wagon. He braked, jumped out, ran around back, flung open the doors and hustled them out. "*Rapido, rapido.*" He pointed at the Ford.

Alvaro, as well as the lady, helped Rolf out the rear of the panel truck. When his feet touched the dirt, he lurched forward. He looked destined for a landing on his face before Alvaro caught him.

The driver of the Ford was well-fed, light-skinned, and fiftyish. His mustache curled up like a modest smile. *"Ándale! Ándale!"* he shouted.

He and Alvaro guided and boosted Rolf into the back seat. As he slumped toward the window side, Rolf lifted his face and turned on Alvaro a look men often give one another, as if they're not yet rivals but suspect they soon could be.

The lady ran around the car to the far door, to save her brother from needing to move any farther. She slid in and across to the middle. Alvaro sat beside her, behind the driver. The guitarist rode shotgun. Before either of them had shut his door, the Ford was spewing dirt. The panel truck disappeared behind them.

The driver said, *"Señores y señorita,* call me Ismael." After a chortle, he patted the guitarist's shoulder. "Who are you?"

"Noah."

"Aw, another famous man of the sea. And why are you attacking these *federales?"*

"He shot my *amigo."* In the mirror, Alvaro saw Noah's chin crinkle. A tremolo entered his voice. "The big guy in the cowboy suit. Who is he?"

"Paco Monreal," Ismael said.

"Oh no."

"Why you say 'oh no'?"

"Carlos told me about him," Noah said. "Some things."

"And where do you know Carlos?"

"From Good Willy's Market. He came there asking everybody where to find Raul. I took him to Raul's house."

Alvaro had thought the lady was attending to nothing except her brother, but she interrupted. "Who is Raul?"

Noah turned to face her. "He is the queen of heaven's boyfriend."

Alvaro hadn't yet told them that Lupe, and probably this Raul, were in jail. Unless Monreal had shoved them out of the copter.

The driver asked Noah, "How do you know Raul and Lupe?"

"They like my songs," Noah said. "In Malibu. I sing my songs for people who like them, outside Good Willy's Market. I didn't know she was the queen of heaven, not until the newspapers." He twisted around for a look at Lourdes. "Unless the queen of heaven is you."

Lourdes shook her head and turned back to tending her brother.

"But I should've known Lupe was the queen. She's so beautiful, and so kind. She stayed with me for a whole week. Raul went somewhere. She cooked for me and listened to my songs. She liked the pretty ones best. And she hugged me goodnight, every night. We were in my cave. It's back in a canyon. I'm not supposed to tell anybody which canyon. You need to climb the rope ladder to get to my cave. But she told me it was as good as Hearst's castle. And she couldn't look at Gretchen without smiling and going to pet her. And when Rabbit and Fritz drove their Harleys up the canyon to check her out, she kept still through their drunken cussing and all that."

"Rabbit and Fritz?" Alvaro asked.

"Just these two bikers I know. And even after they left, she didn't say a bad word about them. You ever meet somebody and from about a minute after, you feel sure you have a friend forever?"

"Not often enough."

"Sometimes people think I'm stupid," Noah said, "or a little crazy, but I'm not. I only got sent to the home because making up songs is awfully hard. But I went there, and I'll tell you, even inside that place, where the most beautiful people live, nobody is so beautiful and kind as the queen of heaven." He turned for another look at Lourdes.

Alvaro asked, "And Raul introduced you to Carlos?"

"No. Carlos only came, let's see, the day before yesterday."

As though speaking from out of a dream, the lady asked, "Tell us about Raul, please."

"He was a student. He didn't go to Pepperdine. I know lots of students from Pepperdine. But Raul, he went up to UCLA. He didn't come by Good Willy's very much, but sometimes. He had lots of friends. Students, and everybody. Lots of them were Mexican, but not everybody. Raul is the most generous of all except one actor, Martin Sheen, he's generous, too, but he's got money. I mean I guess he does. Raul doesn't have money. Well, sometimes he does, and whenever he does, he gives some to me, and when he got in trouble, he came and asked me for help."

"What kind of trouble?" Alvaro asked.

"Oh, the UCLA people thought he stole some cameras or projectors or something."

"What kind of cameras and projectors?"

"Expensive ones."

"Any chance they made holograms?"

Noah's mouth crimped and his eyes narrowed. For a minute he sat lost in concentration. "You want to hear my song about Raul?"

"*Cántate*," the driver said.

"Okay."

"Hold on," Alvaro said. "One more question. When was the last time you saw Lupe?"

"Well, at the party, at that house just up the beach

from that trailer park where Jim Rockford lives. A friend of Martin Sheen owns the house, and Martin got me the job. That's some house."

"I said when?"

"Oh yeah, Memorial Day. Lupe and Raul came with me. I think they wanted to ask some rich people for money for the their *Partido*. Can I sing now?"

"Sure." Alvaro was thinking about Raul and Lupe in Malibu the day before Hans Shuler got killed.

"Here goes," Noah said, "*Raul, my amigo, was a champion, he fought for the weak and the poor…*"

While Noah sang, his voice eerily smooth and melodious, Alvaro thought, Now you can add a verse about how Raul was like Robin Hood, or Pretty Boy Floyd, only stole from the filthy rich to use his loot in the good fight. And a verse about how he turned his girlfriend into a Virgin and, with space age holograms, gave her to *la gente*.

Chapter Twenty

Alvaro thought, now that he knew the essentials about the Virgin and her mission—that Lupe was real and backed by *El Partido de la Gente*—all he needed to accomplish was to rescue her and Raul, unite the sisters, and deliver them all to safety. "No sweat," he whispered to himself, "if I was Superman."

Where the dirt road intersected Highway 1, he sat tall watching for police cars. The driver had slowed. He made a full stop then turned north toward Ensenada. Up the highway he cruised at a leisurely speed, as if they were a carefree band of picnickers on their way home after a fun-filled day. Alvaro leaned back into the seat, his head close to Lourdes' shoulder, wondering if *he'd* gotten shot, would she kiss and pet him like she did Rolf. He let himself imagine she would. Which helped his mind slow down. Just before fatigue caught up and knocked him out, he was thinking, *Call Clifford.*

He awoke in a place he recognized. A tract of

budget homes that looked about half as substantial as his flimsy duplex, on the southern outskirts of Ensenada. A few blocks into the tract, the wagon pulled into the carport beside a green house. The Fairlane motor gasped and stalled. Ismael jumped out and ran around to help first the lady then Rolf, who by now had gone vampire pale. He breathed in rapid sips while he staggered and got led toward the door by Ismael and Alvaro. Fresh blood oozed from his wound and ran down the right thigh of his dark slacks. The rag Lourdes held over the wound had disappeared beneath the blood, some of which bubbled between her fingers as she clenched the rag.

The front door to the house swung open. A plump, dark woman stood aside, fingers pressed to her mouth. She looked a few years older than Ismael. Her jaw was about four inches wide. After Ismael and his fugitives plodded through, she nudged the door almost shut, peered through the crack that remained, then pushed it closed. She turned the lock-knob and slid a dead bolt into place. Over her shoulder, she yipped commands for Ismael. Secure the curtains. Bring everyone water and snacks.

The living room, so long and narrow it looked like a wide hallway, was furnished with pressboard shelves, a TV hutch and a coffee table, all painted fire-engine red as if to purposely clash with the lime green walls.

Wooden chairs faced the white-leather loveseat over which the woman spread an old blanket before Ismael led Rolf to it and helped him lie down. He curled into a ball. The lady cradled his head with her hands until Ismael's *señora* brought a pillow and a clean rag.

Then Lourdes knelt beside her brother. She pressed into place the new rag. Her left hand was stripping dried blood off his wavy hair when she looked up at Alvaro. Her eyes flashing, her mouth opened round, she looked young as a cherub. "He needs a transfusion, I believe."

Alvaro nodded and pointed at the doorway through which Ismael and the *señora* had disappeared. Noah found a battered guitar leaning against a wall in a dark corner. He sat beside it and plunked one of the dead strings.

When Ismael returned, Alvaro pointed to Rolf. "He needs blood, probably."

Ismael frowned. "A hospital?"

"Or a doctor with plasma or something. How long can you hide us out?"

His head drooped as though he needed to confess something shameful. "Maybe already they are coming here. I am known as a conspirator, a comrade of *el Partido de la Gente*."

"*Señor* Ismael," Noah said, "can I tune your guitar?"

"Please do." Ismael stepped closer to Alvaro as though to pass a secret, and his voice dropped nearly to a whisper. "*La Virgen*, as I think you know, is Lupe Shuler, wife of Raul Meza."

Lourdes turned a startled look on them. "Wife?"

"And," Ismael said, "if the *federales* don't already know about us and *la Virgen*, all they must do is catch one of the *hombres* who rescued you from them, and torture him a little while. And you know they will catch somebody."

"How do we know this?" Lourdes snapped.

"Men drink, men talk," he said as though reciting a proverb.

Noah, having rough-tuned the guitar, strummed a C chord, winced, and reached again for the tuners. The dissonance made Alvaro smile in spite of everything. He knelt beside Lourdes, thinking that in company of a political gang dedicated to ousting the PRI, they had as much chance of hiding in Mexico as the Beatles in their prime would've in Liverpool. "We need to get over the border," he said.

The lady looked at him and nodded then turned back to Rolf.

Alvaro stood and took Ismael aside. "We're going to make a dash for *el norte*. The three of us." He pointed to Noah and the lady. "Rolf won't make it. He needs to stay, get to the hospital or wherever."

"Did you tell her she will be leaving this brother behind?" Ismael asked.

"That's a problem."

As he was returning to Lourdes, hoping to convince her, Alvaro thought he heard Rolf mention gold. And he did hear the lady reply, "I don't know if I believe in this curse."

Alvaro knelt beside her. He waited to hear more talk about the gold, but stares from Lourdes and Rolf notified him the talk had stopped, at least while he was near.

"Rolf needs to go to a hospital," Alvaro said.

The lady appeared to ponder. "All right. And I will go with him."

Alvaro glanced at Rolf and thought he detected a hint of triumph in the midst of the man's agony.

Back with Ismael, Alvaro said, "The lady wants to stay with her brother. She'll fight to stay with him, I'll bet. You don't have any sleeping pills, do you?"

"No," Ismael said. "I could go to the *farmacía*, but right now I am going to call the doctor."

The guitar looked like a toy model tourist shops priced at fifty dollars but sold for twenty after the slightest bartering. Noah finger-picked the chords and melody of "Ode to Joy," a favorite tune of Alvaro's. He thought Beethoven might've composed it to calm and offer hope to folks in as frightful a plight as he, Lourdes,

Rolf and Noah had gotten themselves into. He went to the lady and touched her shoulder. Because she leaned slightly into his touch, he reached up and stroked her hair. She glanced up, then recoiled as though he were a strange lecher.

Rolf attacked with his eyes, which were watery and a darker blue than his sister's. He coughed then managed to ask, "Are you stealing our gold?" Then he coughed again.

Alvaro replied with a bitter sigh and a shake of his head. Then Ismael returned. "The doctor is coming."

◇◇◇

On one issue, Alvaro felt clear. Their chances of reaching and crossing the border on their own totaled zero.

He asked to use the phone. Paying close attention because numbers had always been an enemy of his, he dialed all ten of them correctly. Clifford answered the second ring. "X?"

"Oh man, I'm glad you're home."

"Like I'm glad you're alive? Where are you? Underwater or on a crummy phone, I hope. Tell me you're not still in Mexico?"

"Can't do that."

"Ah, *'mano*, you're in deep. Listen, Pop squeezed some details out of a G-man. It looks like the smoke and mirrors the Virgin uses came out of equipment stolen from UCLA film school."

"Yeah," Alvaro said. "By Raul Meza. Did they get the news that the Virgin is in custody?"

"If they did, they didn't tell us. So now you're coming home, right?"

"Not that easy. We're in Ensenada. The Chevy got left behind, down south of here. I'll get it back, don't you worry."

"Oh right, like I'm not going to worry when you're stuck down there holding hands with a Virgin look-alike. And when a guy who's reputed to be meaner than Godzilla is up from the Capital in charge of the Virgin operation."

"Paco Monreal," Alvaro said. "We saw him in action. So, do you owe me any favors?"

"No doubt. What do you need?"

"Get ahold of Augie Q., tell him to hire a *coyote* with a hot rod four-by. We need him in Ensenada, an hour ago. Have him tie a bandana to his antenna and cruise down Avenida Todos Santos. I'll have somebody pick him up. We'll need him tonight and all day tomorrow, maybe longer. We can pay, don't sweat the money. Whatever he wants, he gets. *Comprendes?*"

"Yep."

"*Hermano*, if you can't find a guy tonight, let it go. No way do I want you coming down. Promise."

"Depends."

"On what?"

"If I can locate the right guy."

"Don't get *loco* on me, brother. Look, if both of us get killed, I won't miss you and you won't miss me, unless we're in opposite climates, which I guess is likely. But Ava, Feliz, Little Tommy when he gets here—I'm not going to let you die without seeing your son. And Pop. Without you and me, he wouldn't have enough to worry about. The relief would kill him. I'm serious, Clifford. You can't find anybody, I've got a back up plan."

"What's that?"

"I send a kid down to Playa Estero, where I had to leave our Chevy. We hide out till tomorrow night, get the Chevy, head for the desert on the back roads, and jump the line. *Coyotes* do it every night. No problem. You don't find anybody, call me here."

Alvaro gave him the number on the phone then waited through the silence, wondering how he could risk his life when death could mean he'd never again see Clifford, the most loyal human alive. When Clifford said, "I'll keep my head, brother. You won't catch me down there unless it's the only way." Alvaro knew that was the closest to a promise he could hope for.

"Anything else?" Clifford asked.

He wanted to say, Yeah, in case I don't make it, remember I love you, man, and tell Pop the same. And he might've added, if I don't make it, buy me a tombstone and if you have it in your heart, engrave it with my name, dates, and *A True Hickey*. And he wanted to tell his brother about the gold bars under the duplex, in case neither he nor the lady survived. But if he said any of that, Clifford wouldn't hesitate to run to his car and speed to Ensenada.

He said, "No, that's all."

"Then I'll get busy. X?"

"Yeah, brother?"

"Whatever you do, don't die."

Alvaro tried to answer but couldn't get a sound to pass the goose egg lump in his throat. He shook his head and dropped the receiver into its cradle.

◇◇◇

When Ismael's *señora* came out of her room, Alvaro was on the floor, back against the wall. His eyes were closed. He felt desolate, stumped by a maze of dangers and desires. He longed for even a few minutes of oblivious sleep.

The *señora* made a soft hiss and waited until Noah, the lady and Ismael looked up at her. Then she stared at the floor as she passed along the news. She said the radio had reported that Carlos Meza, a prominent architect from the Capital, had been shot and killed by a man believed to be *norte americano*. And the same man was suspected of killing two expatriate members of *el Partido de la Gente* at their headquarters in Long Beach, *Alta California*.

She looked up and her face jutted forward and shot glares from Alvaro to Noah and back, as if she was trying to decide which of them was the killer.

"Did they give a description?" Alvaro asked.

"No, *Señor*."

Alvaro scooted closer to Noah. "Are they talking about you or me?"

"It was that *federale*," Noah said.

"Yeah. Monreal shot Carlos. But the other guys, in Long Beach, who killed them?"

"*Federales*," Noah said as if the answer were obvious.

"How do you know?"

"Carlos. He came to the states looking for Raul, and when he went to Raul's house, he found the two dead guys."

"And how did he know the *federales* killed them?"

Noah shrugged and picked up the guitar.

Chapter Twenty-one

While Clifford dialed the phone, he stared out his living room window at the moonlit bay and watched a speed boat pull what looked like a naked water skier.

If Feliz had been well, he wouldn't have even attempted to call Augie Quartilho. But her temp was still over 100 and the headache wicked enough to make the brave girl whimper.

Clifford had interviewed Quartilho a few times for *Epitaph* articles. He called both home and work numbers but heard only rings, didn't even reach an answering machine or service. He tried to think of who else might know a reliable *coyote* if such a creature existed. All he could think of were the lawyers for whom his brother worked as a clerk, and they wouldn't soil their own hands dealing with a *coyote*. Any they knew of would get handled through Augie, their fixer in Tijuana. Clifford knew several border patrol agents, but not well enough to ask for a referral to an outlaw.

Feliz was sleeping, Pop dozing in the chair beside her. Clifford tiptoed into the bedroom where Ava lay tossing as though in a nightmare, lately a common occurrence. He opened the closet and fetched jeans, a sweat shirt, and his Converse sneakers. From a night-stand beside his bed, he grabbed the .45 automatic Pop had given him—and helped him convince Ava to allow it in the house—after the college girl next door got murdered.

He stuffed a few essentials like dental floss and aspirin into his medicine kit and tossed it into a TWA flight bag along with the gun and a pouch full of ammunition. At the front door, he stopped long enough to thank God Pop was here. If he hadn't been, the choice between his brother and his baby girl might've torn him apart.

He climbed into the old Volvo he'd bought a week after Feliz was born. A tow truck driver he'd interviewed told him Volvos could get run over by trains without their cargo getting scratched. He drove to Dr. Fred's house.

Fred owned an acre in a cleft of Mount Soledad, overlooking La Jolla Shores. The house was more like a pagoda than like the mansions that surrounded it. Though midnight wasn't far off, Fred was awake. Clifford supposed most guys stay up late when they're on trial for attempted murder.

Fred greeted him with a scowl that disfigured his beach boy face. His curly hair looked tangled. "Hey, pal. I didn't see you in court." His voice was so hoarse, talking must've hurt.

"Yeah," Clifford said. "Feliz is down with a brain-threatening sinus infection and Alvaro's in a mess, in Mexico. Which is why I need to borrow your Bronco."

"Back up. Alvaro's where, in what kind of mess?"

"He hooked up with the Virgin, the one in the papers, and the FBI and *federales* and every other thug in creation is out to get him. Honest, I can't spare a minute. Give me the keys."

"Jesus, Clifford, tomorrow I get called to testify."

"I'll get back by tomorrow, if you hurry up and give me the fucking keys."

Clifford didn't usually swear, and it was the first time Fred had known him to look and sound homicidal. "Okay, okay," Fred croaked. He reached for the keys on a hook on his wall near the door.

◇◇◇

After a stop for gas and a thermos of coffee, in Fred's Bronco on I-5 south, over the 12 mile stretch to the Mexican border, Clifford lamented that he'd forgotten to leave a note for Pop and Ava. And he reviewed all he knew about the mess Alvaro was in.

The *federales*, from the top, were out to disprove the claims of this Virgin, using whatever means, because the *federales* were in reality a branch of the PRI. Comes a new government, the crooked among them might have to learn new ways to steal. And if the Virgin could turn the *pobres* against the PRI, since the vast majority of Mexicans were poor, without their votes the PRI would become no more than a smudge in history. They could only fix ballots to a certain degree. A landslide would take them out.

The FBI, and probably the DEA, had agents in Baja, he had learned from Pete Carillo. And those agencies must be in cahoots with the *federales*, because no matter what kind of filthy banditos a good many *federales* were, *gringo* lawmen needed their cooperation. So the FBI, in turn, was cooperating. Meaning Kevin Pratt, though he'd passed along insider knowledge, was at least half-way in the pocket of the *federales*. Meaning Clifford had to get his brother, and probably this lady who would otherwise get him killed, out of Mexico, preferably before daylight.

"Yeah," Clifford muttered as he passed a sign, *Mexico 1 Mile,* "I'll do that." Provided, he thought, the Mexican customs police up ahead were too busy dozing or arguing sports or dreaming of the big *mordida* to bother searching his bag.

◇◇◇

As the dark Chrysler pulled in beside Ismael's wagon, Alvaro stood peering between window curtains. The man who stepped out had come alone, carrying a doctor's bag. Alvaro positioned himself so that when the door opened, it would hide him. He'd asked for a gun, but Ismael claimed not to own one, which Alvaro found suspicious, and which in turn made him wonder if he was slipping toward paranoia.

The doctor was tall and stiff. He had a knob-like chin and bushy gray hair. Without a greeting or question, he squatted beside the couch where Rolf lay gripping his sister's hand. She let go of the towel pressed onto his belly and moved down to sit beside his knees. The doctor opened his bag for a stethoscope.

Ismael's *señora* hustled to the kitchen and returned with a chair. The doctor declined to sit. He took Rolf's pulse and blood pressure, listened to his heart, peered into his eyes, removed the towel and stared at the bloody wedge a 5.56 millimeter bullet had chopped out of his side. Then he gazed around the room until he saw Ismael in the doorway to the dark bedroom. "He needs more than plasma. He needs whole blood and surgery. I can't do it here." Pointing to Ismael then to Alvaro, he said, "You will please carry him to my car."

Rolf tried to stand, and would've collapsed except Alvaro caught him around the waist. Slowly, flashing back to Vietnam, the last time he had carried such a fragile burden, he walked toward the door and out, letting Rolf's legs take steps even while they couldn't hold any of the weight. He heard the lady behind him, and felt her breath on the back of his neck. As he guided Rolf into the Chrysler, she hurried around, meaning to climb in beside him through the other door. But Alvaro followed and grabbed her arms, pulled her back, and kicked the car door shut. He stood between the car and the lady. "You're not going."

She sidestepped, lowered her shoulder, and drove into him. He stood his ground. "No, no, no," he said while he reached around and pinned her arms to her side. He squeezed her so tight, it could've cracked ribs. She kicked him in the shins and kneed him too close to his groin. She thrashed with every limb and other part of her.

The Chrysler must've had power windows. Rolf had somehow rolled his window down. In a voice stronger than Alvaro would've thought him capable of, he said in Spanish, "*Querida*, do as they say until I come for you. And then, if they hurt you, or steal from us, they will pay." His eyes turned the threat into a pledge.

Still the lady didn't give up her thrashing. Alvaro wrestled her around the front of the car to the doctor's window. As the window lowered, he asked, "Can you give her a shot of something?"

"I won't," the doctor said, and started the car. The lady ripped one arm free and groped for the car.

Ismael caught one of her hands in both of his.

"Pardon me, *Señorita*, but if they see you with him, they will call the police and learn who he is, and they will believe he is an associate of your sister and Raul, and they will take him to jail where he will die. But without you, the hospital staff has no reason to distrust the story Doctor Magaña tells them, about the robbers who stole this poor man's money and his watch and rings and shot him when he tried to run away."

Lourdes shook her head as though trying to make it fly off. And she kept lunging toward the Chrysler's rear door.

"This way," Ismael continued, "after the election, you can send someone for your brother. Until then the doctor will not allow the hospital to release him. You have my promise."

Even after the car pulled away, Lourdes threw herself at it, until the Chrysler turned the corner and disappeared. Even then, Alvaro sensed that if he let her go, she would chase after the car.

◇◇◇

The third roadblock checkpoint Clifford saw was at the turn off to the Bajamar resort. All three checkpoints were on the northbound side of the toll road. Going south, he hadn't gotten stopped except at the toll road entry. Even there, the only cops were questioning and searching northbound vehicles.

All the way down, two hours from the border,

he'd listened to XRRR, Tijuana's radio news station, and wished he'd perfected his Spanish. The fast-talking commentators required too much of his concentration. And they told him nothing he didn't already know except that the *federales* were blaming the double murder in Long Beach on a *gringo* they also blamed for a murder at Playa Sin Olas.

"Not X," Clifford mumbled. "Please not again." The other time Alvaro was accused of murder, what followed got Clifford sentenced to purgatory.

He pulled into a vista point to refill his coffee cup from the thermos. He used the opportunity and peed over the edge of the cliff, at least a hundred meters above the surf that whacked and swallowed the rocks. The moon and stars that hung west of the cloud bank cast enough light so he could see the reason for the many shrines and crosses along the cliff-side highway. Smashed and rusted cars littered the rocks. Mexico, land of the dead, he thought.

On the next downgrade, when XRRR became static, he found an Ensenada station broadcasting news. He listened to the election coverage, the latest polls from the Capital and southern states, hoping they'd segue into an update on the Playa Sin Olas appearance of the Virgin. They did.

An on-the-scene reporter sounded dizzy with excitement when he declared, "The honorable *Coman-*

dante Monreal of the Federal Police…" The voice blurred into an uproar of shouts that only silenced when Monreal began his proclamation. In a spit-polished baritone, he said, "We have in custody the actress who masqueraded as a prophet many of our citizens take comfort in. The imposter is Maria de Guadalupe Shuler of Alta Tierra in the state of Durango. At the age of eighteen, she ran away, lured by the glitter of Hollywood. The masquerade was planned and orchestrated, in Hollywood, by the anarchists who call themselves *el Partido de la Gente*."

From the background racket, Clifford made out jeers and loud objections. The *federale's* voice raised a notch. "Moreover, she has admitted that the anarchists were financed in this fraud by a coalition of political parties that stand in opposition to the PRI…" He paused and waited for the hisses and taunts to subside. "…who have found themselves in a desperate position, with all reliable polls showing the entire slate of PRI candidates poised for certain victory."

"Maybe last month," Clifford mumbled. "Not today."

Monreal continued, "Whether she willingly participated in the conspiracy or was coerced, we have yet to determine. Tomorrow," he said with the reverence Mexicans give that word, as if it meant heaven. "*Mañana*, she will make her public confession. Until we know whether she is a criminal or a madwoman, we are treating her kindly." Jeers and laughter sounded in the background.

Monreal advised the reporters to go home, write their stories, and return midmorning, when he would meet with them again. Until then, he promised, neither he nor any other official would respond to any questions.

A minute later, while Clifford was guessing what the *federale's* claims meant for Alvaro, he reached the foot of the grade and the outskirts of Ensenada. A quarter mile ahead, he saw the first southbound roadblock.

Chapter Twenty-two

The two army officers backed up by half a platoon of soldiers cradling automatic rifles must've been looking for someone in particular. Maybe Alvaro. Or Lourdes Shuler. Or both. They only made Clifford open his rear doors so they could see the floor and peer under the seats.

Two blocks after he veered right on Avenida Todos Santos, he spotted a sky blue '61 Chevy low rider with gold plating where chrome used to be and a bandana flying from an antenna that looked tall enough to pull in a signal from China. The driver, an over-aged *cholo* wearing a sleeveless t-shirt that left his tatooed arms bare, raised a fist in his direction then waved for him to follow.

Clifford obeyed. He hoped to God it was the right *cholo*. Otherwise, he might end up at some after-hours car club rendezvous, whorehouse, cockfight, drug buy, or *Rebel Without a Cause* game of chicken, where they'd command him to race Fred's Bronco at the cliffs and dive out only at the last instant.

They continued through the city on Todos Santos past dark tourist boutiques and cafés, past the harbor with its sport fishing wharf and seafood grottos. They drove so slowly, the speed wouldn't register on the Bronco speedometer, which made Clifford pound the seat in frustration, though he realized a low rider going much faster than an idle would be suspicious indeed.

Beyond the harbor, the low-rider turned inland. Clifford followed, through a dizzying maze of commercial and industrial streets and into a zone of duplexes and two-story apartments with balconies and planter boxes. Near the dead end of one such street, the low rider slowed to a crawl. Then it stopped long enough for the driver to hook an arm out the window and point over the roof of his car at the green stucco box house with no front yard and a purple door. As the Chevy pulled away, its air-shocks bounced a salsa rhythm.

The house looked blacked out. A curtain parted and revealed a streak of light about as wide as an eyeball. Clifford jumped out of the Bronco, ran to the front and stood in the beam of his headlight, facing the window.

The curtains fell shut. The front door to the house eased open. Alvaro called out, *"Ándale, hermano."*

After they embraced, Alvaro said, "What the hell brings *you* here?"

"I decided to moonlight as a *coyote*, since I can't support my girls as a scribbler."

Alvaro wagged his head. "Jerk."

"Pop came to babysit Feliz and Ava."

"That's good anyway. So, rest a minute then we've got to fly out of here before our host comes back. He's gone on a errand and he's liable to pick up a tail on the way."

"I don't need to rest."

"I do," Alvaro said. "Some bug got into me."

Clifford recognized the woman wedged into a corner of the sofa, reclining like the voluptuous mistress in an old master's painting. Her fleshy but firm body, her face plump and creamy, haloed with long and wavy golden brown hair and jeweled with sea blue eyes, were so exactly like the sketch of the Virgin, Clifford thought she, not her sister, could be the one.

A thin and scraggly fellow was on the floor, leaning against the wall. On a guitar with a crack that ran across from the edge of the box to the sound-hole, he was finger-picking a weary, complex melody that sounded vaguely familiar. Probably one of the classical pieces often used as cartoon sound tracks.

Alvaro sat on the arm of the sofa, opened his mouth and pointed to the guitarist, then, without a word, jumped up and scooted toward the bathroom, stricken by a sudden case of the runs.

A woman Clifford made as their hostess brought him an Orange Crush and a sugary cookie. To his thanks, she replied, "*De nada*," and asked if he could eat fruit or a taco.

He declined. The woman adjourned to another room, where the radio played voices talking just loud enough for Clifford to hear but not understand. From the parting look she had given him, he imagined her praying for saints to come and rid her home of these wicked visitors.

As Alvaro left the *baño*, the *señora* leaned out of her room and beckoned to him. Alvaro went to her. The lady in the corner had crooked her face toward the sound. Clifford stood and stationed himself near the bedroom door, hoping to overhear. He only caught the murmur of disjointed words.

When Alvaro came out, he found his brother standing mid-room. He wrapped an arm around Clifford's broad shoulders and walked him to the chair. Clifford sat. Alvaro remained standing. "I say we speed to the border, slip across, go to my place and sleep until Sunday, then turn on the tube and watch for election results."

Noah stopped playing mid-note and shifted as though to rise and head for the car, but Clifford said, "Before we rush off, there are complications, like road-blocks."

"So we take trails instead of roads."

"And hope the trails aren't all washed out. But there's something else. Did you hear Monreal on the radio?"

"No." Alvaro looked toward the bedroom. "The *señora's* monitoring the radio. She comes and goes, in and out, must've missed it. What'd he say?"

"He said Guadalupe Shuler confessed to masquerading as the Virgin. Tomorrow, he says, she'll go public."

Lourdes folded her hands across the crown of her head and pushed as though to hold her brains in. She threw a fierce glance at Alvaro. "They are torturing her." She sounded assured as the voice of prophecy.

Alvaro went over and knelt beside her. He looked like a worshipper. "My guess is, they're torturing Raul."

"Raul?" Clifford asked.

"Lupe's husband, the Virgin's producer. They might have his *cojones* in a meat grinder and be waiting to turn the crank the first time she misreads a line of their script."

"Yikes," Noah said, his face contorted as if he felt the pain.

Clifford glanced from his brother to Noah and back. "Tell me neither of you guys is wanted for a double murder in Long Beach."

"We didn't do it," Noah said. "*Federales* did."

Clifford nodded. "So we do what?" He watched his brother and Noah turn to the lady. The lids closed over her splendid eyes. Her lower lip quivered. She placed the fingertips of her hands together and held them between her breasts like somebody deep in prayer or meditation.

She said, "Paco Monreal is subservient to my oldest brother. Andres will not let them torture Lupe. Kill her perhaps, but torture her, no."

"Not even after she killed your father?"

The lady shot Alvaro a look so hard it backed him away.

Clifford turned to the lady. "Then how about Raul? Will Andres let Monreal torture Raul?"

"I don't know."

"Let's think," Alvaro said. "Suppose you call your brother and—"

"I will not call Andres." The men stared at her. She stared into space, her eyes and mouth hardened. Only after minutes, she said, "Perhaps Andres believes I am the one who killed our father."

"What's his phone number?"

She didn't even glance his way. "I don't know."

"Look," Alvaro said, "whatever Andres thinks, we've got a million dollars that says we can stop him from letting anybody get tortured any more than they've already done. I'm going to call Pop. He'll find a way to Andres." He watched the lady for a hint that she might relent and give the number. No hint came.

"A million dollars," Clifford said. "Last thing I knew, you were eating Top Ramen."

"I had a turn of fortune. Andres will know where it came from. I'll call Pop, then we're out of here."

"Let me talk to him first," Clifford said. "I owe him an apology."

◇◇◇

Tom Hickey wasn't pleased with his son. Not that getting called at 3:40 a.m. bothered him. What had riled him was Clifford's running out without waking him.

After Tom vented his annoyance, Clifford said, "If I woke you, you would've knocked me down and come yourself."

"Maybe," Tom said.

"Tell me Feliz is okay."

"She's doing fine," Tom said, not willing to let on that her temperature was back up to 103 and might've gone higher if Tom hadn't spent the last hour in the tub with her, in cool water, because she wouldn't stay there alone. The cool tub was a trick he had learned when Clifford was younger than Feliz. "She's tougher than either of us. Girls are like that. You've got news or a job for me?"

"For that, I'm putting Alvaro on."

Alvaro made a mistake. He asked, "How are you feeling, Pop?"

"My prognosis is way better than yours," Tom snapped back. "Let's don't waste time here."

Alvaro gave him the necessary details. Two Shuler

sisters. Lupe got banished, by her father, to die in a storm. Ten years later, the father got his due when somebody killed him. Then Lourdes ran off with a bunch of gold, and came looking for her sister who, just yesterday, landed in federal custody, somewhere in Ensenada. What they hoped Tom could do was find a way to contact Andres Shuler, convince him to order the safety of his sisters. And, if Andres proved less than an ogre, to arrange for the safety of his sister's escorts.

"By the way," Alvaro said, "if somebody tells you that I or a guy named Noah murdered a couple fellows in Long Beach, set them straight."

"Tell him it was *federales*," Noah said.

◇◇◇

Harry Poverman wasn't pleased to be awakened at 3:50, even after Tom explained he had no choice, that it was almost six in Mexico City and those mountain folk rise early.

"So what I need," Tom continued, "is a chat with your man in whatever Mexicans call their White House."

"What for?"

"I need him to get me a phone number, is all."

"Guy ain't listed?"

"Andres Shuler. A big shot, I hear."

"Yeah, well Jaime ain't going to be pleased when I ring him up at dawn. But I owe you a couple, right?

Or do you owe me? I'm so damned old I forget things. Hold on." He must've cupped his hand over the phone. Tom's ear suffered no damage when Harry shouted, "Hey, Maria, get that phone book out of my desk and bring it, will you? Tom, see, Jaime's going to ask you what you want with this Nazi? You tell him the wrong thing, some guys might show up while you're eating breakfast, ask you to take them to this Virgin gal."

"Andres Shuler's a Nazi?"

"He's got the blood for it," Harry said.

"You know the family?"

"I hear things."

Chapter Twenty-three

Clifford and Alvaro had both spent time in Ensenada. Between them they knew the layout. Clifford drove. They avoided the main streets and still arrived at the eastern outskirts where the street turned onto a gravel ranch road that pointed north east. From here, beyond the squatters' villages, they would follow whatever trails appeared to carry them into the Sierra Juarez, where the largest communities were *pueblecitos*, and *policia* of any species were scarce.

Over the mountains, the craggy black clouds looked restless, shifting and changing shapes. The only breaks in the darkness were from sporadic fits of lightning, which Alvaro welcomed. This Bronco was rigged with struts and extra leaf springs for rocky roads, sand and mud. As long as they could find a trail, the storm would offer them cover. Alvaro's thoughts had begun to lighten when the lady broke the spell.

She said, "We can't leave Lupe here in jail."

"We've got Pop calling Andres," Alvaro said. "If anybody can convince him to lay off, it'll be Pop. And if Monreal can't torture Lupe, or Raul, she's not going to confess anything. So we cross the border, and from the other side we make plans how to spring her. Some of your gold ought to do the trick, after the election."

The lady made a dismissive puff sound. "And today or tomorrow the people see my sister on television, and then they believe she is no Virgin, no matter if she confesses or she does not. And the PRI wins, as always."

For a minute Alvaro only gaped at her. Before now, he hadn't gotten a clue that she cared a whit about the election. "So risking your life to break your sister out would be what? A gesture of love toward Lupe?"

She looked away. He said, "Or do you care so much about defeating the PRI? I don't get your motive, that's all."

She turned back, but her eyes didn't meet his. "Does it matter? What you call my motive?"

"You bet it does. Because without knowing it, nobody's going to help you do something stupid. Not me anyway."

"I'd like to know your motive," Noah said.

"Then I will tell you. Yes, I want to help my sister defeat the PRI. No, this is not a gesture of love for Lupe." The lady and Alvaro locked eyes. "This, I want to do for you," she said, her voice a pitch higher than ever before. The tenor of it made Noah, riding shotgun, stop finger-picking the guitar he had promised to return when he came back in a few days to find Gretchen. He turned and stared at her. Her fiery words made Clifford ease his foot off the gas and Alvaro reach for her hand. It was hot and moist.

He would've traded all he owned, some equity in a duplex with gold bars stashed underneath, and a half interest in a souped up '55 Chevy wagon that might've gotten stripped and parted out by now, for an inspired plan with even a slim chance of breaking Lupe out of jail. "Nope," he said. "We've got to trust Pop and Andres."

With her lips still parted, the lady sat perfectly still, her eyes fixed on the carpeted floor, as though she had slipped into catatonia. When she raised her chin, she stared so hard at Alvaro, he wondered if she was accusing him of cowardice. But she said, "Then I shall become the Virgin."

Alvaro smiled. Murderous, devious, whatever she might be, this lady held the reins to his heart. "Okay."

"Okay?" Clifford asked. "X, did you say okay?"

"Yep."

"He sure did," Noah said.

Clifford lifted his right hand off the steering

wheel and rubbed his temples. "If I wasn't a writer, and therefore devoted to avoiding clichés, I might ask you doesn't that mean we're jumping out of the frying pan and into the fire?"

◇◇◇

Besides dodging ruts and rivulets and attempting top speed without putting the Bronco into a slide, Clifford squinted into the dark beyond the headlights, on the lookout for parked cars. If the feds had mobilized all the various breeds of Baja lawmen, federal, state, and local police, they might have set checkpoints even along goat paths and foot trails.

In the shotgun seat, Noah picked a riff that droned over and over, the way Clifford remembered Alvaro used to play during the first months after his discharge, when he smoked a lot of grass.

On a gravel straightaway where he could split his attention from driving, Clifford argued, "Suppose the Virgin thing works better than anybody could dream, say practically everybody votes against the PRI, and suppose they unite behind one of the opposition parties, the PRI is going to rig the vote count and win. The only difference is, a bunch of *pobres* will go nuts over the fraud. I mean, not that they don't expect fraud, but maybe they'll think this one went over the top. They'll probably revolt, and get slaughtered. See, if Lourdes goes out and plays Virgin tonight, instead of being the savior of the *campesinos*, she might become the mother of a bloodbath."

Alvaro said, "So, because something we do might backfire, we shouldn't do anything, right?"

"Yikes."

Clifford swerved, but not fast enough to miss the wide and knee-deep rut that jolted the Bronco so hard the lady slipped off her seat and onto the floorboard. Noah got a finger stuck between guitar strings.

After he helped Lourdes back to the seat beside him, Alvaro said, "I'm not saying we're smart enough to predict cause and effect, *hermano*. Only, if we've got a chance to do something, we'd better take it. I mean, how are we going to feel every time we come down here or look at the news and see a beggar or a sick orphan, when we know that just maybe we could've helped fix things."

Clifford recalled when Alvaro decided to enlist in the army even though he questioned the Vietnam war. He reasoned that people in the States lived better than people in communist countries, and he'd feel like a bum if he didn't help defend the country that had taken him in. Then he ordered Clifford to stay home, go to law school, make Tom and Wendy proud. When Clifford noted his brother's double standard, Alvaro said, "It's because I'm disposable. You're not." Clifford demanded to know when their folks had failed to love their adopted son as well as their natural son, Alvaro only said, "Hey, it's my life."

Only three years later, Alvaro was a civilian, Clifford a felon serving time. Now, seven years farther along, Alvaro would soon be a lawyer. Clifford, in Ava's terms, was unemployed. Those thoughts helped him defer to his brother's judgment, even though he saw tragedy rushing at them.

◇◇◇

As eight o'clock came and went, the world appeared stuck between night and day. The iron gray clouds rarely allowed a patch of blue. A hint of the ozone that foretold a storm came on the dusty air.

Alvaro used a map he'd found in a pouch hooked to the Bronco's visor. He consulted the compass on the dash. His best guess had them traveling about ten degrees northward of due east. If that proved accurate, the road they were following over the foothills toward the mountains might deliver them to a rancho called El Faustino, some twenty kilometers north of Agua Dulce where a gifted *niña* had sketched Lupe.

Noah snoozed in the shotgun seat, hugging Ismael's guitar. The lady had fashioned a pallet on the floor in the rear using blankets they found under the back seat. She had fallen asleep. Alvaro leaned over the seat and hovered there, staring mostly at her profile, the pale half-moons of her eyelids, the generous parched lips and strong dimpled chin with her hands folded beneath for a pillow. Title her face *Innocence*, he thought. And what would he title those curves, he wondered, the rise of her hip and the long, curled up legs. *Magic* was the only word that came to him.

Clifford had watched him in the mirror. He said, "*Dígame algo, hermano.* Tell me you're not going to let her play out this Virgin thing just because you're stuck on her."

"Who says I'm stuck on her?"

"Hey, you're not a good enough actor to hide from me who you're stuck on."

"That so?" Alvaro muttered. "Well, here's one for you. Would I let a woman I was stuck on risk her life on this crazy mission?"

"Maybe, for *la gente.*"

"Yeah, maybe." Alvaro leaned forward and squeezed Clifford's shoulder.

Then he stealthily cajoled the guitar out of sleeping Noah's arms. He played a ballet suite from "Swan Lake" while Clifford drove up a foothill and slowed at the crest.

"X, look here."

In the valley ahead lay a rancho. A long adobe house, three barns and three Quonset barracks, a small orange grove and beyond it a dozen horses roaming on a grassy knoll. On the next hill, which appeared to be the last before the *montañas*, hundreds of longhorn cattle grazed.

Alvaro would've preferred to avoid big ranchos where the *patrón* was most likely PRI and might command his *vaqueros* to lasso and hog tie them while he called the feds. But he needed to make a call and this place was connected to power lines and might have the only phone they would find between here and Agua Dulce.

The valley was dark, under storm clouds, and the road a maze of deep puddles Clifford zigzagged through, past a pair of old *campesinos* standing beside a small tractor, staring into the motor compartment. He skidded the Bronco across a muddy parking area. Red chickens scattered.

When the Bronco stopped, Lourdes awoke and asked, "Where are we?"

He handed her the map and pointed to the spot where he believed they were. "I'm going to call Augie, tell him what we're up to, while you lay low, don't let anybody see you."

She agreed, but as he opened the side door, a plump *señora* walked out of the house. Though taken by surprise, Alvaro tried to block the woman's view in case the lady hadn't hid in time. He attempted to shut the car door casually behind him. He greeted the *señora* with his best smile. From her apron and round *Indio* face he supposed she was a servant. After apologies, he said, "My brothers and I, and our lady friend, are going to the *montañas,* catch some fish if they'll bite in the rain. But, stupid me, I forgot to call someone." He supposed an affair of the heart would be more likely than a business matter to persuade the *señora.* "She'll be awfully worried."

Before he could offer to pay for the call, she had shown him inside and across a dark parlor. The sofas and even the chair looked as if moving them might require heavy machinery. The phone was on a nook in a hallway that led to the kitchen. She left him there and went on to the kitchen.

Alvaro dialed Quartilho's number on the rotary phone. Elena, the lawyer's secretary, answered with a muffled, *"Bueno?"*

Probably snack time, Alvaro thought. "Hello, beautiful."

"Equis?"

"Shhh." If anybody in Tijuana had a tapped phone, the rogue Quartihlo would have one. "Listen, I wish we could talk, but I'm borrowing a phone. Is Augie around?"

"Not yet today."

"You can reach him within the next couple hours, with a message?"

"Pues sí, he has an appointment pretty soon. He will be here."

"Okay, this is going to sound *loco,* but tell him to meet me at a village called Dos Lobos. At dusk, and bring a TV news cameraman. Not a team, just the camera guy."

The *señora* passed behind Alvaro, carrying a plate of something hot and savory. Elena asked, "Are you going to play your guitar for the *campesinos*?"

"Yeah. A friend and I are going to put on a show. But we only want Augie and the cameraman, *entiendes*?"

"Not me too?"

He wished he could tell her the truth instead of conning his *amiga* into thinking he would be in Dos Lobos with Carlos Santana, whom Elena idolized. She had asked Alvaro more than once for a chance to meet him. "You can come, but not a whisper to anybody else. Remember, Dos Lobos. It's about forty kilometers southeast of Tecate on a rough road. Okay."

"We will come."

"'Bye, beautiful." He trusted her discretion. If she didn't know how to keep a secret, Quartilho wouldn't employ her.

He hung up, looked around for the *señora*, then dialed Clifford's number, but got stopped by busy signals as soon as he completed the country code.

As he crossed the dark living room, he noticed that the far end was a trophy wall, festooned with heads and antlers. The *señora* opened the front door, entered and handed him a paper plate with a *chile verde* burrito the size of a football.

He thanked her for it and for the phone. "I wonder if you might have a spare Bible. Just any old one."

She nodded and walked down a hall, turned into the first room. He used the opportunity to eat. She soon returned with a *Santa Biblia*. Since Alvaro didn't mind interrupting his Saturdays for a lively discussion with strangers, he recognized the Bible as the Jehovah's Witness variety. He groped for his wallet. She waved him off. He held up the burrito, bit into it, and praised her cooking with a rapturous groan.

She wished them happy fishing. But her eyes, hard with suspicion, clued him that she'd seen Lourdes. When he got to the Bronco, Clifford told him she had.

Alvaro climbed in back and sat beside the lady on the rear seat. "Did she sneak up on you?"

"Noah got out," Clifford said. "The woman poked her head in. She brought us food."

"I left the door open," Noah muttered. "Don't blame anybody but me, okay?"

"No doubt she thinks we're abducting the Holy Virgin," Alvaro said. "And she's got the phone. She might be on it already."

Clifford laid his plate and half eaten burrito on the cup rack. "*Vámonos.*" He spun the Bronco and skidded past the *campesinos* seated and eating on the hood of the tractor.

Chapter Twenty-four

Tom wouldn't make his calls from home. Any pal of Harry's whom Tom didn't know and trust as well as he knew and trusted Harry was somebody he didn't want to know his or his family's whereabouts. Or even who he was, if he could help it.

So, for most of an hour, he'd been sitting on the block wall beside the Jack in the Box on the corner of Pacific Beach Drive and Coast Boulevard, a short block from the beach. He had called one Mexico City number, then the next, and twice waited for return calls. He'd been referred by one so-and-so to another so-and-so who told him to call another one in order to get through to Andres Shuler. In addition, he'd spent the hour finding that the beach girls who sashayed by wiggling their bikinis had such curves and supple flesh they could render momentarily speechless even a 73-year-old. Even a codger who was busy trying to save lives, including those of his sons, and also to help rescue Mexico from the tyranny of the PRI.

At last he reached Andres Shuler and got asked in a deep commanding voice, "Who are you?"

"Call me Tom, that's good enough."

"Then call me Doctor Shuler."

"Doctor?"

"Economics. Princeton. What is your business?"

"Actually," Tom said, "I'm calling about *your* business. Your family. It seems the *federales*, led by one Paco Monreal, have captured someone they believe was posing as the Holy Virgin. I've been told she's your sister."

"Tom, I believe I keep as well informed as you do with the actions of our federal police. And so, I expect you are going to ask me for money in exchange for you not telling the world that the 'Virgin' is my sister. Correct?"

"Nope. I'm going to ask you to tell Monreal to keep his mitts off your sister and her husband, that's about all. Because he's got something else in mind."

"My sister and her husband? You have a bad source of information. My sister has no husband. My sister lived with my father, essentially imprisoned at home, until only one month ago. How can she have a husband?"

"Lourdes?"

"Of course."

"Wrong sister," Tom said.

"I only have one sister."

He spoke with such conviction, Tom half believed him, and wondered if this gal of Alvaro's had fed him nothing but lies. "The way I hear it, there's Lourdes, who's accused of killing her father, and then there's Lupe, who considered herself unwelcome at home, and made herself scarce for a long while."

In the silence, Tom thought he heard Andres drop the receiver. "Are you there?"

"I am."

"Now, I don't suppose you want the family's dirty laundry to become the topic of a mini-series entitled 'The Nazi Who Sent His Daughter to Die in A Storm.' Right?"

"Keep talking."

"You could probably avoid that by having a word with Monreal. Who, by the way, murdered a fellow named Carlos Meza. Shot him in the back from fifty yards."

"We have a different report. Carlos Meza, according to my sources, was shot by a North American. Paco Monreal is determined to capture this man. You see, he and Carlos Meza were *compadres*." Shuler sounded like a different man than only minutes ago. This new fellow was distracted, talking by rote, at least half his mind far away.

"Maybe that's why Paco shot Carlos in the back," Tom said. "Didn't want to look his *compadre* in the eye while he killed him."

"*Señor*, we have spoken long enough."

"Not quite. I can tell you why Monreal shot Carlos Meza, and I can tell you where to find your father's missing gold."

"Tell me," he said as if he only vaguely cared.

"Carlos Meza's son Raul is Lupe's husband, and maybe the mover behind the Virgin. Monreal figures, kill Carlos, and when his son comes to avenge him, grab him. Which he did."

"I see. And the gold is where?"

"I've got it."

Tom bid Andres *adios* and hung up.

He called Ava. "How's the wonder girl?"

"Squirmy, which I guess is a good sign, right?"

"Let's hope. Temp still below a hundred."

"Just barely."

Though quite aware that Feliz' temperature could rise again, like before, he said, "Since she'll be okay without me, I'm going to the USD library. I'll call again in an hour."

"What's at the USD library?"

"A good collection on Mexican politics."

"Pop, do you think Clifford even cares that him going off like this scares me to death?"

"You want the truth, right?"

"Sure."

A woman of Tom's vintage passed by in a bikini fit

for a ten-year-old. He shut his eyes. "I think he believes you don't much care what happens to him."

◇◇◇

Instead of climbing the next foothill, the road cut around it as if to allow vehicles a chance to rest before the next ascent. The road was rutted and slippery, one car wide and so steep, even after he shifted into four-wheel-drive, Clifford needed to hold his foot steady on the accelerator to keep the tires from spinning. The road leveled, climbed, leveled, and climbed onto a mesa of rocks big and gray as the prows of Navy ships. From his map, the Bronco's odometer and the landscape, Alvaro guessed they weren't many kilometers north of the national park that surrounded Laguna Hansen. An arrow and lettering on a boulder pointed the way to Las Pilitas mine. "We're probably less than ten miles from Dos Lobos," Alvaro said. "We'll find a place to hole up a few hours."

Clifford preferred not to take the Bronco far off the road, which was slick but hard-packed, into the forest where they might sink into humus or clay. He drove a mile or so before a garage-sized boulder and a stand of cedar offered cover between them and the road. He slogged the Bronco over needles, sticks and rocks, through black mud, and parked behind the boulder just before a shaft of sunlight cracked the volcanic clouds and touched down in the clearing beside them.

All four of them climbed out and stretched. Alvaro stayed with the Bronco while the others fanned out and crossed the clearing to explore or relieve themselves. Or, Alvaro thought, they might be pretending they were on a holiday instead of running from the Mexican state and federal police and on their way to commit a fraud that could land them in a prison they might never leave short of dying.

His papá wasn't the only person he'd known who died in a Mexican prison. The brother of a drummer he played with supplemented his take from the band selling tubes of benzedrine in the clubs along Tijuana's Avenida Revolución, until a rival sold him to the *policia*. He died in a prison brawl. A classmate at community college who picked up a hitchhiker outside Acapulco got charged with murder when the fellow had an epileptic fit, swallowed his tongue and died. The kid who got charged overdosed on a variety of pills, probably on purpose, before his folks could raise the *mordida*.

The Hickey brothers might surface one day, wrecked but still walking, but the lady wouldn't survive. Strong as she was, some imprisoned and repentant backslider would waste her. Or a Bible study group would conspire to catch her when she was asleep, lash her to her cot and set her on fire, inspired by tales of the Inquisition.

And Noah, who appeared to have not a dash of

meanness to him, without a guitar to hold onto might last a day or two, no more, before he toppled into darkness. In Mexico, only the rich, the crafty, and the hardened survived disputes with the law.

The walk across the clearing looked treacherous. At the tree-line, Noah stepped into a pit of soggy mulch and sank his right leg past the knee. While he was still tugging it free, the lady yipped. Alvaro was already a few running steps toward her when he saw through the trees. A bobcat had bolted from hiding and startled her before it hissed and fled.

When Noah returned to the Bronco, Alvaro decided to leave him with the lady and follow his brother. He wanted to get Clifford alone. He wanted to talk about normal stuff, such as Pop and women, to lift himself out of this madness for a while.

He found Clifford resting, seated with his back against the trunk of a piñon, knees drawn up close. "You look like that guy on the postcard taking a *siesta*, only you need the sombrero."

"How are you holding up?"

Alvaro yawned. "Who needs sleep when you've got adventure? So, do you think I'm nuts?"

"Sure."

"Because I've got an itch for Lourdes? Or because I'm going to let her try to fool the whole world, and maybe get us killed?"

"A little of both. But then, she's some woman. And I can't think of many better causes than sticking it to the PRI."

"Yeah, but I don't want to get you killed, or Noah either, for *la gente* or anybody. So, you drop us off at Dos Lobos and get out of town before we put on the show. We'll find some barn to hide in for a couple days. After the election, we'll jump the line on foot. If *la migra* picks us up, all the better."

Clifford rolled around, onto his knees. "You wouldn't get a mile without me."

"Hey, who's the outdoorsman in the family?"

"Me."

Alvaro shook his head. "Nope. Besides, you've got kids, a wife."

"Kids, no wife."

"That bad?"

"She gave up on me. Won't even laugh at my jokes. Every chance she gets, she's taking piano lessons from Pastor Joe. She never asked me to give her guitar lessons. And, when I ask her if she wants a piano, she says we can't afford it, with my not having a real job."

"Then get one. Why don't you try that?"

"Maybe I would if I thought it would work. But look, she's going to walk out. I feel it coming. So, that's enough making me talk about what I'm thinking about all day and half the night. You tell me something, like how stuck on the lady are you."

"Hmmm. Okay, it feels like I've got a dervish in my head, and a conga line hopping through my stomach."

"You're in a jam, all right," Clifford said.

The shaft of sunlight retreated. Thunder boomed. Lightning struck, maybe half a mile east. Alvaro gave his brother a hand, helped him up.

Chapter Twenty-five

When Tom returned from the library he found Feliz asleep. Ava was at the loom where she created the wild and vivid tapestries that adorned most every wall of the bayside cottage. Today she didn't look inspired.

"Got a few minutes?" he asked.

"Uh huh."

He helped her out of the chair. She followed him out to the patio, but didn't sit. "Too early for Scotch, right?"

"Yeah. How about one of those fruity teas of yours?"

She nodded and went inside. While he waited, he watched the action on the bay. He and Madeline, his first wife, bought the place when they moved down from L.A., forty-some years ago, when the Depression was lifting on account of the industries that provided for the wars in Europe. They paid $500 down for the cottage, and $60 a month. Since then, he had seen the bay, his back yard, transform from a sewage dump and a haunt for guys who fished out of rowboats to a resort. Big hotels sat on lots where vagrant Okies used to camp. Grown kids with so much money they'd never need any sense whizzed back and forth in speed boats, Catamarans, and now these Jet Skis. He understood the craving for speed. But people needed someplace they could find peace. So he limited his walks around the bay to nights.

Ava came out, delivered tea, and sat in the Adirondack chair beside his, the one he'd made for Wendy when she was nearly as pregnant with Clifford as Ava was now with Tommy.

"You should know more about what's up in Baja."

"Okay," she said. "I can handle it, I think."

"It's got a long history, like most things that happen. Here's the way I piece it together. Before you were born, at the University of Mexico, Carlos Meza and Paco Monreal were known as *existentialistas*, what we called beatniks, before Paco went on to law school, Carlos into architecture. Paco found his place in the PRI. Carlos didn't, and he raised his son Raul as a free thinker.

"When Raul Meza got to the University, he wrote pamphlets blasting the PRI, which I'm guessing is why he fled, came up here to UCLA. Where he met Lupe Shuler, I don't know. But after somebody got the idea to cast her as the Holy Virgin, Raul must've stolen some fancy equipment that has to do with lasers from the film school. Now he could make what they call holograms. So Lupe becomes the Virgin, which her sister Lourdes discovers and comes knocking on Alvaro's door."

"Like so many women do."

Tom gave her a wink. "Now, Raul and Lupe are in an Ensenada jail, and Clifford has gone down there and picked up Alvaro and Lourdes. He's bringing them home. They ought to show up tonight."

From the hard set of her face and a little sniff she probably didn't know she made, he suspected Clifford might feel in deeper, hotter water when he got home than he did on the run in Mexico.

"Clifford didn't skip out on you and Feliz. He sent for me to cover. If I hadn't come, he wouldn't have budged. That's how families work. They cover for each other."

She sniffed again. "Mine didn't."

"Well, the family you belong to now does cover for each other. You'd be wise to remember and adjust."

Ava turned and stared, clearly appraising whether he meant the comment as a suggestion, a criticism, or an order. "I'll remember."

Tom knew this was an awkward time to talk to her about marriage. Still, he said, "I gather the honeymoon's over."

"So," she said, with more than a hint of defiance, "it's my fault and you're going to set me straight, right."

"Yeah."

He'd surprised her. She froze for a moment, then set down her tea and clutched an arm of the chair.

"Sure," Tom said, "I don't know the whole story. I do know there's never been a Hickey without a mind of his own. We're stubborn. And we're dreamers. Clifford might be the dreamiest of us all. He's an artist, Ava. You fell for him at least in part because he's an artist. You married him knowing he was an artist. Right?"

"Okay."

"If you marry an artist and expect him to become a banker, what kind of expectation is that? You're an artist too. Imagine yourself as a wage slave and ask, 'Would I want to live with me?'"

She was breathing so hard, he wondered if Clifford would come home to a new baby. "And suppose he manages to become something he's not. The sad truth is, he won't be good at it. Nor will he be as good a husband, or dad, or man. So, if what you want is prosperity, the best course you could take is to help him get successful doing what he loves."

A little smile softened her face.

Tom said, "Pretty."

"Huh? What's pretty."

"You."

Now she smiled wide. "Making a play for me?"

"Girl, if I was young and we were single, you'd

have to hire an army to keep me away."

"Pop, did you bring your clarinet?"

"Nope. You want to get serenaded, you're going to have to wait till the boys get home."

"Too bad. I was going to suggest that a chorus of 'Stand By Your Man' would've added some punch to your lecture."

He laughed, picked up his tea, sipped it and grimaced. "Awful stuff," he said. "A guy my age has earned a Scotch whenever in the hell he wants one, don't you think?"

He stood and walked a few steps before she called to him. He turned, and she said, "Did Alvaro tell you Clifford and I were on the outs because of money?"

"He said you'd prefer a bigger house. Which I interpreted to mean prosperity in general."

"I don't think money's what I want."

"What do you want?"

Ava bowed her head and sighed. "I don't know."

◇◇◇

For an hour, reclined in the driver's seat, Clifford stared at the rain that lashed one way then the other as the wind whirled. He wondered how Dr. Fred had handled himself on the stand, and if he would survive until Monday so he would witness the closing arguments and write Fred's story. And he thought about Feliz.

A few weeks ago he'd met up with a college friend

who sold his first novel to Hollywood. Clifford hadn't yet finished the novel he'd started five years ago. But he wouldn't have traded his precious little girl for a dozen Oscars. In Feliz, he'd been given a blessing of inestimable worth. A favorite Bible verse of his mom's was, "I will pour out my spirit upon all flesh." To Clifford, Feliz was a great spirit come to life, a miracle.

He wanted to get home to Feliz. Only a small part of him was glad to help his brother with this scheme of masquerading Lourdes as the Virgin, which appeared half-baked, doomed, and vaguely blasphemous. The rest of him wanted to call the game, speed for the border, and when Alvaro objected, reply, "Look *hermano*, this is only another one of those times when your hormones are getting in the way of common sense."

Noah, in the shotgun seat, was finger-picking melodies of mostly low notes that harmonized with the rain that clopped on the Bronco roof. In back, Alvaro consulted with the lady to decide what the Virgin should tell the people of Mexico on her final visit before the election. He tapped his brother on the shoulder. "Help us write the script here, would you? Do you know offhand any Bible verses that will inspire *la gente* to race to the polls and flush the PRI down the pipes to the sea?"

"How about in Isaiah. Fifty-nine, maybe. About fasting."

Alvaro looked in the Jehovah's Witness Bible and browsed a few pages. "Here's some stuff about fasting in fifty-eight. Let's see, 'undo the heavy burdens,' 'let the oppressed go free,' 'feed the hungry' et cetera. What else have you got?"

"How about Mary's song, in Luke, where she says, 'He has put down the mighty and exalted the lowly, filled the hungry and sent the rich away.' Or look at Psalm Five. There's some good stuff in it."

Alvaro turned the pages and read the Psalm. "Here we go."

Clifford turned far enough to catch the lady's eye. "Somewhere, Christ tells his disciples that when they're in front of the magistrate, to let the spirit speak through them. Try doing that, you'll do all right."

"You sure will," Noah said. "That's how I write my songs."

Alvaro asked his brother, "Is that how you scribblers work?"

"On the good days," Clifford said. "So, what if the rain keeps up all day and night?"

Alvaro glanced at the lady and turned back to his brother. "Then the TV audience gets to see their Virgin sopping wet."

Which, Clifford thought, might be enough to talk the Pope and the College of Cardinals into dropping their attachment to celibacy.

Chapter Twenty-six

Alvaro had chosen Dos Lobos because he knew the layout. He remembered an arroyo that followed the eastern base of the hill about two kilometers outside the village. From the hill, the arroyo cut straight south, on a parallel to the dirt road, past the shrine at the site of Lupe's visit.

The storm clouds had broken and scattered while the van slogged through mud pits and over slick caliche on the public road. Alvaro showed his brother where to turn onto a trail that looped around the village to the east. It was all silty mud, slower than the public road, pocked with the tracks of goats and cattle as well as truck tires. Some of its potholes were big enough to swim across. But they couldn't let the Bronco be seen, by the TV newsman or any skeptic, approaching the place from where they would start the lady down the arroyo.

As they passed straight east of Dos Lobos, the sun tipped behind a silver peak. Alvaro wondered if it was divine providence that had stocked Fred's Bronco with not only the makings of a Virgin costume, but with binoculars. Probably not, he reasoned, since the costume was only a sheet and every doctor he knew bought plenty of toys.

He made out a cluster of five or six vehicles in the meadow beyond the shrine. One was a motor home that had probably arrived before the last rains and now was condemned to stay until the road dried. The other vehicles were smaller, one of them a Jeep. None looked appropriate for TV news.

They drove past the hill until it blocked the view of the vehicles and the shrine. They cut across a pasture where the only way Clifford could hold traction on the four wheels was to crawl in the Bronco's granny low gear.

Lourdes had fashioned a frock out of the sheet in Fred's bedroll and the needle, thread, and safety pins in his emergency kit. She climbed out of the Bronco, walked around back, slipped out of the yellow dress and into the frock. She glanced at her image in the rear window, then walked around to where the men stood waiting.

They all peered like critics. Noah clapped. Clifford nodded. "For sure."

But Alvaro fretted, because she looked years younger and centuries less confident than how he remembered the Virgin, both from the sketch and from her image in the sky over Playa Sin Olas.

◇◇◇

Alvaro wore a black T-shirt from a bin of Dr. Fred's camping clothes. His jeans were dark enough. The lady was wrapped in a dark gray woolen blanket, part of Fred's bedroll.

Unless he used the penlight he had found in the Bronco glove box, the fading light of a day whose brightest moments were gloomy only allowed them to see clearly a meter or two ahead. Even where the ground looked safe it was treacherous with pudding-like mud. A pair of rocks beneath the surface snagged the lady's foot between them. In freeing herself, she gave up her sneaker, which she would have to discard before climbing out of the arroyo anyway. Then, rather than walk lopsided, she kicked out of the other shoe and went barefoot, stubbing her toes and gouging her soles on the rocks. All the while she committed to memory Psalm 5:9, mumbling first in the English Clifford gave her. "All your promises are insincere; your heart is bent on destruction, your throat an open grave." Then she translated into Spanish.

"Does your brother know the whole Bible by heart?" she whispered to Alvaro.

"He remembers that verse because our mamá used to quote it, when she told us about some men she'd known. Guys she hadn't quiet managed to forgive. Did I tell you she got kidnapped by Nazis?"

"You did not."

"Ask me later."

She stopped and grasped his shoulders. "Alvaro, do you think I can do this?"

He pondered a moment before he said, "I suspect you were born to do this."

"Do you think a trap will be waiting for me?"

"If it is, I'll come in with guns blazing."

"You don't have a gun anymore."

"Then I'll come with hands and feet blazing."

She gave him the first real smile since early yesterday. "Do you believe in me?" she asked, her voice quavering.

Alvaro nodded, too choked up to speak. The lady raised onto her toes and kissed his chin. Then she peeled the blanket from around her and gave it to him. She turned and walked the rest of the way without a single groan or grumble about the sharp stones on her bare feet. Near the end of the arroyo, just beyond the south base of the hill where the pilgrims were gathered, she stopped again. "Here is the place."

"Uh huh."

"Please go now."

For an instant Alvaro believed he wouldn't see her close up again, that she would address the pilgrims then vanish into the sky.

He wrapped the blanket around his waist. He jogged fifty yards back the way they had come, then climbed out of the arroyo and ran up the hillside.

◇◇◇

Alvaro ran, dropped and belly crawled up and around the side of the hill to the crest. He found cover behind a shrub.

In dusk, Fred's binoculars helped little. But in the picnic area villagers had cleared and outfitted, around the shrine to the Virgin's first visit, most of the seventy or so pilgrims had lanterns or battery lights.

He spotted Clifford standing in the glow of a lantern. As they'd planned, Clifford had driven around the far side of the hill and down the road from the north, pulled in, and parked. Alvaro saw the Bronco parked next to a motor home. Then he saw Noah, already playing his guitar, sitting on a stool beside a small campfire, surrounded by *niños*.

But he didn't see Augie Quartilho, Elena, or any cameraman. He whistled twice, in his ballplayer's loud whistle, the signal to the lady to wait.

The scattered clouds had reformed and darkened, blocked out the moon and stars. Thunder rolled down from off the eastern range as though to herald the approach of a shiny black pickup that topped a rise on the road a kilometer north.

As it neared, Alvaro watched most of the pilgrims

turn toward the pickup. It swung onto the trail that led off the gravel road and came rumbling toward them. He glanced down at the arroyo where the lady had been hiding. He saw her climb out of the arroyo. Whether she'd felt prompted by some spirit to move, or got too anxious to wait any longer, or decided on taking a calculated risk that the pickup was bringing the TV cameraman, he didn't have the leisure to speculate. Whatever her motive, it served their purpose. The pickup distracted the pilgrims. When they turned back and looked toward the hillside, she must've appeared to have materialized out of nowhere, rather than dashed through about twenty meters of darkness from the arroyo.

The pilgrims rushed the hillside. At the rear of the crowd, a cameraman scurried out of the bed of the pickup. All 200 pounds of Elena crawled out after him. Augie climbed out of the shotgun seat. The driver came last, a bald man carrying something Alvaro guessed was a pocket tape recorder. "Damn," he muttered, sure he'd told Elena to bring no one but the cameraman and Augie.

By the time the Quartilho contingent had caught up, the kids and pilgrims including Clifford and Noah had started up the hillside and stopped about ten meters from the lady, in obedience to her upraised hand. As little Augie and fat Elena approached Clifford, arm in arm like honeymooners, Alvaro saw his brother shake his head, warning them not to greet him. Better to give the pilgrims no cause to suspect a conspiracy.

The lady called three children forward. They walked her way using short and tentative steps. In a voice that carried all the way up to Alvaro and was so rich he could've been listening to opera, the lady blessed the children. She bent and kissed their foreheads. She held their hands, all three at once pressed between hers, and gave each some words of prophecy. The little boy with a birthmark on his cheek she promised would become the papa of many happy boys and girls. She told the *niña* in a blue dress sizes too large that she would go away to college and become a doctor. The youngest, a squirmy girl with sunken cheeks, would be a worker of miracles, the lady said. When a feeble gray haired woman in a cowboy shirt got pushed across the line behind which the other pilgrims stayed, instead of chastising, the lady went out to meet her. She placed a fingertip between the woman's eyebrows. The gray woman beamed as though she had already landed in heaven.

The lady backed up a few steps, reached and held her arms splayed out like Christ's on the cross. Without giving any sign she'd seen the cameraman, in mournful Spanish she reported that the PRI had too long betrayed the trust of *la gente*. "*No hay sinceridad en lo que dicen;/ destrucción son sus entrañas,/ sepulcro abierto es su garganta."*

She gazed into the eye of the camera and implored, "'Declare them guilty, O God! Let their intrigues be their downfall. Banish them for their many sins, for they have rebelled against you. But...'" she returned to the *niños* and fingered the little boy's hair. "'...let all who take refuge in You, my God, be glad; let them ever sing for joy.' Let them give thanks without ceasing for the blessed day that is upon us when the gentle, the patient, those who have no desire to oppress or revel in the fruits of their greed, when the meek will inherit the earth, without bloodshed, but with their simple power to object, to refuse to participate in oppression."

What amazed Alvaro, not only had she quoted the verse Clifford gave her, but she had recited another, though during these last two days and even during Clifford's coaching, she hadn't given a clue that she'd read the Bible, let alone memorized any of it. And then she spoke on her own, with poise, passion and charisma that equaled her sister's.

She didn't go back to the arroyo but walked up the hill. Another inspired move, Alvaro thought. The farther into the darkness she withdrew, the more vaguely the pilgrims and camera could see her final exit.

The cameraman followed her, disregarding the shouted objections of several pilgrims. But with the heavy camera, he couldn't keep up. She gained distance from the camera as she neared the crest, yet in white she remained visible until sheet lightning flashed all across the eastern sky.

Lightning struck the plain beyond the arroyo, about halfway to the eastern peaks, near enough so everyone including the cameraman startled and looked. The camera turned with the man, Alvaro noticed. And when, after no more than a second, they looked back up the mountain, the lady was gone. She had dashed past Alvaro. She was already running down the back of the hill.

◇◇◇

Clifford watched the pilgrims. Most of them stood frozen in mid-gasp. The feeble gray woman was out of her chair, around back of it, leaning on the handgrips. The *niños*, who had stood politely still and silent while the lady took her leave, broke from their reverence and whooped.

Clifford went to Noah, toward the rear of the pilgrims. He was strumming and crooning "Ave Maria." The driver and the cameraman were already hustling Elena and Augie to the black pickup. Clifford had expected them to interview witnesses. Maybe they needed to race to make the 10 o'clock news. Or maybe Quartilho had sold out Alvaro and the lady, and their driver was a *federale*, already on his radio calling in airborne troops.

The pickup spewed reddish brown mud. The truck fishtailed out of the meadow. Clifford wanted to speed around the mountain and meet up with Lourdes, praise her performance, her mind, her spirit and her beauty, and deliver her out of danger. But he couldn't let himself act suspiciously. Better to stick around, let Noah do another couple songs, and watch the crowd for activity that might portend danger.

He noticed that one of the pilgrims, a golf-attired fortyish *gringo* with a drooping face, strode to a Ford sedan and pulled out. The Ford raced north as though late for a tee time.

The sight made him rescind his plan. He called Noah away after the first song. The golfer, employed by some gang like the FBI or DEA with whom the *federales* traded favors, could be on his way to set up a roadblock.

Chapter Twenty-seven

On his evening walk, from the bayside, Tom cut through an alley to Mission Boulevard. He picked up the evening edition for Friday, June 29, and carried it into Jub's Tavern. He sat at the bar. Behind him a gang of middle-aged jocks roared about various sights, such as a topless jumping jack endurance contest, they'd seen at the annual over-the-line tournament.

Tom ordered a Dewars, then opened the *Sentinel* to the World section. At the bottom of page one, he found the headline, "SAN DIEGO MAN WANTED FOR MURDER IN BAJA." He hadn't brought his glasses, couldn't make out all the small print. But he found the name Alvaro Hickey.

He waved at the bartender. When she arrived, he said, "Let me use your phone." He didn't say it like a question, and she read him well enough so she didn't take it as one. While she went for the phone, he dug out his wallet for the slip of paper on which he'd written two numbers, one for the FBI, through which he could reach Kevin Pratt, and the direct line to Andres Shuler.

◇◇◇

Clifford found his brother and the lady crouched behind a boulder alongside the road, wrapped in Dr. Fred's dark gray woolen blanket. Lourdes' teeth clacked. She trembled and quaked. She looked as if she might topple and writhe on the ground if Alvaro let go of her.

He hoisted her into the back seat, jumped in and held her from the side, almost cradling her. She grasped her knees to her chest and whimpered. More lightning hit the plain. Rain came in flurries.

When they had turned north on the public road, Lourdes raised her head and stiffened into a posture that told Alvaro to back off. He obliged. She stared at her legs and arms in the dirty white frock, as though it were a jail outfit tainted with vile memories. She said, "Please, look away. Let me put on my own clothes."

Alvaro leaned into the front, between the seats, and stared out the windshield. "Some performance."

"Oscar quality, at least," Clifford said. "We'd better get off the road before too long. I'm betting there's a roadblock up ahead."

Alvaro heard the lady rustle out of the wet frock and wad it up. It thumped on the floorboard. When she said, "Okay," and he joined her on the seat, she was wearing her same yellow dress. She tucked the hem around her knees. "Take me to Rolf," she demanded.

"Huh?" Clifford said.

The lady stared at Alvaro. He said, "Her brother. He got shot, he's in the hospital, and there's no way we're going back to Ensenada."

She leaned so close to his face he could feel her words. "I am the boss, no?"

"Not anymore."

"The gold belongs to me. I am paying you."

Alvaro would've shouted at her, if not for the sparkles that came from her eyes and the kindness he saw in them, even while they defied him. He said, "Lady, I don't want your gold."

"Then what do you want from me?"

He wasn't about to field that question. "Look, if you came looking for somebody who's only an employee, like a P.I., you should've made that clear. I would've found one for you."

"Then, if you are no employee, what are you?"

He tried to connect that question with her saying she would help defeat the PRI for his sake. Like so many inconsistencies he'd heard from women, this one left him clueless. "A friend."

"A friend would take me to my brother."

"Not this friend."

She backed away from him, slid up against the

door. "Let me out of the car."

"Speed up," Alvaro told his brother.

"Now you are holding me captive," she said.

"Okay. We can do that. Listen, the guy who owns this truck is a doctor. He can send a helicopter down, bring your brother up to his hospital." If Rolf's alive, he thought. "Augie Quartilho can make the arrangements, take care of the *mordida*."

While they waited for her response, Noah silenced his guitar mid-strum. He leaned forward and squinted to peer through the rain. "Car coming."

Alvaro said, "Take the next farm road east, *hermano*."

"Why east?"

"West of here they'll be on the lookout. They know I'm from San Diego."

◇◇◇

On the farm road Clifford chose, they rattled and banged over ruts and dips past a cluster of shacks in a willow grove and another dozen shacks in a circle like a wagon train barricading against Indian raids. Out of an unfenced pasture, a drenched goat charged at them head-down as though imagining he could butt them to the south pole. At the last instant, he swerved. He missed the rear bumper by inches.

The trail they followed dead-ended. Clifford skidded to a stop with the bumper out over a bank. He and

Alvaro climbed out to explore. In the headlights, they saw a riverbed down the middle of which a fast stream ran, wide as a football field and too deep to ford. They climbed back into the Bronco and reported to the lady and Noah. The lady must've realized they had entered wilderness, and wouldn't encounter any phones. She began pounding her leg just above the knee in a staccato rhythm like Alvaro's second mamá used to do when she was slipping into catatonia.

◇◇◇

They had crossed the divide. Or so Alvaro calculated, with no help from Fred's map of Mexico that showed only Baja's main highways. He supposed the river flowed southeast toward the Sea of Cortez, bisecting the northeasterly course he hoped would lead them to the Tecate-to-Mexicali highway west of La Rumorosa.

The trail split in two. Clifford asked, "Which way?"

"Make a right. Like some president said, if it doesn't work, we'll do something else."

"Jimmy Carter?" Noah asked.

"Some older guy, I think."

"Truman," Clifford said.

A half mile southeast, they reached a bridge, like a dam with large drain pipes running through it. But it had collapsed in the middle.

"So we go to the next one," Clifford said. "No big deal."

Another mile and a half brought them to a widening of the riverbed. Clifford stopped the Bronco. He and Alvaro got out and waded through the mud, wiping rain out of their eyes, down the bank and across the silt, which felt imbedded with stones that made it firm enough to drive on. They waded into ankle-deep then knee-deep rushing water and peered ahead.

"Stay here," Alvaro said.

The water was hardly colder than the Pacific off Coronado where he swam and surfed. He waded with arms up as if they carried an M-16, out of old habit, and stretched his legs and hips to their limit, to keep from drenching the pack he wore so long in Vietnam he hadn't expelled it from his imagination. Soon the force of the stream made him walk full-footed. Even then he toppled twice. But he crossed it and returned to Clifford and traced a line across his upper belly. "What do you think?"

"Your call?"

"Maybe there's a better place up ahead."

They walked back to the Bronco and climbed in. Alvaro would've told his brother the alternatives he saw, but fatigue had made talking into hard labor. Instead of talking, he thought, while off in the night a pack of coyotes yipped and howled.

They could backtrack to the Dos Lobos road, take their chances going north on the road that had brought him and the lady south only 60 hours ago. Or they could backtrack far enough to meet up with an unpaved road that led them south to Highway 3, the main route across the mountains. Then, if a road-block on Highway 3 hadn't ended their journey, they could follow trails or even go cross country through the desert and on the salt flat, Laguna Salada, all the way to the Tecate to Mexicali Highway. Yesterday, first light arrived around 5:20. He checked his watch. A few minutes after midnight. No way could they do that in less than five hours. He longed for the detailed Baja map he carried in the Chevy wagon. "Let's cross the river."

"Yeah, let's do *that*," Noah said, as if seconding the choice for a Disneyland ride.

The lady was slumped, her head leaned back, staring upward. She said nothing.

Clifford drove them back to the wide place. He approached the river as though to plunge straight in, sideways to the current. But at his brother's suggestion, he nosed the Bronco slightly upstream to compensate. After a minute staring like a pitcher at his target, Clifford checked to see that his passengers were belted or braced then revved the motor and eased the Bronco down a draw and into the riverbed. The Bronco slid sideways before the rear tires caught a little traction. Then it started bucking. All across the shallows, the front wheels never gripped. When they hit midstream, the Bronco teetered to the right, bucked twice, stalled, and flopped onto its side.

Alvaro and the lady had gone down to the floor and braced themselves between the seats. With the Bronco on its side, Lourdes was lurching upward, grasping for the door handle. As she caught hold, Alvaro managed to stand, one foot on a headrest. He pushed on the door while the lady yanked the handle. The door cracked open far enough so another heave and jump started him through. He hoisted himself out and lay on the rear quarter-panel while he reached back in for the lady.

They slipped off the Bronco into the river. In deep water, Alvaro held tight to the lady's waist. Her hip and thigh pressed against his groin. He didn't want to let go. He saw Noah thrashing downstream, chasing after his guitar. But he saw Clifford nowhere. He hollered for his brother. Heard nothing.

He couldn't both hold onto Lourdes and climb onto the Bronco. He tried to let go of her hand but couldn't make himself, for fear she'd go tumbling downstream, light as she was. Instead of letting go, he towed her, while she heaved and thrashed as though he were an attacker, ten meters closer to the far bank and into thigh deep, slower water. Then he let go and ran, dove, and swam back to the Bronco. He scrambled up and dove in through the front passenger door.

Clifford, gripping the wheel in both hands, stared at him as though awaiting the answer to a dread riddle.

"What?" Alvaro demanded.

"Fred's truck. We can't just leave it here."

"Hey, it's a Ford," Alvaro said. "It would've broken down soon anyway."

Clifford drooped his head onto the steering wheel. Then he pounded his head on it. At last, he let go and accepted his brother's outreached hand.

While Alvaro pulled, he yelped, "God, you must weigh three times as much as Lourdes."

On the bank, while catching his breath and peering downstream for Noah, Alvaro asked, "So you would've gone down with it, like a ship captain?"

"Ship, truck, what's the difference?"

They heard a dissonant strum of Noah's guitar before they saw him plodding along the bank. When he reached them, he gave each of the brothers an exasperated frown. "Now what?"

"First, tune that thing," Alvaro said.

The four of them stood a minute, watching each other shiver in the balmy rain, as though each sought an answer from the others.

"I need my bag," Clifford said.

"Leave it."

"I'm not leaving the gun. It's Pop's old gumshoe forty-five."

While Alvaro watched his brother wade and swim back to the Bronco, he recoiled at the thought of Clifford carrying a gun. Because he knew Clifford's conscience hadn't yet forgotten the biker he'd killed.

"Hey," he called out, "while you're at it, grab that box of snacks."

Chapter Twenty-eight

A half hour's walk brought them back to the rim of the canyon. Along the edge of the canyon, they spent another half hour searching for a trail before they gave up and made their own. Alvaro, partly raised in the Sierra Nevada, trained and tested as a Vietnam infantry soldier, was best equipped to lead. But since Clifford was also a competent mountaineer, Alvaro turned the point position over to him and kept for himself the honor of chaperoning the lady.

Though she never complained, he saw her grimaces and tentative steps. Sneakers weren't made for climbing, and stone bruises from Dos Lobos made her every step a torment.

Noah followed Clifford, the guitar strapped to his back with a length of the nylon cord Alvaro had fished out of the sunken Bronco, to use if they encountered cliffs and needed to rappel down them. The lady followed Noah, with Alvaro close behind. The slope was steep though manageable as long as the trail Clifford blazed cut sideways along it, but the mud made it slow. In places it was slippery as ice. In others the mud stuck like cement and caked their shoes. Rather than trudge straight along the slope, Clifford made zigzag trails. Whenever they encountered a boulder they could lean or sit on, he stopped the procession and gave them a minute to kick the mud off. At least the rain had softened to a drizzle.

Halfway down, the obstacles multiplied, with more boulders, yucca and mesquite, and jumping cholla to circle widely around. Cholla could spike its needles through boot-leather. All four of them wore canvas shoes and had crammed their wet socks into the lady's canvas purse or Clifford's TWA flight bag.

Around four a.m., they reached what remained of the canyon floor alongside the torrent that gushed and churned, cluttered with branches, weeds, and cacti, down toward the desert floor. Alvaro guessed their elevation as a thousand feet. A three thousand foot climb over fifteen or so miles would bring them close to the border, on the plateau north of the canyon. He hoped that in daylight they still could travel, dashing from cover to cover, at least two miles each hour, which would allow rest time before nightfall. The way they staggered along the slope told him they couldn't go much farther up the canyon without more rest than the brief stops.

The sky, in breaks between the clouds, turned silvery. A chorus of doves sang their plaintive coos, one of Alvaro's favorite sounds. He stretched and breathed deep of the rain-washed desert air.

Noah was the first to hear the motor. A second later, detecting its hum, Alvaro shouted, "Run."

They were a hundred meters short of an oasis, an outcropping low on the west slope and edging into the stream's path, so the water detoured around it. Alvaro thought they could hide beneath the stubby palms or in the shadow of the boulder, tall as a boxcar, on the river edge of the oasis.

Clifford ran with his big loping strides. Noah almost kept up until his back foot tripped over his front foot, which the mud had caught. He toppled forward onto the muddy slope, flipped sideways, and zoomed like a toboggan into the rushing water.

Alvaro shouted to the lady, "Follow me. If we get even a glimpse of the plane, we go under water." He dropped to sitting and eased down the bank after Noah.

The airplane looked like a Cessna, two propellers, probably a four-seater, Alvaro noticed in the instant it took him to react after the first wing appeared and before he and the others plunged into the knee-deep, fast and foamy water. Alvaro counted to seventy before his lungs demanded air. Then he rolled onto his back and attempted to only let his face surface. The plane glided away, straight north.

The air must've been tepid but, as wet and fatigued as they were, the chill reached into their bones. In a straight but shivering line, they plodded along the water's edge to the oasis and cover underneath the edge of the mammoth boulder, which was disc-shaped, like fry bread. Clifford said, "Hollywood could paint this monster and cast it as a flying saucer."

"I'll tell Martin Sheen about it," Noah said. "He always comes to Good Willy's."

They collapsed on the sand, white as a tropical beach. The boulder gave them a few square meters of dry shelter. Alvaro lay on his back with hands folded beneath his head. The lady was next to him, not touching but close enough so he could feel her warmth. Clifford and Noah lay crosswise at their feet, between them and the stream.

As the sun rose and their shivering subsided, all but Alvaro dozed. He knew better. No matter how secure you felt, somebody had to stand guard.

He watched a shaft of sunlight gild the foamy rushing water. He wondered if the clouds were breaking. When a dull roar commenced, it sounded as if he held a conch to his ear. Every second the noise came louder.

He'd never heard a roar like this one. But he knew what made it, and he bolted upright. He knocked his head on the stone ceiling, and yelled, "A flood. Get up. This way."

He led them crawling out of the uphill side of their shelter. Clutching Lourdes' wrist, he scampered on two legs and one hand, straight up the muddy hill. "Don't look, just move," he shouted.

They gained a few yards, slid backwards, grabbed shrubs and sharp rocks that jutted out of the hillside, until the roar came louder than inside the curl of a monster wave. The uprooted trunks of piñons and desert willow crashed against the oasis palms, knocked them loose and shoved the small ones into the current like rebels on the march enlisting forces along the way. Alvaro and the others clawed and crawled up the slope until he looked back and saw that the water had already begun to recede. Then they sat and panted, watching the water roil.

Noah sprang up. "Look, there's my guitar." He pointed downstream to a cottonwood that grew at an angle out over the stream. One of its branches had caught the guitar by its strap. He slid down, ran and jumped to grab it. The branch was too high. He had to go hand over hand along the tree trunk. When he reached the guitar, one hand let go of the branch. The other hand lost its grip. He plunged back-first into the stream. The guitar fell on him. He flailed, grabbed the guitar, waded ashore and staggered toward the others.

When he reached them, he gasped, "It's not a very good one, but I promised to return it."

The hillside offered no cover. All the boulders, most of the brush, and the few clusters of trees the flood hadn't uprooted were near the canyon floor.

Noah spotted the cave, forty meters up the eastern hillside. Alvaro climbed there to scout. From below, the entrance had looked no bigger than his head, but he managed to squirm his shoulders through, then the rest of him. Inside, he dug in his pocket for Fred's penlight then used it and groped his way deeper into the cave, on the lookout for snakes and scorpions. At the end, he estimated that the space about equaled the interior of a sports car with a smashed-in roof.

He found a loose rock and used it to chip at the entrance, widening the hole to allow Clifford's big shoulders through.

They fit in the cave like four prisoners in a torture hole meant for one. The floor was concrete hard, mossy, textured like a bed of nails. The cave smelled like the acid Alvaro had used to open clogged drains. But he hardly minded while he lay snug against the lady, his arm across her upper hips. She dozed and breathed shallowly between ragged gasps that quickened his resolve to protect her. Twice she talked in her sleep. Both times, amidst phrases that sounded like innocuous childhood memories, something about a horse and another something about climbing a hill, she said, "*No te preocupe*, Rolf."

◇◇◇

Alvaro changed from his gym shoes, which had lost half a sole somewhere along the riverbed, to the moccasins he had stashed in the lady's canvas purse. Then he tried to rest and ward off thoughts of doom, but they gripped him tight, like skin diving weight belts around his head and chest. He felt monstrously careless for bringing them all to this place. For killing or ruining the lives of a lady he admired above any, his brother who had always stood beside him and always forgiven his excesses, and Noah, a gifted and most gentle fellow.

Clifford dug out the box of soggy granola bars. Alvaro passed around the wine bag Clifford had salvaged from the Bronco and filled with grainy stream water. He managed to rest and daydream that all four of them would cross the border alive.

◇◇◇

Thunder and lightning woke them. The hillside quaked. The rain came so hard, the view out the mouth of the cave looked like what Alvaro imagined he'd see from behind a waterfall.

Noah, still lying on his back, crooked the guitar on top of him and began finger-picking a bluegrass melody.

Alvaro asked for a few minutes with the guitar. He riffed scales and chords until his fingers limbered enough. Then he played and sang something he vaguely recalled from his father. He'd found it on a record soon after the Hickeys took him in, and had played it ever since. It was a Christmas song to the tune of Greensleeves, the most enchanting melody Alvaro knew. He sang softly, on account of the cave's acoustics. *"Que niño es este que al dormir en brazos de Maria…"*

While he sang, through the dark he caught glimpses of the lady. She was giving him a look he could choose to interpret as love, or at least fascination. When he finished the song, Noah said, "Beautiful, beautiful. Can you teach me those words?"

Alvaro handed the guitar back to Noah. "We have to go."

"Why?"

"It's only a few hours till dark, and they won't fly in this storm. Trust me, the farther we can go while the storm lasts, the better."

Outside, in a train with Alvaro in front, they inched on their rears down the hillside. They trudged alongside the streambed, the rain pounding sideways into their faces like a warm blizzard. They tried to peer through it, awaiting the next flash flood. Clifford shouted, "Can somebody tell me, are we walking or swimming?"

Chapter Twenty-nine

After the storm relented, they kept hiking, past flowering ocotillo besieged by hummingbirds and a trio of sidewinders slithering fast from rock to bush to rock. For a spell, Alvaro nearly forgot about danger and fatigue. Hawks gliding above the canyon made him feel as if this were only another day. Noah stopped and pointed to the fruit on a prickly pear cactus. "Can we eat these?"

The fruits were green, but the people were hungry. Alvaro said, "Try one out."

Noah picked one, bit into it and made pinched face. "I wish we had a watermelon," he said, then ate another bite before he threw it down.

Then they heard voices. They crossed the stream on a natural bridge of rocks and driftwood, and climbed about thirty meters up the sloping canyon wall and to the cover of brush and scrub oaks above the flood line. Hustling from brush to tree brought them to a place where they could look down upon a campground. The Hickey brothers knew the place. They had spent more than a few weekends reading, drinking beer, and lounging in its hot springs. Alvaro had supposed the storm would keep weekenders away, yet he saw at least a dozen cars, pickups, camper vans, and a motor home with its generator chugging.

Noah said, "Hey, I could go down there and play some music for people. They would give me food, for all of us, I bet."

"Stop and think a minute," Alvaro said.

Noah appeared to ponder. "You mean there might be cops down there."

"Wait," Clifford said. "Suppose Noah holds off till we get a half hour farther along, then he goes down and finds *gringos* who'll take him in, feed him, lend him a spare sleeping bag and tomorrow or Sunday will take him over the border."

"No sir," Noah said. "I'm with you guys."

Alvaro sneezed. All afternoon, his eyes had been watering and his head filling with mucus. He said, "Besides, Noah might be the *gringo* they're saying murdered Carlos Meza."

"But I didn't do it," Noah said.

"Right. Monreal did. But he's PRI, remember."

◇◇◇

At the first pass of the helicopter, Alvaro and the others

were in the open and too far from cover. They would've gotten spotted, except lightning struck piñon on the canyon rim. The pilot, apparently spooked, circled to the east and only returned to swoop low above the canyon a half mile behind them. By that time, they were hidden beneath a jutting ridge.

The helicopter was a CH-46 Sea Knight, a vehicle Alvaro knew all too well. He'd been transported, dropped into jungles and picked up by them. This one, though olive drab, had no insignia.

The storm had brought an early dusk. Alvaro guessed they were two miles from the canyon's upper outlet, but Clifford, who had hiked it more recently, guessed twice that far. Either way, Alvaro believed that unless the storm grounded the aircraft, they wouldn't cross the border tonight. The high part of the canyon used to offer the cover of brush and trees, but the flood would have stripped it bare.

The Sea Knight made another pass, flying north and making perilous dips below the rim of the canyon. A few minutes later it returned, rocking and wobbling in the rain and wind. It turned north. The whup of blades had gone out of their hearing for many seconds before it came again, lower than ever and so close to the canyon wall that Alvaro couldn't tell what happened next. From under the ridge, he only saw the Sea Knight go straight right like paper caught by a crosswind. When a rear blade hit the canyon wall, it must've stuck in mud. It stopped dead, which stalled the motor. The copter tipped sideways. Then it rolled and thundered five turns before it landed in the stream with a mighty thud.

Clifford and Noah crawled out from beneath the ledge and stood, numbed by fatigue, gazing at the wreck a quarter mile upstream. The lady remained under the ledge, shivering with her arms wrapped across her breasts, her chin tucked into her arms.

Alvaro told the men to get under the ledge with Lourdes. Then he rummaged through Clifford's bag for the .45 automatic.

Though he saw no sign of life around the copter, he circled up the hillside to the south and approached from the rear. He crept down the slope to the tail, came around the pilot's side and found one man lying half in, half out of the cockpit. Red hair, freckles, and the grayish jump suit and arm patch of a U.S. Navy Lieutenant J.G.

The Lieutenant didn't move. His neck had fallen sideways so an ear rested on his shoulder. Alvaro picked up his limp arm and found no pulse. He groaned and genuflected, a habit he'd taken from his papa and never had the heart to kick. He tiptoed around to the other side. The second man slumped over the co-pilot's controls. Breathing. Now and then he gasped, but most of his breaths came regularly. Alvaro peered into every cranny of the cockpit but found no weapons. He squatted in the stream beside the wreck and leaned close to the co-pilot. "Hey, man. Are you there?"

He heard a gargling sound that turned into something like, "Yeah."

"What are you doing down here? In Mexico, I mean."

The man's head crooked toward him. "We're supposed to rescue some guys."

Chapter Thirty

Clifford had left the shelter beneath the ledge and followed his brother. He'd trudged from one boulder to the next, ducked behind each of them and listened. He rounded a boulder shaped like a dull arrowhead and saw his next stop would be the wreck.

Alvaro sprang from behind the copter, his pistol raised.

"Did you miss Pop's lesson about pointing guns at people?"

"What'd he say?"

"Don't do it. Are they both dead?"

"One is. The other just conked his head, I hope."

Clifford heard the man groaning and saw his head move enough to indicate his neck and spine were probably intact.

"Look at the uniforms."

Clifford chose to look at the living man, whom he would've called a boy if he hadn't worn a uniform.

He had the haircut of a rookie, probably not long out of flight school.

The man stopped groaning. Clifford waited for him to speak, but his head slumped to the side. Clifford knelt and felt his wrist. "Nice and strong," he said. "So what's our Navy doing here?"

"Beats me. *Hermano*, you and the others move out. I'll do what I can for this guy, get what I can out of him, see if the radio's working, and catch up."

"If the radio's working, then what?"

"I'll meditate on that. You move out before their backup shows."

Clifford slogged through the mud to the ledge where the lady and Noah waited. To Lourdes' questioning gaze, he shook his head. "Two *gringos*. U.S. Navy. One's dead."

Noah watched the lady with a look Clifford believed meant he was waiting for her offer to revive the dead man. He must've given up. His face turned mournful. "Now what shall we do?"

"Let's get moving," Clifford said. "If the bad guys saw the chopper go down, they'll be coming after it." He watched the lady for signs of terror or weakness. But he saw in her eyes the grit of a soldier's heart.

When they passed the helicopter, Alvaro was in the pilot's seat. He had pulled the dead pilot out, positioned him face up on a bed of sand beside the wreck, and laid his flight jacket over his chest and shoulders. Now Alvaro was tinkering with the radio. He circled his arm like a base coach waving a runner home. "Don't stop until you're far away and under cover," he called out. "I'll catch up."

A thousand or so muddy strides ahead, Clifford led them into a cleft in the canyon's east wall. "Maybe it'll take us out of the canyon," he told the others.

But after the cleft crooked one way then the other, they met a dead end. The lady sat on a log. Clifford and Noah joined her, one on either side. "I guess we should pray," Clifford said. Lourdes looked over, watched him and waited, until Clifford said. "I meant you."

She didn't speak, but she reached for his hand and Noah's.

◇◇◇

They were still on the log when Alvaro came stumbling. He looked about to collapse, but he reached the log and sat beside Clifford. He rubbed his temples and muffled a cough with the back of his hand.

"Rest a while," Clifford said.

"Yeah." After a minute, he said, "The guy's going to make it. He's got a concussion and a busted leg, at least. If they haven't picked him up already by the time we get to wherever in hell we're going, we'll send somebody."

"No radio?"

Alvaro shook his head. "It's all busted up."

"Did he say anything?"

"Plenty. I asked what's the U.S. Navy doing working for the Mexicans. I questioned whether that was by the book. He says he never read any book, he only takes orders, and sometimes they help out the border patrol, sometimes the DEA. And this time it's the FBI."

"Oh oh," Noah said. "I don't trust the FBI."

"So I said, 'What's the FBI got to do with anything, I mean now that they've already caught the one they think was the Virgin?' He says, 'Well, they're not so sure the one they caught is the right Virgin. Since she showed up again yesterday.'"

"Oops," Noah said.

"And then he says, 'And there's something about a murder up in Long Beach.' I asked him what about it. Like who does the FBI think did the killing. He said he didn't know, and I'm betting he's way too broken to lie very well. Then he says, 'Anyway, we're not exactly down here looking for the Virgin. We're supposed to rescue some United States citizens. I guess you're them, right? A couple brothers and some lady that's with them.' And get this. Just before they crashed, he radioed the FBI, gave them our location. Which means that any minute now, I'm betting we'll have visitors."

The lady sat quiet through all this. Clifford thought back and noted that she hadn't spoken for hours. He couldn't quite decide if she looked like a drone or like a fasting saint. Either way, only part of her remained with them.

"You know what I want?" Noah asked.

Clifford turned to him. "What?"

"A hamburger."

Clifford smiled. Then he thought of Feliz. His gut cramped and his legs itched to move on, get this trial over with, whatever the outcome. He stood and asked, "Now what?"

His brother pointed at Noah and the lady. "You two are going to stay put. *Entiendes?* I'll go look up ahead. *Hermano,* you follow me, about fifty yards behind."

"I'll go first," Clifford said.

"Why you?"

"I'm a better talker."

"Not in Spanish. Anyway, who's the lawyer here? Besides, this was my idea. I get to be the one who screws it up." He laughed then turned solemn. "And if things go south, it won't be a fight like you've ever seen. It'll be jungle warfare."

◇◇◇

While he plodded toward the narrow waterfall he supposed marked the head of the canyon, he sharpened with a stone and spit the fishing knife he had salvaged out of Fred's Bronco. He stopped and adjusted the gun so it didn't gouge his back with every step. He listened for the slightest sound a human might cause. And, between strokes of the blade, he keened his eyes on the top of the cliff on both sides of the waterfall.

He supposed, from what he'd already known and what the co-pilot told him, when the Mexicans or the FBI appeared, they would want the lady. He, Clifford, and Noah were incidental. Maybe, like the pilots' mission implied, the Mexicans would grant their freedom and even safe passage to the border in exchange for the lady. They needed her as well as Lupe to prove the Virgin was a fraud.

So he could deal with them. And then, once he crossed the line, he could jump on the phone to TV, radio, and newspapers on both sides of the border and give the whole story. With that plan, the odds of them all surviving were fair. If her brother Andres helped, and if Alvaro offered to return the family gold, the lady would get pardoned if she weren't the murderer. She might get pardoned even if she were. Not that he imagined Andres Shuler cared a lot about his sister. But he must know that families prosper or don't on the reputations of them all. If Andres wouldn't cooperate, Alvaro could find a way to launder the lady's gold, turn it into *mordida*, and arrange for her acquittal.

By playing that game, all he might lose was a chance to win the heart of the lady and help sink the PRI. Neither of which was he willing to give up.

He wrung out Dr. Fred's San Diego State University baseball cap, which felt even heavier than his sopped shirt or jeans. He sneezed into cupped hands and wished he'd snatched the cold medicine and aspirins out of Fred's emergency kit. He thought about the lady and how she had risked everything by choosing to become the Virgin, when they could've crossed the border yesterday. And she'd claimed she did it for him. Though she might've lied to assure he would help, he remembered how he felt when she said it. As if he'd gotten knighted.

A flare shot up from near the top of the waterfall. It overlaid the lumpy black clouds with sparks. Alvaro stood and slapped his hat on his knee, placed it on his head, pulled it low and straightened it. He leaned into the rain, so the Aztec on his cap led the way. He turned and saw what looked like his brother's shadow, fifty meters behind. "You with me, *hermano*," he called out.

"*Ándale,*" Clifford said.

Gray and purple splotches were beginning to color the lower sky as Alvaro reached what appeared to be the final slope before the head of the canyon. He scouted and found a path up, beside the narrow and stingy waterfall. He took a few steps, then heard a deep voice call out, "Heeckey, you got visitors."

He waited. A minute or so passed, then two men appeared at the top of the path to the east of the waterfall, in a shaft of moonlight that found a way through the clouds and mist.

Alvaro reached around behind, gripped the .45, lowered himself into a shallow ditch, and squatted there.

The men started down walking, but the one in the rear slipped. His feet flew out in front and kicked the other fellow, who then tipped backward. They both slid the rest of the way down.

At the base of the path, the men threw their hands out high and wide. The blondest one hollered, "Hey, you must be one of the Hickey brothers."

"Who says?"

"We're FBI. Word gets around."

Enough moonlight seeped through the clouds so that Alvaro recognized them. He'd seen them at Playa Sin Olas, escorting a handcuffed fellow he believed was Raul Meza's partner. "Okay. Before you come any closer, you're here to do what?"

The darker blond said to his partner, "Don't go yelling it out, or that chump will shoot us in the back."

"What chump?" Alvaro demanded.

"*Comandante* Monreal," the blonder agent said. "He already shot one guy. I'm Special Agent Pratt."

"What are you doing here, Pratt?"

"Hey, that's what I'm telling you. We've come to help." He pointed to his partner. "This is Special Agent Ross Clinger."

"Swell. Who sent you?"

"Our A.I.C. sent us to Monreal. Monreal sent us to you."

"Why?"

"Well, we're in Mexico chasing the killers of some *Partido de la Gente* guys in Long Beach. Monreal thinks the killer is you."

"He doesn't think that," Ross Clinger said, "but that's what he's saying. He says you killed the guys in Long Beach before you shot Carlos Meza. So we're supposed to make a deal. That's why he sent us to you."

Pratt said, "We're supposed to get you to surrender to us, so you can spend life in prison in the states rather than in Mexico. I mean, the Mexicans allow conjugal visits, but the prisons are mighty grim."

"Did he say why I killed these guys?"

"He says you're a shooter for the Ornelas mob, and some large smuggling deal between Ornelas and *Partido de la Gente* went sour."

Listening to their story felt like hearing a cancer diagnosis. The agents kept quiet while Alvaro listened to the screeches of lost gulls and recovered enough to say, "And you'll escort me and the lady safe across the border?"

"That's the deal we're supposed to offer. How about if we come closer, so we can give you the whole setup without yelling?"

"I don't mind yelling."

"Okay then," Kevin Pratt said. "We're going to bring you, in custody, up to *Comandante* Monreal. He's got Lupe and Raul Meza right there with him. We're supposed to get you the heck out of Mexico, so they can get on with their election in peace. It's the day after tomorrow, you know. Your brother's with you, right?"

Alvaro was thinking, these characters knew so much, they might soon convince him to believe the legends of the FBI's virtual omniscience. He was about to ask whether Monreal had put Lupe on television. If not, he might assume that Pop had dealt with Andres Shuler. But he saw the one called Ross underhand what looked like a grenade.

The thing hit the dirt a few feet short of Alvaro's ditch. He dove to his right and landed face first with arms folded over the back of his skull. The thing was still rolling. It plopped into the ditch.

After a half minute, Alvaro rose to his knees and shone Fred's penlight on the thing. Then he reached out. It was a paper wrapped around a rock. A note. With the moon behind the wispiest of clouds, he made out the big letters, "X, TRUST THE G-MEN."

From Pop. Or an expert's imitation. He reached for the .45 and climbed out of the ditch. "Come closer."

The agents walked single file, Clinger behind Pratt. At the ledge of the ditch, they squatted.

Alvaro rested the gun on his knee and laid his hand

on top of it. "Why's Monreal using you?"

"Credibility," Kevin Pratt said. "I'll bet you have no idea how many newshounds are covering this Virgin affair. And somebody told Monreal to lay off the sisters. But you Hickeys are the brains behind the Virgin. That's what the *federales* are saying, that you cooked up the scam and hired Lupe Shuler to play the part. If the FBI backs their story, who's got the nerve to call it a lie, besides some commies?"

Alvaro declined to reply. Pratt said, "We didn't get to be Special Agents so we could help kill innocent people."

"Yeah," Clinger said, "that's the CIA's job, not ours."

Alvaro raised a hand, palm out. "You're supposed to help kill somebody?"

"Uh huh," Pratt said. "We're supposed to set you up. Monreal thinks he's going to shoot you and your brother when you try to escape, like he did to Carlos Meza?"

"We heard him talking with another guy," Ross Clinger said. "They think because we're *gringos* we can't understand Spanish unless they shout."

"And you're supposed to what?"

"Get you guys up into the meadow, then hit the road."

"By ourselves," Clinger added.

"And what you're actually going to do is?"

"Get you all across the border," Pratt said.

"How's that going to work, with Monreal planning to kill us?"

Agent Clinger pointed to the gun on Alvaro's knee.

Chapter Thirty-one

When Alvaro was nine years younger, fresh out of training and programmed for robotic actions, he'd been capable of rapid and deadly response. But even then, he was no expert with a pistol, nor had he gone deprived of sleep quite this long without amphetamines.

"Okay," he said. "What I'm hearing is, you want me to shoot a *comandante de federales*."

Pratt said, "That's the only solution we see. The thing is, he thinks he's got backup, but he doesn't. He thinks the army's on his side, but the Colonel in charge has a different idea."

"If Monreal draws on you, shoot him first," Clinger said, looking confident as though Alvaro were Billy the Kid.

"And if he doesn't."

"All the better," Pratt said. "Either way, our next stop's the border. Tom Hickey's waiting for you there."

"It's your only chance," Pratt said. "At least as far as I can see."

He might've asked what if a mob of *federales* came out of hiding to back up or avenge Monreal. But "what ifs" could be endless. And the note from Pop had convinced him these agents were on the level. Still, he knew he could mistake wishes for reasons and believe all wrong. Especially while fatigued and in desperate pursuit of his two fondest dreams, the woman who might fill in the last piece and make him feel complete, and the ruin of the PRI. But he couldn't stand thinking anymore. He needed to move. "Listen up. If you're lying, don't underestimate me."

"So we heard," Pratt said.

◇◇◇

Leaving the agents to wait, Alvaro ran stumbling back to where Clifford crouched behind a piñon.

He passed the agents' proposal along to his brother who hadn't missed quite as much sleep. And he showed Clifford the note. Like Alvaro, only when Pop came into the equation did Clifford begin to think their offer to help might be something besides a ruse.

"If they were conning us," Alvaro said, "how would they know to use Pop? I mean, how would they know he's like our hero unless they went to the office and rifled through your boxes, and dug out one of those stories you've written about him."

Clifford said, "Were Pop so foolish as to get himself in a jam like we're in, what would he do?"

"Beats me."

"Me too."

Alvaro said, "Then how about this. We trust the G-men, and if they've conned us, we try our best to die laughing."

When Clifford took him by the shoulders, Alvaro let himself collapse enough to lean his head on his brother's shoulder.

"You've got a fever, *hermano*."

"No big deal," Alvaro said.

Chapter Thirty-two

The Hickeys gave the others a choice. Come along to meet Paco Monreal, or leave Alvaro and Clifford and hike back down the canyon to the hot springs in hopes that some camper would make like a *coyote* and carry them over the line. When the lady and Noah opted to stick with the Hickeys, Alvaro felt some pride, some relief, and a terror deeper and closer to panic than he'd ever known.

◇◇◇

The agents went first. Alvaro next. Then Clifford, the lady, and Noah at the rear of the line. The path beside the waterfall was at least sixty degrees. They all stumbled and slipped backward on the decomposed granite. The agents scrambled over the ledge and stopped. Alvaro saw why when he peered around them. Through the mist, he made out the cowboy. Paco Monreal, with a long barreled revolver held up beside his face. In his left hand, Alvaro noticed.

Agent Pratt shouted in Spanish. "You want our cooperation, you better put that gun away."

To Monreal's left stood the lady's sister and a young bearded fellow Alvaro had seen through binoculars near the Santa Inez mission and again, at Playa Sin Olas when he came gunning for Paco Monreal.

Raul Meza. Up close, he looked Spanish, intelligent, with a round, pale face, and eyes that could be lasers, and a jaw that appeared locked and ready to receive a blow. He was a soldier not only made intense by desire for survival, but also by devotion to his cause. Even on patrol in Vietnam, or going into a battle, Alvaro hadn't witnessed anyone more fierce or determined.

Lupe wore a smock that looked moss green through the mist. Her posture was bent, as if they had broken her in two. Her hair stuck out as though she had teased it into a golden frame.

The meadow beside the stream at the top of the waterfall sloped upward toward a rocky bank. Beyond the bank was an oak grove.

Monreal stuffed his gun into the holster beneath his armpit on the right side.

Agent Clinger said, "Let's go."

Alvaro and the others followed the agents until they were less than five meters from the cowboy, who had fixed a savage gaze on Alvaro. He looked like some opponents in Tae Kwon Do tournaments tried to, attempting to open a crack in your spirit. After they all stopped, Monreal turned to the uniformed *federale* beside him. "These two," he said, waving his right hand toward Alvaro and Noah, who stood between the Hickey brothers, "nobody told me anything about them. The man tells me, don't kill these two Virgins." He snarled the title. "Or this one." He nodded toward Raul.

He pointed a thumb in Clifford's direction. "I don't know this one. But these two, I know." He swept his glare back and forth between Alvaro and Noah. "This one." He aimed his right finger at Alvaro. "He killed my *compadre* Carlos. He is behind all this trouble, and he keeps breaking away from us. He's a crafty one. We don't want him making trouble in our prison."

All through that speech, while using his left foot to help his right foot out of its mud-caked moccasin, Alvaro had watched the cowboy's eyes. And now, he sensed more than saw Monreal's left hand ease toward the holstered gun and then grab and yank it out.

Alavaro wasn't going to bet on his quick draw. If the man were right handed, he would've tried a front snap kick, his strongest and quickest. But to disarm the southpaw, he chose a round house. And since the big, long-barreled revolver would weigh half a ton and might break his foot, Alvaro aimed at the elbow.

But the kick hit Monreal's forearm and broke nothing, except the man's grip. The gun fell.

Monreal dropped to his knees. He was fast. Almost before he hit the ground, the gun was back in his hand. And he was aware. He must've seen Raul Meza snatch the sidearm from the holster of the *federale* beside him, while the *federale* was busy slinging the M-16 around from where it hung on his shoulder.

The cowboy's big gun rose in both his hands.

Raul was no gunslinger. He had to use his eyes as he fumbled to get his finger inside the trigger guard.

Monreal's first shot hit Raul in the chest, dead center. Lupe screamed like a diva in hell. Raul dropped. First to his knees. Then, as the blood spread into a circle that covered his chest, he fell forward. He coughed, rolled onto his side and lay still, as if he he'd been tired to death anyway, and anxious to lie down. Lupe dove on top of him.

Alvaro had pulled the .45 from under the back of his t-shirt and jeans. But as the cowboy's big gun wheeled toward him, something in his mind tweaked, and imagined the gun failing him. It was old, long unused, now dunked in the river, and though Clifford had dried it and said the bullets looked dry, Alvaro declined to trust it. The gun fell from his hand. He threw a wild kick.

Paco Monreal slumped and went to his knees, and his gun fell slowly until the barrel rested on the ground. Still the cowboy's eyes blazed. They gazed around with an arrogance like some soldiers Alvaro had known, who could see death every day but still not imagine it might come to them. The gun barrel rose off the ground, and Alvaro poured all the strength and precision he could gather into a front snap kick. It landed square on the cowboy's chin.

Monreal's eyes crossed. He fell straight back. His big gun boomed. Only then, the soldiers came running. They ran out of the oak grove and down the bank, M-16s raised in front of them.

Agent Clinger had a hand on the shoulder of the uniformed *federale,* who stood bewildered, holding his weapon in a grip so loose, the barrel waved back and forth.

Clifford had hustled Lourdes and Noah back to the top of the waterfall path. He was holding the lady's arm pulling her toward the path while she fought him. She acted mad, and wild, as if she might run in any direction, into a bullet or over a cliff.

Alvaro went to Lupe. But Agent Pratt was already on top of her, his arms beneath her, between her and Raul. She held onto Raul as if the FBI agent were assigned to be her escort to the gallows. Alvaro grabbed one of her arms, Pratt the other. It took all both of them had left to pry her from the corpse of her lover. They dragged her to the path. As they started down she relented. Then Pratt led her by one arm.

Alvaro squatted at the top of the path and watched the soldiers crowd around Raul and Monreal. The cowboy was sprawled on his back, arms splayed and palms up. His revolver lay just beyond his reach. Agent Clinger kicked it farther away.

The uniformed *federale* stood consulting with an officer Alvaro presumed was the colonel in charge of the soldiers. While Alvaro looked around for Pop's .45, he saw a soldier pick it up then go for Monreal's revolver. And when he saw Agent Clinger starting down the waterfall path, he followed. At the base of the path, he found the sisters squatting in mud beside the waterfall's pool. They held hands. Their eyes made them look like cornered, feral creatures. The agents squatted nearby. Pratt leaned toward his partner. He pointed at the Shulers. "Look."

"Wow," Ross Clinger said. Both Virgins appeared crazy, strung out and disheveled. One looked as if she had bathed in mud, and the savage eyes of both seemed ready to launch out of their heads. "I never saw anything that scary."

"Beautiful."

"Yeah, that too."

◇◇◇

An amplified voice called in Spanish, "Come up here, *hombres*. We need to talk, I guess you know."

"I'll go," Pratt said. He turned toward the path.

Alvaro jumped up and caught him. "Whoa. I'm going."

"Why not me?" the agent asked. "I'm not a fugitive. I didn't just kill the *comandante*."

"Is he dead?"

"I don't know," Pratt said. "Maybe. Anyway, they've got no excuse to shoot me. And I speak Spanish. Ross and I spent two years in Queretaro, on our mission."

Alvaro sighed and got in return a defensive look, as if Pratt suspected the sigh was meant as a slight against Mormons. "The other reason," he said, "is I don't want you talking to any of those guys without me there to listen."

Pratt scowled. "Cripes, you still don't trust us?"

"Right."

"Okay then, may I go along? In case I can help, that's all."

Alvaro shrugged. "Hey, up there," he shouted in Spanish. "We're coming."

They scrambled up the path and back into the meadow. The colonel, a barrel shaped fellow with jowls and a tiny mouth, stood ankle deep in the grassy mud between Raul's body and Monreal, who was still on his back. But now his hands lay on his belly.

The uniformed *federale* and half the platoon of soldiers stood close by. The rest of the soldiers squatted farther off, in a circle like men throwing dice, while they chatted and smoked.

The colonel turned a deep frown on Alvaro and

held out Tom Hickey's old .45. "This is your gun."

Without thinking, Alvaro said, "Yeah," then wondered if he'd just spoken his doom.

"Okay," the colonel said. He turned toward Monreal, genuflected with his left hand then used his right to aim at the cowboy. "*Lo siento, comandante.*" He raised the gun into both hands, took closer aim, and fired. A geyser of blood spewed from the cowboy's chest.

Alvaro looked away. He heard the colonel close behind him. "I don't like this. Killing this man is not so good. But we can't have him alive anymore. If he is alive, you see, he can tell the *presidente* about this fight. That is no good, for the *presidente* to hear his story. You know, *señor*, you put me in a hell of a position. You want to know what I'm thinking?"

Alvaro nodded, supposing this colonel was one of those folks, mostly women, who could only think out loud, and whom you don't want to interrupt or they'll never reach a conclusion.

"I'm thinking this. Today, I get orders straight from the office of the *presidente*. The orders, you keep an eye on Monreal. If he does like we tell him to and makes sure those two Virgins and these Hickeys go safe across the border, then okay. If he tries to do something else, you take over, and you make sure the Virgins and these Hickeys are okay and over the line, then you bring the *comandante* back to the Capital where his future will be decided. Now, why the *presidente* would send me orders like this, I don't know."

Alvaro could've told him. Agent Pratt probably also knew, having spoken to Pop. But to give up the secret that the Virgins were the sisters of Andres Shuler would've betrayed the man who appeared to be helping them all.

"Look here," the colonel said, "if anybody knows it was me that let you shoot this *comandante*, maybe some *pinche* brother of his will kill me. But if I arrest you, maybe you want to fight, maybe some FBI gets killed, or maybe one or two of these Virgins. For such an offense, I will lose my rank or my life. You put me in a noose here, *hombre*."

Alvaro shrugged his apology. The colonel rambled on. "No, the only chance for me, I must go home and pray the PRI loses. My only hope is a different party. Maybe they will forgive me for this." He hitched his thumb behind him, toward the soldiers who were wrapping blankets around Monreal's corpse. "I need to keep your gun." He turned and walked to the *federale* standing over Raul. Alvaro followed and listened. The colonel told the *federale*, "You make sure the prints are good from the killer's hand…" He pointed at Raul. "…on this gun here. And when the investigators ask where this kid got the gun, you tell them maybe somebody that saw General Monreal shoot the kid's papa got to the kid and slipped him the gun somehow."

After a minute giving more instructions, he turned back to Alvaro and Pratt. "Now, you and your Virgins and those other guys are going to get the hell out of Mexico. Fast. *Entiendes?* But first, tell me now where is the U.S. Navy helicopter?"

Alvaro gave directions to the Sea Knight. The colonel called his troops. When they had gathered around him, he instructed them to take their vehicles out to the highway and station themselves on the roadside, a kilometer apart, one vehicle for every kilometer all the way to Tecate and the border. "As these Hickeys pass each car, that car must follow. Be ready with your weapons. We are not the only ones chasing these crazy Virgins. And we don't want them to make some speech at the plaza in Tecate. You know?"

Chapter Thirty-three

Alvaro didn't believe they were free to go. The soldiers and their colonel might be on the level. But whoever was leading the *federales* with Monreal gone might well disagree.

Clifford followed Agent Clinger up the path. Then came Lourdes, Lupe and Noah in the rear. Alvaro and Pratt joined in behind. They trudged single file, arm's length apart, across the meadow. At the far side, the colonel stood beside one of his soldiers. Alvaro stopped and faced him. "If you aren't the only ones chasing the Virgins, who else is?"

"Maybe the ones who killed the men in Long Beach. You heard about that murder, yes?"

Noah, a few steps ahead, called over his shoulder, "*Federales.*"

The rocky bank was an easy climb into the dark oak grove where fallen leaves hardened the mud, so the walking was easier and the noise of footsteps less harsh as the leaves were too soggy to crunch and crack. Alvaro watched and listened, with the supercharged mindset he had used padding through dark jungles.

Halfway through the grove, Lupe fell. Noah tripped over her, and still she lay motionless. Alvaro thought she might be down for good, taken by grief to some purgatory like Wendy used to enter, what doctors labeled catatonia, what the Hickey men believed was simply a sorrow beyond dreams. But Lupe gripped the hand Noah offered, heaved herself up and staggered on, holding tight to gentle Noah's hand.

In an oak grove camp area littered with plastic bags, cans and bottles, several *federales* stood smoking beside a travel trailer. Two campsites over from the trailer was an old Datsun sedan. Agent Pratt pointed to it. "Sorry we're driving my junker. They won't let us bring a bureau car down here."

Noah offered to sit on somebody's lap. Ross Clinger volunteered, leaving the back seat for the Hickey brothers and the ladies.

As the car sputtered to life, Alvaro said, "Look, even if they disregard that I might've killed a *federale*, no way they're letting us out the gate and back to my place, to a million in stolen gold Andres Shuler has got to know about."

Pratt said, "A million in gold?"

"And you're just now telling us?" Clinger added.

"I was busy. Had things on my mind, you know what I mean." He glanced at Lourdes beside him on her sister's lap. She looked only present in a bodily sense, her mind and spirit gone to another dimension. From her expression, she might not have heard them talking about her gold. But she said, "I won't leave Mexico without Rolf."

Alvaro snapped, "The hell you won't."

The lady reached across Clifford for the door handle. Alvaro grabbed through her golden hair and caught the scruff of her neck. "Keep your hands on your lap." He wanted to apologize, explain that killing and watching people die roused his latent temper. But excuses meant nothing, and apologies could wait. They had arrived at the Tecate to Mexicali highway. He spotted a *policia* cruiser parked across the road and another a hundred yards east. "If they're on the level, why the escort?"

"You heard the man," Clifford said. "They don't want us to stop and let these Virgins prophesy along the way. Every vote counts, they say."

The Datsun, a sluggish automatic, killed minutes reaching a top speed of 75 mph. By then, they had already passed two more cruisers and several army pickups parked on the roadside. The cruisers had fallen in behind. Clifford said, "Noah, if you've got room, play us a song. I'm getting nervous."

Between watching the road ahead for roadblocks, Alvaro snuck glances at the sisters and saw that they became more identical as some of the mud that covered Lourdes smeared on Lupe, and some of Lupe's anguish appeared in Lourdes' eyes.

He doubted he'd ever met a person over a year old that looked less capable of shooting someone than Lupe did. Besides, according to Noah, Lupe and Raul were in Malibu the day before the Hans Shuler murder. And Lupe was in Baja as the Virgin the day after. She and Raul could've flown down, raced in a car from the closest airport to Shuler's mountain town, killed the old man, raced back, and caught a plane to Tijuana or Mexicali. Alvaro doubted they did, yet he wanted a chance to question Lupe. But that could wait until they crossed the border. For now, he needed to watch for a double-cross, in case the FBI had somehow tricked Pop or dug up clues about the family that allowed them to fake the note, or the colonel had used Pop's .45 on Monreal to frame one of the Hickeys.

The Datsun bottomed out with every rut. A deep, wide pothole knocked off the tailpipe. Now the little car sounded like a convoy of Peterbilts. As it neared Tecate, civilians rushed out of shacks, cantinas, and junkyards. Some of them grinned and waved, mostly women and *niños* to whom the news must've spread. Alvaro imagined them thinking, The blessed Virgins are racing past. Two of them. What a miracle this is. Maybe even more of them will come from heaven, enough to make that heathen country up north turn from its devilish ways.

They passed what looked like an ancient strip mall of nothing but corner groceries and entered downtown Tecate. Alvaro leaned toward the front. "Don't slow down until we cross the line."

"How far to the gate?" Kevin Pratt asked.

"A mile or so. I'll tell you where to turn."

On the sidewalks at around ten, drunks leaned against shops and whooped encouragement. Teenagers chanted slogans that relegated the PRI to hell. Women crawled off the sidewalk, into the road, their hands clasped or gripping beads. The splash from the Datsun blasting through a puddle drenched a gang of *señoras* who then lifted their hands as though in praise. Alvaro imagined they had stationed themselves in that place, hoping a touch from the tires of a car in which the Virgin or two of them rode could turn the muddy water holy.

"Make a right up here. At the yellow sign."

At the speed Agent Pratt made the turn, the Datsun might've flipped if the overload hadn't held it down. "Look," Ross Clinger yelped. "Look up ahead. Oh man."

Chapter Thirty-four

"*Federales*," Noah said.

They stared at a row of shiny dark Ford and Chevy sedans around which stood a half dozen uniformed men, several others in suits, and two in sport shirts and jeans. A stocky man in uniform stepped out into the road and waved for the Datsun to pull over.

As Agent Pratt pulled in beside the sedans, his partner said, "Kevin, here comes Uncle Donald."

Alvaro recognized the fellow with a dour face who had crossed the border through the walker's gate and was headed toward them. A younger, taller man followed him.

"Your uncle's FBI too?" Clifford asked.

"No, but when our boss talks—"

"Which he never stops doing," Pratt interjected.

"—he sounds like Donald Duck."

"We wouldn't call him names," Pratt said, "except he's always ragging on us about being Mormon. Offering drinks, sending us to strip clubs on surveillance assignments. But he's okay."

The agents climbed out of the Datsun and opened the back doors. As Clifford stepped out, he said, "Brother, their Uncle Donald's not the only one waiting to greet us. Check out the Cadillac."

But Pop's Cadillac was on the other side of the line. "Yeah," Alvaro said. "That's the good news. Here comes the bad." By now, the *federales* began surrounding them.

The *federale* in charge wore a suit and a look cold and haughty, like some wicked king. He came straight at Alvaro, leaned until their noses almost touched. "*Su nombre,*" he snorted. Alvaro gave his name. The man sidestepped to Clifford and repeated his question, then moved on to Noah and repeated it again. Then he backed away. In a voice to low for Alvaro to make sense of, he consulted with one of his uniformed men.

Uncle Donald had taken agents Pratt and Clinger aside. Alvaro heard him quack a request for the facts about the meeting with Monreal. And he heard the agents, alternating lines, giving the story the way the colonel had told it, with Raul as the murderer of Paco Monreal.

Then Alvaro heard the *federale* in charge instructing several of his men, telling them to show the ladies to his car. Alvaro knew that, given Mexico's Napoleonic law, once the *federales* had the ladies in custody, they wouldn't let go. Either the ladies would rot in prison until a court found them innocent—Lourdes of stealing a million in gold, Lupe on some conspiracy charge—or *federales*, prosecutors, judges, prison wardens, and others behind the scenes would require their piece of the *mordida*. Unless Andres Shuler rescued them, which Alvaro wasn't willing to count upon.

So he slipped his right arm around Lupe's left, his left arm around Lourdes' waist. His right hand went under the front of his shirt, to where someone might have a small pistol tucked beneath the waist of his jeans.

"*Vamos*," he said, and started backing away, into the road.

"Hey, *alto*," a *federale* shouted. The rest of the *federales* turned, gawked, and reached for their weapons.

"Keep walking, keep walking, keep walking," Alvaro chanted as he steered them. He didn't need to push or tug. By the halfway point between the *federales* and the border gate, they were going sideways so Alvaro could watch both the Mexicans and the U.S. customs agents at the gate. The *federale* in charge was yelling for them to come back. At least three of his men had guns leveled at them.

But the customs agents stood aside and stared as if they'd gotten to witness the Second Coming.

Chapter Thirty-five

Alvaro waved to Tom, who was only a few car lengths away, leaning against the fender of his Cadillac. If he hadn't probably killed a man tonight, Alvaro might've felt something like ecstasy. But even his mild joy got dulled when he saw Uncle Donald, followed by his helper then Agents Pratt and Clinger, come through the gate. And when Uncle Donald came straight to the ladies, quacked an introduction, a thank you to Alvaro, and a stern request for the ladies to come with him, even the relief at having brought them all across the border got snatched away.

As he watched the ladies get escorted to a dark blue Ford, Clifford and Noah came to join him. Then Noah said, "I'll go with the queens of heaven and keep an eye on those FBI guys. I don't trust them."

Clifford chucked Noah in the arm. "Better hurry." Noah hustled away.

"So, *hermano*," Clifford said, "you were going to

make off with the ladies, leave Noah and me in Mexico to take the wrap?"

"What wrap?" Alvaro said. "Nobody accused you or Noah, did they?"

◇◇◇

While the Cadillac smoothed the bumpy road, on the plush and wide rear seat, Clifford held Feliz on his lap and wrapped her in his arms. His heart was so full of the blessing he'd been granted, being home with his baby who seemed bouncy and well, he had to keep reminding himself not to squeeze quite so hard.

Ava was beside him, massaging his neck, something she knew he loved, which he supposed was why she hadn't done it in months. When he'd first seen her in the car, he imagined she would either bawl him out or express through the chill in her voice that any man who terrified his wife by disappearing in the middle of the night was scum. No matter if he'd helped save the blessed Virgin from disrepute or brought his brother back home alive.

But he heard no chill in her voice. All she said was, "Thank God you're back."

With his girls in his lap and at his side, with Pop in the driver's seat, and Alvaro riding shotgun, he thought of this ride as a preview of heaven.

Tom said, "X, that Mexican standoff you made us watch was darned risky."

"Naw," Alvaro said. "I was betting not a one of those feds was going to risk shooting down the Virgin."

"Did you boys run into Paco Monreal?"

"Yeah. Raul Mesa offed him," Clifford said, figuring offed was a word Feliz wouldn't know. When his brother looked around, he raised a finger to his lips. He could've counted on his fingers the times he had lied to Pop. Maybe he would tell Pop the truth someday, but not while Ava, who could be quick to judge, was near.

At the Highway 94 junction, Tom pointed to a roadside cafe. "You boys hungry?"

Clifford looked at his brother, probably sensing he had matters other than food on his mind. And Alvaro wasn't going to tell anyone, even Pop, that he'd rather starve than stop, that he needed to get somewhere alone. Somewhere he felt free to grieve, rationalize, scheme, or whatever his mind required before it would find a way to give him peace, about the death of Paco Monreal and the flyer, and his feelings for Lourdes Shuler. Besides, he wanted to check on Lourdes' gold.

Ava produced a bag of Doritos, the snack she most craved over the past months. And Tom reached over to the glove box for a can of the Spanish peanuts he was rarely without. "Yeah," he said, "Let's just munch and get on home."

"Pop," Clifford said. "How'd you save our butts this time?"

"Don't blame me. All I did was talk."

"Come on, Pop. Tell us the story."

◇◇◇

He gave the short version. "Harry knows a guy. Call him Miguel. This Miguel and Harry Junior are working on a Baja racetrack and casino deal. Well, as I'm sure you all know, except my super girl—"

"I'm not super, Papá," Feliz said.

"Want to bet?"

"Yep."

"You're on. I'll prove it to you when we get home. Anyway, the kinds of gambling you do at casinos hasn't been legal in Mexico since Cárdenas in the thirties. So this Miguel's got a liaison, you might call him a lobbyist, working on the *presidente*, legislature, judicial side and all. As you might guess, this requires a virtually unlimited fund of pesos. Much of which comes from Harry. So this liaison, call him Jose, on account of the loot he's quite willing to part with, he's got access to the *caballeros* at the top. Including Andres."

Tom wasn't ready to give them all the details. Alvaro would no doubt go visit Lourdes Shuler. Better that he didn't know right yet that Andres had appeared at least as interested in gold as in his sisters. Besides, that was just Tom's conjecture, on the level of gossip. Neither did he tell them that the story Clifford related about Raul Meza killing Monreal didn't accord with the one the *federales* at the border had passed along just before the old Datsun appeared.

"So does Andres want his sisters back?" Alvaro asked. "I mean, who does he think did the job on their father?"

"Beats me," Tom said. "Who do you think offed the old man?"

"What's 'offed,' Daddy?" Feliz asked.

"It's like when you sock somebody in the nose, real hard. Which is not okay, right?"

"Right," Feliz said severely.

Tom said, "Whoever the guy was that did the offing had got hold of the old man's Luger."

"Benito," Alvaro said. "Hans Shuler's bodyguard. He was after the gold. Or maybe Rolf. Lourdes' brother. He came looking for her and got shot. Or maybe he came looking for her gold."

Clifford asked, "Why would he worry about a few gold bars when he stands to inherit gold mines?"

Tom crooked his head to catch a glimpse of Clifford. "Gold mines?"

"Hans owned a bunch of them," Alvaro said.

"Who told you that?"

"Lourdes."

"Funny," Tom said. "All I read says Hans Shuler was a financier. Nothing about gold mines."

Over some miles and several minutes, Alvaro's

weary and overwrought mind recalled Lourdes' questioning if the gold might be cursed, and she and her brother discussing the same question. "Oh God," he mumbled.

"What?" Tom asked.

"I think I know where the gold came from."

Chapter Thirty-six

Instead of going into his duplex, Alvaro stood in front of the carport and watched the Cadillac glide away. Then he walked straight through the carport, pulled his key ring from his pocket and opened the kitchen door. From the only drawer that hadn't been dumped, he took a flashlight. He clicked it on to check the batteries. He went outside and into the back yard. After a quick look and listen, he bent and opened the hatch to the crawl space under the house. He crawled in, flashed, and saw exactly what he'd feared he would see. Nothing.

"Crap," he yelled. He crawled out into the light. "Crap, crap, crap, crap," he mumbled all the way into the house and through it past spilled drawers and open, emptied cabinets whose previous contents littered his floor. While brushing his teeth, he mumbled, "Benito, Benito, Benito. Crap."

He could've slept between the rails of a train track

while a hundred freight cars rolled over him. He cussed himself to sleep in about thirty seconds.

◇◇◇

On Saturday, the Hickey brothers missed their first Pest ball game in the three years they'd played for the team. Aside from fatigue, Alvaro was too heartsick to play anything. Clifford decided he owed his girls the weekend. Neither was he in a hurry to confess to the Pests' starting pitcher that his Bronco was now junk in a Baja river.

Alvaro spent the morning playing mournful tunes on his classical guitar. He killed the afternoon walking the beach along the Silver Strand and past the Tijuana sloughs, all the way to the border and back. Back home, he found a message from Noah, who asked if he could flop on Alvaro's floor and said he'd be at the Coronado ferry landing about six.

Alvaro walked to the landing. When he didn't see Noah, he bought a *Sentinel* and sat on a bench. He turned to an article by Roxie Hewitt, whose sympathy for the Virgin's campaign against the PRI appeared, albeit subtly, in most every line. This Roxie had left several messages for him at Garfield et al, according to the receptionist who had left her own message on Alvaro's home machine.

Soon the 6:15 ferry arrived, with Noah at the rail. Alvaro waited on the bench. Noah came and sat beside him, and gave him news about the ladies. The FBI had placed them in a Holiday Inn on Pacific Coast Highway. And an ambulance and its team had gone to Ensenada, picked up Rolf Shuler, and brought him to San Diego, to University Hospital.

Alvaro cleaned up, ironed a pair of cotton slacks, buffed his best shoes and went there by foot, ferry and taxi.

He wasn't anxious to visit Rolf. He needed to see the lady. He waited in the visitors' area on the third floor, from where he could see anyone using the hallway that led to the private room the FBI arranged for Rolf Shuler. When the sisters came out of the elevator and started down the hall in matching emerald green dresses and with matching gardenias in their long golden hair, Alvaro jumped up. He took Lourdes by the elbow. Lupe gave him her mournful, exquisite smile and walked on.

He said, "You might want to sit down before I tell you something?"

The lady's eyes and mouth rounded. "Rolf?"

"Not Rolf," Alvaro grumbled, then caught himself and softened his tone. "It's about the gold."

"Oh." She released the breath that had stuck in her throat. "Tell me."

"It's gone."

"Gone," she said, as though contemplating the deep meanings of the word.

"Somebody ransacked my house. Probably Benito. He must've got lucky."

"Please tell me you are not stealing the gold?"

The question stung him. "Suppose I'm doing just that."

"Then you will be cursed."

"Yeah," he said. "Your father didn't own gold mines."

From the look she gave him, he knew he'd struck a nerve and wounded her. She said, "I'm going to see my brother now."

Alvaro followed her into the room. Rolf was sitting up. His wavy hair looked recently trimmed and combed, his boyish face just washed, rosy cheeks and all. Lupe was on the far side of the bed. Out the window behind her, on the hillside across Mission Valley, a condo village under construction looked like an ant colony.

Rolf stared at Alvaro as though expecting an argument. He said, "I thank you for protecting my sister," and Alvaro wondered how the meaning of words and the message could be so perfectly opposite.

Rolf reached out for the lady's hand. She sat on the hall door side of the bed. She wore sandals. Her toes touched the floor. Alvaro could've used the visitor's chair, but he stood, watching the lady stroke her brother's arm.

He thought of going to the nurse and saying, That

guy is fine, only playing invalid to get all this attention. But he knew a mean, jealous thought when he thought one. Still, he couldn't stand there and watch while the lady doted on the fellow. He tried sitting, and plucked a magazine out of a rack beside the chair. *Sports Illustrated.* He managed to find the index and decide on a story about Pete Rose as the Phillies' new manager, about his skill at motivating the team. He found the page then shut the magazine and stood.

He tapped the lady on the shoulder. When she turned his way he said, "There's a patio at the end of the hall, the door on the left beyond the elevator. I'll be waiting out there. I need to tell you a couple things."

On the patio, he stood overlooking the valley, watching traffic snarl on the interstate below and wondering what to say when she asked what he needed to tell her. Then the magazine fell from his hand. He slumped over the patio rail.

A while later, how long he couldn't guess, he found himself on the sidewalk in front of the hospital without remembering how he'd gotten there. He caught himself mumbling, "No, no, maybe I'm wrong."

He wheeled around and strode inside. He climbed the five flights of stairs two steps at once. In the hallway, he tried to walk slower. He told himself, "Be cool, be cool."

Lupe was standing, gazing out the window. The lady was still on the bed. She turned toward the door.

Alvaro pointed over his shoulder. "One minute, that's all."

She whispered something to Rolf, then climbed off the bed and walked past Alvaro and out to the hall. Then she turned and waited for his question, her eyes cloudy and cast slightly down.

He took her by the elbow and led her past the busy nurse station, past the elevator and out the door to the patio. The *Sports Illustrated* still lay on the floor. He picked it up and tossed it on a deck chair. He leaned on the patio rail. "Tell me about you and your brother."

She raised fiery eyes to meet his. "I don't want to."

"Don't give me that," he said. "You're one tough lady. And I helped you save him, didn't I?"

"Yes."

"So tell me."

"Why do you make me? You already know."

"Because," Alvaro said, no longer demanding. Now his manner was a gentle plea. "Because if you don't, I'll spend the rest of my life thinking maybe I walked away from somebody wonderful on account of misunderstanding."

She reached to touch him but at the last instant pulled her hand away. It fell limp at her side. "I only love Rolf," she said. "I cannot love anybody else, only Rolf, forever."

Alvaro went to the chair and sat, feeling as if he

had begun to turn into stone. "Why forever? Why nobody else?"

"You know," she said, and her face expressed the answer.

"You mean shame?"

She again lowered her eyes. He said, "Look, we're all ashamed of something."

"Rolf is my life." She went to the rail and faced the valley where a thousand lights were just now blinking on. "I will make no excuses for loving Rolf."

"Then let me guess."

"If you have to."

"After Lupe disappeared, no way would your father give you the slightest rein. He kept you like a prisoner. And for reasons I'll probably never understand, you decided not to run away. And there's Rolf, handsome as the son of Maximilian and Carlotta."

Her eyes were the blue of the lake just offshore from Pop's Tahoe cabin. Alvaro said, "And who could blame Rolf? How could any man not fall for you?"

She turned, wiped a tear from the side of her nose then let the same pretty finger glide down his cheek. "You are wise, my *Equis*."

Alvaro shrugged. Having no more to say, he was turning to leave when a thought came. "You love Rolf even though he killed your father?" He wouldn't have bet a nickel that Rolf was the murderer. But now he knew.

Her face was the proof. And this time she didn't lie.

"I do," she said.

"So Rolf killed his own father for some Nazi gold?"

Lourdes raised her fists and held them beside her face while she screamed. "He killed our father for me."

He stepped toward her. The lady fell into his arms and stayed there all the time she told the story.

◇◇◇

How Benito had learned about her and Rolf, they didn't know, or care. But they weren't going to pay him to keep the secret. So he told Hans, perhaps believing the old man would reward him.

Alvaro saw the old Nazi rise from the chair in his office that looked out on the walnut grove. Hans bellowed for Rolf and Lourdes while he strode to the gun cabinet and reached for the Luger and the bullwhip. Benito backed out of the room, spooked by the fury he'd unleashed. Rolf passed Benito in the hall and walked into the office. He saw the whip in his father's hands and the Luger on the desk. Hans glared at Rolf and spat on the floor then yelled again for Lourdes. When she entered the room, wearing shorts and loose halter, he looked her all over. Then he came at her with his stiff-legged short steps, the bullwhip raised over his head.

Rolf jumped to the desk. He grabbed the Luger and shouted for the old man to stop, back up. Hans turned, saw the gun in Rolf's hand and laughed.

Rolf had only shot targets with a pistol. He lifted the gun in both hands, sighted and fired. Both shots hit the Nazi low on the forehead. As the old man staggered and fell, Rolf threw down the gun and ran out of the office. He saw Benito on the phone, and kept running.

Chapter Thirty-seven

While Ava went to church and a choir luncheon, Clifford played with Feliz. They walked the length of Mission Bay, from their cottage on the north shore, on the sand and along the boardwalk, past the hotels, summer rentals, the sailboat harbor at Santa Clara Point, and on until they heard the screams of roller coaster riders at Belmont Park.

When Clifford returned from carrying Feliz on his shoulders all the way home, after Feliz's first ever roller coaster ride, he found two phone messages from his brother. Both of them railed against the PRI, but not with Alvaro's characteristic fervor on the subject. From the voice on the phone, if Clifford hadn't known it was his brother, he would've suspected the caller was someone who had meant to dial the suicide hotline.

Alvaro's third call came while Clifford ran back and forth on the sidewalk of Pacific Beach Drive, chasing Feliz on her tricycle. He was passing their cottage when the phone rang. He grabbed up Feliz and ran inside. Once again, it was Alvaro, calling to damn the PRI to hell. "They've outdone themselves, *hermano*. Their advantage, based on the early vote count, is higher than it was the last election. Or so the newsmongers claim. One *pendejo* had the *juevos* to say it looked like the people reacted to the Virgin by racing to the polls to voice their loyalty to the PRI. Not a single newscaster's had the guts to even suggest a fix. They're killing me."

The next time Alvaro called, while Clifford was attempting to teach Feliz to play checkers, it was to report less grim news. Winona and Chief had come to visit and brought with them eight gold bars.

"Get this," Alvaro said. "Winona tells me she just happened to be in the back yard bright and early last Wednesday and noticed me going under the house. I mean, it was five a.m., and she's a foot shorter than the fence.

"Okay, so on Friday, they heard noises. They put their ears to the wall and decided it had to be somebody ransacking my place. I asked why they didn't call the law. Winona says, 'Now just suppose we done that and the cops found a stash of some illegal substance. How would we feel, having got you busted?'

"Anyway, they saw the guy. It was Benito. And after he gave up, they went over and snooped and found the gold, and brought it to their house for safekeeping. That was Friday. I didn't bother to ask why it took them until now to return it. From their looks, it was killing them to give it back."

By the next time the phone rang, Ava was home, making spaghetti. Clifford was in the bathroom with Feliz. They were playing catch with a Nerf ball while she bathed. Ava called Clifford to the phone. It was Dr. Fred. "Okay," he said, "I got your boy Rolf to *el norte*. Now where's my Bronco, all washed and vacuumed out?"

Clifford said, "It wasn't as lucky as Rolf. But listen, a check's in the mail. Kelly Blue Book plus five hundred for your gear and your trouble."

Fred didn't answer.

"Hold the check for a couple days. Would you?" Fred still hadn't spoken, or breathed. "I'll see you in court tomorrow." Clifford said.

◇◇◇

Alvaro sat on the sea wall at the west end of G Avenue. He didn't notice even one of the dozen or so girls in bikinis within ogling range. Straight across the wide beach were white capped waves and bright sails rounding the high cliffs of Point Loma. He didn't see them, either.

He was thinking of what the lady's gold could do. One bar could pay off his law school loans and buy Clifford and Ava a home of their own. He wondered for how many years the other seven bars could support the Tijuana orphanage he, Clifford, and Ava always brought Christmas presents to. If a curse came with the gold, feeding orphans might lift it.

As the sun tipped down behind the ocean and streaks of magenta appeared and darkened all across the horizon, Alvaro turned and walked home.

He phoned the Harborside Holiday Inn and got connected to the Shulers' room. Noah had given him the room number. Lupe answered. He asked her to tell her sister to expect him within the hour. Then he called a cab.

A lesson Pop taught and Alvaro had trusted and practiced was, once you've decided on a course of action, proceed with at least moderate abandon, without anymore questioning. The Sunday evening traffic was light on the bridge and up Pacific Coast Highway. The Holiday Inn was across the highway from the northeast corner of the Lindbergh Field airport. Alvaro instructed the cabbie to wait. He crossed the parking lot carrying two canvas shopping bags, one in each hand. The room was on the ground floor, number 107. Rolf opened the door.

Alvaro set the bag on the concrete. He reached out, clasped Rolf's hand, shook it once, and dropped it. "*Adios,*" he said.

Chapter Thirty-eight

Before Clifford arrived at the courthouse on Monday for the closing arguments and perhaps the verdict in Fred's trial, he had gone to the *Epitaph* offices in Little Italy and imposed upon Patrick Tarantino the owner/editor. Patrick and Clifford had shared an apartment their senior year at Pacific Christian College.

Clifford asked for an advance on the next seven cover features he would write. Patrick wanted to know the reason he needed so much money, but Clifford wouldn't give it. He didn't want to lie, and he couldn't tell any of the truth without alluding to the Virgin. And her story, he wouldn't tell anyone at least until after the happy day when Mexico broke free from the PRI. Patrick looked hurt, but he shrugged and jotted a note for Clifford to take to the bookkeeper.

The advance was just enough to pay Fred for the Bronco and to buy little gifts for Feliz and Ava.

As Clifford walked from the parking garage to the courthouse, he saw Noah waiting on the steps, a guitar slung on his back in a soft case Clifford recognized as one of Alvaro's.

He checked his watch and asked Noah to join him for a bagel. In the deli between the courthouse and the Greyhound station, a pair of pretty women in business suits and carrying brief cases clearly preferred Noah over Clifford. Probably the guitar, Clifford reasoned.

Since Mexico, Noah had shaved, gotten new Levis, and washed his sneakers. He looked sharp in one of Alvaro's Hawaiian surfer shirts. But Noah sat watching his feet, and didn't seem to notice the women. He said, "Alvaro's idea is, down by the ferry landing is best place around to set up and sing, with the tourists and all. Old Town's good, he said, but later, around supper time. It'll be sad playing for people till I get Gretchen back. She's my helper."

Clifford waved to a server. Noah said, "Alvaro's plenty bummed, with the lady and her sister gone."

"Gone?"

"Yeah, they disappeared."

"What's that mean?"

"Uncle Donald was going to pick them up this morning. He was going to take them someplace. But they were gone."

"Checked out of the motel?"

"I guess. Uncle Donald called and asked if they came to us. But they didn't. And that Rolf's gone too. And then the radio said the PRI won for sure. So that's when Alvaro picked up that pretty guitar, the nylon string, and started playing the same song, over and over. He played it at least a thousand times. Or two thousand."

"What song?" Clifford asked, though he imagined he knew.

"The prettiest song. There's a sailor, he's from Guaymas, and he gets so lonely when he's out to sea, and there's a bird steering the boat, and the sails get shredded, and maybe the anchor gets stuck on something. It's Spanish, so I don't get all the words. But this sailor, his soul dies. I think. Want me to play it?"

"I know the song," Clifford said. "But I've never known him to play it more than a few times in a row."

Noah said, "Remember you're going to help me find Gretchen?"

"Yeah," Clifford said. "Only Pop thinks I'm not all that welcome in Mexico, so he's going to take you. He went to visit my half sister in Laguna Beach. He's coming back tomorrow."

◇◇◇

Alvaro tried using anger to help him forget the lady. But that tactic failed when a courier arrived at the offices of Garfield et al and brought him a pouch with a thousand hundred dollar bills. On top of the money was a note on Holiday Inn stationary. She had scented it with lilac. The handwriting was graceful and exact as calligraphy. "Dearest *Equis*, if I were free, I would come to you, my brave, kind, loyal man, our savior. Truly, Maria de Lourdes Montenegro de Shuler."

He closed the door of his cubicle-sized office, turned his desk chair to face the window that overlooked the harbor and the Navy base on North Island. He closed his eyes and sat with elbows on his knees and chin in his hands, remembering her at her best, in the white smock made out of a sheet, bringing hope to a small band of *campesinos*.

After some minutes, he left the penthouse suite carrying the pouch. He rode the express elevator then walked up 1st to Broadway and turned east. Remembering the lady their first night together, at Bula's and running in the rain, he moved like a sleepwalker all four blocks and up the creaking stairway to the office with Hickey and Sons Investigations on the door.

Inside, he sat in Pop's old leather chair in the dark with the shades pulled. He reached in the pouch for the note, folded it into quarters and put it into the part of his wallet where credit cards would be if he had any. He continued remembering the lady, and he waited for his brother, who had phoned during the lunch break from the Dr. Fred trial and asked if they could meet for a drink or three.

When Clifford entered the office, he squinted into the dark then flicked the light switch. "Are you okay?"

"Sure."

"Have you been waiting long?"

"I couldn't tell you. Did the verdict come in."

"Yep. Not guilty."

"Excellent." Alvaro stood, picked up the pouch, met Clifford in mid-room, and handed it to him. "A hundred grand. It's too much."

"And it's Nazi gold."

"Who knows? Lourdes only thinks so. Anyway, take what you're going to give Fred for the Bronco, then we'll decide what to do with the rest."

Clifford stared at the money then looked up at his brother. "You miss her, right?"

"No sweat. You know me, Don Juan de Coronado."

Clifford took the pouch to the desk, sat in the visitor's chair, and counted out 140 Ben Franklins. "I've got an idea. We could accept the fact that we're half decent and half mercenary. We keep fifty, and give the other fifty to, let's say…"

"The orphanage."

"Deal."

The bills were in banded stacks of a hundred. Clifford dealt fifty stacks onto a pile. He shoved the pouch with the remainder, $36,000, across the desk to his brother.

"We split," Alvaro said.

"Nope. It's yours," Clifford said, and got in return a scowl that reminded him who his brother was, where he came from, and what he valued most. "Okay, okay."

Alvaro divided the bills into two tall stacks. "How about we give Pop ten grand?"

"Sure," Clifford said. "But you know what he'll do with it is make our wagon all cherry again, if he even finds it."

Clifford put his share into his briefcase. He swept the orphanage money into a drawer. Alvaro took the pouch. "You know, sometimes it's best to give up. Right?"

"I suppose."

"And one of those times is when you only want something somebody else needs."

"Are you talking about the money," Clifford asked, "or the lady?"

Alvaro didn't answer, and his smile was far more brave than cheery.

"Let's get that drink," Clifford said.

"How about I meet you at Rudy's, in a half hour. Old J.T. wants to see me. To bawl me out, I guess."

◇◇◇

In the penthouse suite, J.T. Garfield was still behind the desk he claimed was solid teak but which Alvaro would've bet was press board and veneer. He looked like Scrooge or some other miser in one of the Dickens novels in Clifford's collection.

"Am I mistaken," J.T. droned, "or were you gone all last week?"

"Three days, not counting the weekend."

"You realize, I presume, that your absence reduces my desire to write a recommendation that will land you a job at a prestigious firm."

Alvaro recalled what he'd heard that morning on the radio, some politician contending that in the U.S. of America, people can prosper if they work hard and play by the rules. Maybe that's why we Hickeys haven't exactly prospered, he thought. We work plenty hard, but we don't always play by other people's rules, because we've got rules of our own.

He left the big office and walked down the hall to his cramped one, intending to finish the appeal he'd been working on almost a week ago when the lady first called. He only had a few blocks left to fill in. Instead, he pulled her note out of his wallet and read it again. And again.

Tina, a receptionist, came in. She was a tiny doll with scarlet lips that pursed all day long. Alvaro said, "Do you ever go home on time?"

"On my birthday, I did. Mister Hickey, a woman's called you about a dozen times now. She says she's a reporter. Is she stalking you?"

Alvaro winked. "I'll try her now."

He dialed. Roxie Hewitt answered. He identified himself and apologized for not getting to her before the election. "I was out of the country. I guess the story's old news."

"Who can say for sure?" Hewitt said. "We could hope she shows up in three years. But in the meantime, maybe you'll help me with a follow up, a feature for the Sunday magazine, about the possible long-term effects of her visits. It'll be mostly interviews."

Alvaro refolded the lady's note and put it back into his wallet. "I could meet you at Rudy's on C Street in ten minutes."

"Make it twenty. I'm uptown."

◇◇◇

The Hickey brothers were on bar stools in the saloon wing of Rudy's Hacienda. "You're not going to tell a reporter, are you?" Clifford asked.

"I'll tell her part of it, that a lady came to me and thought the Virgin was her sister, but even after her sister got busted, the Virgin appeared. I'll tell her something like that. I mean, who are we to say the Virgin wasn't for real. We only know that one time she was a fake."

"I'm not even sure about that time. I—" Clifford stopped when a tall woman entered by herself. She wore red slacks and a silky brown top. She had a bush of curly red hair.

Alvaro waved. The reporter waved back. They met halfway and shook hands. She acted shy, as if something had fractured her composure. "So, shall we take a booth?" she asked while reaching into her purse. She pulled out a tape recorder. "A quiet corner, if there is one?"

"Have you ever been to Bula's?"

"Yeah."

"Like it? And are you hungry?"

"Sure. And sure. We'll go Dutch."

"Not if I can help it." Alvaro turned and smiled at his brother.

To receive a free catalog of Poisoned Pen Press titles, please contact us in one of the following ways:

Phone: 1-800-421-3976
Facsimile: 1-480-949-1707
Email: info@poisonedpenpress.com
Website: www.poisonedpenpress.com

Poisoned Pen Press
6962 E. First Ave. Ste. 103
Scottsdale, AZ 85251